Willa Blackmore

Witchwood

Copyright © 2021 by Willa Blackmore

All rights reserved. No part of this publication may be reproduced, stored or transmitted in any form or by any means, electronic, mechanical, photocopying, recording, scanning, or otherwise without written permission from the publisher. It is illegal to copy this book, post it to a website, or distribute it by any other means without permission.

This novel is entirely a work of fiction. The names, characters and incidents portrayed in it are the work of the author's imagination. Any resemblance to actual persons, living or dead, events or localities is entirely coincidental.

Willa Blackmore asserts the moral right to be identified as the author of this work.

Designations used by companies to distinguish their products are often claimed as trademarks. All brand names and product names used in this book and on its cover are trade names, service marks, trademarks and registered trademarks of their respective owners. The publishers and the book are not associated with any product or vendor mentioned in this book. None of the companies referenced within the book have endorsed the book.

First edition

This book was professionally typeset on Reedsy
Find out more at reedsy.com

To my family and everyone who helped me get this story on the page.
You know who you are, but I have to list a name or two...
Anna, Bonny, Farrah, Jake, Rose, Toni, Jacob, HeatherJo
I appreciate everything!

I hope you'll enjoy Witchwood, Book One of The Carolina Files!

Contents

Prologue 1

Chapter 1..7

Chapter 2..13

Chapter 3..17

Chapter 4 23

Chapter 5 32

Chapter 6..38

Chapter 7 43

Chapter 8..51

Chapter 9..56

Chapter 10 63

Chapter 11...67

Chapter 12...73

Chapter 13 80

Chapter 14 87

Chapter 15 91

Chapter 16...100

Chapter 17 111

Chapter 18 114

Chapter 19 123

Chapter 20 129

Chapter 21...136

Chapter 22 144

Chapter 23...153

Chapter 24 162

Chapter 25 168

Chapter 26...173

Chapter 27 180

Chapter 28 185
Chapter 29 190
Chapter 30 201
Chapter 31..211
Chapter 32..217
Chapter 33 227
Chapter 34 235
Chapter 35..249
Chapter 36..254
Chapter 37..271
Want More Carolina Files?................................277
Also by Willa Blackmore 278

1.

2.

3.

4.

5.

6.

7.

8.

9.

10.

11.

12.

13.

14.

15.

16.

17.

18.

19.

20.

21.

22.

23.

24.

25.

26.

27.

28.

29.

30.

31.

32.

33.

34.

35.

36.

37.

38.

39.

Prologue

This story isn't about a demon possessed chainsaw, nor is it about John-John Newberry, whom you're about to meet. I was already well acquainted with the chainsaw. John-John, not so much. But the day they showed up together on my doorstep was the first hint that something might not be right at the vineyard on the edge of town. I didn't think much of it at the time. But I should have.

I was in my office, down on the floor searching for a quarter, when John-John Newberry came in and pulled up a chair in front of my desk. Calling the old converted tool shed an office was maybe a bit of stretch, but that's what I'd been using it for since I'd had the bright idea that a paranormal consultant who intended to charge in cold hard cash should maybe have something borderline legitimate to offer as a face to the world. I'd wanted to set up shop in one of the rooms at our family's inn, but my sisters had vetoed the idea in the strongest possible terms - by threatening to help.

God forbid.

So I'd spent a month or so cleaning out the old shed, slapped on a coat of paint, put in a desk and a couple of chairs and hung my sign on the door. It wasn't much, but since most of my *paid* work came from law enforcement who insisted I come to them, I figured it would do. For a while anyway.

When John-John came calling, I'd been busy with the all important business of attempting to flip quarters into a shot glass full of water. My aim was shit, and I'd spent more time on the floor in search of wayward coins than I had at actual flipping.

So you could say I kind of met John-John from the ground up.

First thing I saw was his feet. Muddy work boots, then about an inch of white sock, followed by long hairy legs, ending in the turned up cuffs of a pair of dirty denim shorts.

My fingers closing over the elusive coin, I got up from the floor and quickly returned to my chair where I got my first good look at the man who'd so rudely waltzed into my office without bothering to knock. I pegged him at late twenties, maybe early thirties. Sort of good looking in a scruffy, can't be bothered with combing my hair kind of way.

"Sorry," I said, "I didn't hear you knock."

"Cause I didn't," he replied, gesturing back over his shoulder toward the door. Which was open wide. "Open door means come on in where I come from. You ought to be more careful. You never know what might take you up on that kind of invitation."

"And where might that be?" I inquired, ignoring his attempt at sage advice. I didn't particularly appreciate strangers telling me what to do with my doors or anything else.

"Where might *what* be?" he asked, revealing himself to be a little slow on the uptake.

"Where you come from," I prompted, letting a bit of impatience creep into my voice.

"More or less right here. Henley-on-Hale, or close enough."

I knew that couldn't be true because there wasn't a living soul in Henley that I didn't know on sight. Well, other than the tourists, of course.If this man was a tourist I'd start eating quarters instead of flipping them.

His drawl was a good match for my own though, and that alone told me that even if he wasn't from Henley-on-Hale, he was at least from this same neck of the woods.

"I live out by the county line," he continued. "Over by The Hole."

The Hole was kind of a no-man's-land. A forested area that sat right on the county line, it was a place where things we ran out of Henley-on-Hale sometimes ended up. Things that mostly consisted of bad tempered supernatural entities that we hadn't seen the need to kill but still didn't want on our doorsteps. We tried not to be too bloodthirsty if we could help it.

Honestly, I wasn't sure what roamed around those woods, only that everybody – including us Whitlows – stayed the hell away from them.

"Nobody lives by The Hole," I told him. "Not in years."

"Funny thing then. Seeing as that's where my house is. And that's where it's been since my momma squirted me out into the world. And my own daddy was born in it. So I guess you better run over there and tell my place it ain't real."

"Okay, let's start with the basics." I was quickly tiring of this man and anxious to get back to flipping quarters. "Why don't you start by telling me your name and what you think I can do for you?"

He introduced himself as John-John Newberry II, Junior for short, and then stated that he didn't expect I could do much for him one way or the other, but he figured he might be able to do something for me.

"I got this chainsaw outside," he began. "*Your* chainsaw, to be exact. I reckon I stole it, but I don't exactly remember." He looked at me as if he hoped I might be able to shed some light on the situation. "Unless one of you Whitlow girls gave it to me?"

I shook my head. Much as we all hated it, we were stuck with the thing, except for the rare occasions when the chainsaw - we called it Larry Joe - magicked some poor fool like John-John into busting it out of the cage we'd locked it in.

"I don't remember taking it, but I guess I did," John-John continued. "I remember walking by y'all's place, wondering why you folks had a chainsaw in a cage. I think I probably walked over to it. It ain't everyday you see a chainsaw in a cage, you know, so I don't think I was being nosy. Anybody'd want to get a better look. After that, things get kind of fuzzy. Next thing I remember is wakin' up from a drunk and there it was. Right at the foot of my bed. Anyway," he said, pointing his thumb toward the open door, "I brought it back."

"You can keep it," I told him. "It can be one of those things like when you're a kid, and you take something and then when you own up to it, whoever you stole from is so *impressed* by your honesty, they let you have it anyway? This can be one of those situations. I'll even give you his cage." In truth, I was just runnin' off at the mouth. Larry Joe was so mean I wouldn't wish him on

4

my worst enemy and wasn't about to give it to this man. Thief or not.

"Thank you anyway," John John demurred, "But I got no use for power tools that are liable to creep up when your back's turned. It did that you know. Twice."

I figured he was lucky if that was the extent of the chainsaw's mischief. It was capable of worse.

My mother named the chainsaw Larry Joe after a boyfriend she'd come to particularly despise. Not an ordinary chainsaw, Larry was possessed by a demon so violent it was almost rabid, and was so hard to control, we had to keep the thing in a cage we had specially built.

It had occurred to me that maybe the chainsaw wasn't possessed by a demon at all, but instead might house the spirit of the actual very nasty but undeniably *human* Larry Joe. He'd disappeared shortly before my mother came into possession of the chainsaw, after all. Getting mad and sending somebody's spirit into a power tool was the kind of thing mother might be apt to do if she was mad enough. But she would have had to kill him first, and I'd like to think she'd draw the line at murder.

My visitor seemed as if he was about ready to take his leave, so I thanked him for bringing back the runaway chainsaw. Maybe he was a thief, maybe he wasn't. But I put a lot of stock in being polite to all kinds. At first, anyway.

Before leaving, John-John had one more thing he wanted me to know.

"You know that vineyard out near The Hole? The fancy one with the little restaurant and all?"

I told him I knew of it, but not being remotely interested in wine, I'd never visited.

"Something strange is going on there. Dancin' around in the middle of the night, singing songs. People wandering around the roadside in front of the place like they're drunk or lost, or both. I dunno. It's got a bad feel to it. Worse than usual, even for The Hole."

"Probably just a bunch of tourists livin' it up," I said. "It's a vineyard. They serve wine. I reckon you can get drunk on wine, same as any kind of booze."

"Maybe. Maybe not. I figured you bein' a Whitlow I ought to mention it. I know you folks keep an eye on things."

After he left, I thought about what John-John had said about my family. How we kept an eye on things. It was true, we did. Most of the time I felt like we did a pretty good job. But just because we were witches didn't mean we were infallible. Once in a while, we dropped the ball.

I thought about a lot of things that day. None of it very important. I thought about how bad I sucked at games of any kind. I thought about how it sucked that I was going to have to lug the chainsaw home all by myself. I thought about how growing up wealthy should have ruined me but didn't. I thought about the dumb shit that flits through your head when you're feeling lazy but know it's okay cause nobody needs you for anything right that minute anyway.

The one thing that never crossed my mind was that vineyard.

That was me, Tula Whitlow, dropping the ball.

Chapter 1

Trout's Tavern was located right in the middle of the township of Henley-on-Hale, and had been a landmark of sorts for more than a hundred years.

That is, of course, if you believed the brass plaque that hung beside the entrance. As a local, I knew better. The claim was entirely fabricated, just another bit of fluff to please the tens of thousands of tourists that flocked here during most every season of the year.

I couldn't blame them, really. Henley-on-Hale was kind of a jewel in the crown of the state of North Carolina. Or maybe more like a pearl, in that we were blessedly hard to find. And rare in that we'd somehow managed to keep ourselves small, despite the temptation to build a zillion mountain cabins, chalets, and riverfront condos. Unlike many other parts of the state, so far anyway, town elders had resisted.

That was in part because Henley-on-Hale happened to be populated by those of us from the realm of magic. Not everyone, of course. Some were mortals who over time had come to not only tolerate, but to also see the advantages of having neighbors who were a little bit "extra."

Many of the magical residents of our town were witches, like those of us from the Whitlow line. But there were others as well - shapeshifters, banshees, at least two werewolves, and then those of the Fae. No, let's not

7

forget *those* assholes. I'd been engaged to a Fae, and he'd proven himself to be little more than a womanizing, low down piece of trash. So right now, the whole damn bunch was on my shit list.

And why not? They *had* closed ranks to protect the asshole when I'd thrown that disappearing penis spell his way. Honestly, I don't know why they'd gotten so bent out of shape. It was only going to last a week, at which time his penis would have been good as new. Which in truth, hadn't been all that good to begin with.

Anyway, Henley-on-Hale, in spite of, or maybe because of its magic population, was a quaint and charming little town. It could be said that some of our over-exuberant merchants had extended the faux cozy mountain theme to an extent that bordered on ridiculous, especially here in what was referred to as "old town," but in many ways Henley-on-Hale was a genuine relic. Most of the families of Henley had roots that went back at least two centuries. Some, like us Whitlows, could boast nearly three hundred years in the area, pre-dating even the Revolutionary War.

I pushed open the big wooden door and entered the tavern. We were currently in early summer, so the place was literally teeming with tourists -so many in fact – you'd have to look pretty hard to find a familiar face within the crowd.

Unless you happened to be looking for my sisters. As was typical, they were the center of attention. Alafair because she was currently performing magic tricks to a group of half a dozen men and women, all of them gathered round the far end of the long, polished bar. Also, she was lovely. Even when falling down drunk, which seemed to be where she was currently headed. Long, golden hair rippling in waves down her back, eyes as blue as cornflowers, dimples to die for. And tiny. Let's not forget tiny. Barely five feet tall, Alafair was often described as doll-like. Disgustingly so.

And then there was Emmery. She seemed to have attracted an even larger crowd of admirers without the help of magic tricks or anything else. They were there because, well – she was Emmery. The short white dress she wore made her dark brown skin and jet black hair literally gleam. I had to work pretty hard not to be annoyed by Emmery's unending perfection. Should one single individual have been blessed with just basically everything? Wasn't that almost criminal?

Yes, I wasn't above a bit of jealousy where my sisters were concerned. I think that's kind of a given.

The three of us were so different in terms of appearance, that those who didn't know better would never peg us as sisters. My hair, for instance, was red, of the flaming variety, my eyes green, and my skin was so pale people were forever asking after my health. *"Are you well dear?"* I heard that at least once a day. Our vast differences however, were quite easily explained.

We all have different fathers.

Not that any of us know who those fathers might be, nor do we care. In our lineage, fathers haven't played much of a part. Not to say we wouldn't have enjoyed having a father around. Maybe we'd have loved it. Benefited from it even. But our mother was against the whole idea of sharing her children with anyone, most especially a man. She viewed the opposite sex with suspicion and more than a little derision. In her view, men were just uncommonly deficient.

Poor Mother. Right now she was off in Paris living with an uncommonly deficient man half her age, spending our inheritance just about as fast as she could manage.

Poor Mother indeed.

Thinking of Mother and our ever decreasing bank account, I was on the verge of turning around and leaving the Tavern. Surely I needed to be working. As a consultant with the US Marshals, I had a few cases that could use some attention. Nothing that would generate a huge amount of cash of course, but a paycheck was a paycheck. Alafair and Emmery could afford to dawdle, they'd pretty much made it an art form, but I could not. One of us had to at least try to be normal.

As if she sensed the resentment in my thoughts – and she probably did, being very good at the whole sensing thing – Emmery turned her head in my direction and motioned me over to the bar.

"What are you drinking?" She asked, unceremoniously shoving a besotted fellow off the bar stool to her right. "Sit."

"Why do you even ask me? You know I'm having tea."

"Bullshit, Tula. You're having a beer at least."

I *never* drink, never have, never will, but Emmery insists on pretending she doesn't know that absolute fact. In the universe of Emmery, I *should* drink, therefore I do.

Lucky for me though, Johnny, who was currently working the bar, knew exactly what I preferred and sat a steaming cup of Earl Grey down in front of me.

10

"Johnny, my dear sister Tula will take some Bailey's Irish with that. Go and fetch it please," Emmery told him.

"No she won't," he said.

"You guys are just boring," Emmery sniffed. "I honestly don't know why I bother."

But I was no longer paying attention. My eyes were focused on Alafair, who, to uproarious applause, had just pulled a rabbit out of a hat. Alafair, especially drunken Alafair, doing actual magic right in front of a barroom full of tourists, was the stuff of nightmares.

"Oh hell's bells," I said, as I watched her toddle from her stool and take a deep and stumbling bow. "She's using real magic."

"Leave her alone, she's just a little tipsy is all."

"Yes, and what's she gonna yank out of that hat next? An elephant?"

"In her dreams. You know she couldn't pull that off."

It was true. None of us were really adept – though if we worked harder we could be, according to Granny Whitlow anyway – and Alafair was especially clumsy. Which is what worried me. She could pull most anything out of that hat without even meaning to. A crocodile for instance– crocodiles terrify me, almost as much as alligators– or a rattlesnake, or a wild boar. Or worse.

I was just about to head over to my doll-like little sister and put a stop to her nonsense when I felt my phone vibrate.

I reached back and after a bit of jiggling and tugging, freed the device from my back pocket. It was unusually difficult to do, and I wondered if I was maybe putting on some pounds. The last thing I needed was a larger ass.

Why does fat never, ever seem to make it to the boobs? It's like against the laws of nature or something. Maybe I needed to make a sacrifice to the Boob-Gods or something.

I glanced at the screen.

Shit. It was Vicki.

If Vicki was calling me from the inn, it probably wasn't good. For the past six years, she'd basically run the place, so not much happened that she couldn't handle on her own.

I swiped and answered.

"What's up?"

"You probably want to get down here," she said.

"Tell me."

"You know that alarm that you showed me way way back when you guys first hired me? The one you said not to worry about cause it'd never go off?"

Oh no, that's not even possible...

"Well,   it   just   did."

Chapter 2

I figured it would take me less than five minutes to walk from the tavern to the front door of the inn. Since the matter was so urgent, I'd debated taking my car and had determined that I'd reach it even faster on foot, because even though it was nearing on 10 PM, the narrow streets were still hopelessly clogged with vehicles and cyclists, presumably going from one bar to the next. Had to be – nothing else was open.

Our inn, The Manor House, was what had once been, for lack of a better word, our ancestral home. Everyone in town just called it the Whitlow mansion, and by any definition that's what it was. Naming it The Manor House was simply our nod to the whole tourist trap thing – though we'd never, ever, book a room to one. A tourist residing there? Never in a million years.

Wow. *That would be something.* For a minute I imagined a family from Iowa rubbing shoulders with an actual imp. I had to admit I was a little bit intrigued by the idea of it. But no. Such a scenario was out of the question, even though it *would* make for some great entertainment.

The mansion had been converted to an inn during the 1990's. After a short stint as a museum, which my mother found incredibly dull and costly, dear Mother had happened on a phenomenal sheltering spell and had the really brilliant idea of an inn that would offer a safe zone to those from the realm of magic who found themselves on the wrong side of one thing or another. Providing they were willing to pay the price.

Which was hefty, to say the least.

Not only in terms of dollars. There was that, sure, a nightly stay at The Manor House came at a price that would put The Four Seasons to shame. But there was more. The cost in power was substantial as well. Our guests, be they vampires, fae, or any others from the realm of magic, also paid with bits of their various powers. Every passing minute spent within the walls of The Manor House meant a siphoning of their power, until the quota they owed to us was fulfilled.

In exchange, they were one hundred percent safe from the magic of others. But they also couldn't practice it themselves. No magic could be performed either inside the inn, nor on the grounds themselves. Not a single spell, incantation, transformation. Nothing.

Any creature or being entering the premises immediately forfeited all their power for the duration of their stay. And it wasn't voluntary. It was, due to my mother's spell, simply impossible.

Except for us, that is. As Whitlows, we were immune. Luckily Mother had thought of that little loophole.

Though certainly a much more talented witch than any of her daughters, it had been more than a little amazing that my mother had come up with the absolute most effective sheltering spell on the planet.

How that came to happen was still an open question. My mother had about as many stories about her famous sheltering spell as she had purses, and she had so many of those they required an entire closet just to house them. So who knew.

Sometimes she'd say the spell had come to her while under the influence of Turkish hashish, aspirin, and absinthe. And maybe a little antihistamine thrown in for good measure. I didn't doubt it. Mother was nothing if not inclusive. The more the merrier.

Another way she told the story was that she'd been delivered the spell by magic (of course) after reading a series of romance novels about vampires who were all bright and shiny and apt, at the drop of a hat, to throw a woman down for the purpose of mad, passionate lovemaking. The very idea of these bright and shiny vamps had alarmed her so much that she'd felt the need to construct a space that would render the lot of them powerless.

Vampires be damned!

My mother could not be convinced that the books were merely a work of fiction. The writer, she'd said, had penned the stories with nothing short of naked certainty, so much so that she was positive said author had obviously run up on one or three such creatures, and that if they did indeed exist, then the world as we knew it would end.

I kind of saw her point. None of the vampires I'd met would have ever made it to within twenty feet of my bedroom, and the only thing they shone with was blood.

Well, there was the one... but he wasn't your garden variety blood sucker.

From what I knew of vampires, I found them to be disgusting creatures, and if the sexy-beast version existed, I'd certainly never met one. Well, other than that single exception.

C'mon people! Why do you think they need a glamouring spell?

But supposing my mom was right, the dangers posed by a herd of shiny style vampires would just be inconceivable.

So her absolute horror at the possible existence of shiny vampires could very well have led to the spell – maybe. Like I said, either that or an absinthe cocktail induced inspiration. Depending on which version of her story you decided to believe. For now, I was leaning toward the vampire thing.

Regardless of how she'd come to have the spell, it did in fact render vampires powerless and had shown to have the interesting side effect of rendering all creatures of the magic world powerless as well. Within the confines of the Whitlow mansion, and the one and a half acres of manicured grounds that surrounded it, there was zero possibility of magic.

But she'd insisted on the alarm anyway. Just in case.

The alarm that had me even now running down the street in a mad dash to reach the inn and...

Do what exactly?

No one had ever said.

And it wasn't like I had an instruction manual.

I was going to have to call Mother.

Damn.

Chapter 3

I arrived at the inn drenched to the bone thanks to a pop up thunderstorm, a common occurrence in our part of the state. Throughout the summer months, these storms were frequent, but at least blessedly short.

These reliable little downpours were good in that our lawns and gardens were generally always verdant, but it also meant that you never really knew when you'd need an umbrella.

Note to self - always.

Though the downpour had lasted all of maybe three minutes, it was furious enough to plaster my hair to my skull and completely soak my thin summer dress.

I used my keycard, punched in the six-digit code to unlock the outer door, then crossed the tile vestibule, where I had to repeat the process in order to unlock the french doors that led to the lobby.

I was a little annoyed by this extra step because I knew that Vicki could have unlocked the doors using the automatic release button behind the desk. But she never did. And this night was no exception. I had a sneaky feeling that she rather enjoyed seeing me jump through all the hoops in order to enter.

Vicki had been with us for going on six years. She'd been a Dean's list senior at the University of North Carolina when she'd discovered her pregnancy, abruptly dropped out, and returned to Henley-on-Hale. None of us had ever understood why she'd taken such a dramatic action - there had been alternatives to just giving it all up - but she never spoke of it, and we never asked. My mother had hired her on the spot, pregnancy and all. She was smart as a whip, reliable as day turning to night, and had an attitude that commanded instant respect. Even, as it happened, with *our* kind of guests. Everyone paid attention when Vicki had something to say.

Once inside the lobby, I could see Vicki's five-year-old son Caleb curled up on one of the plush sofas that surrounded the huge river stone fireplace. The child was fast asleep, his blonde hair fanning around his head like a sweet golden halo. Vicki was sitting behind the check-in counter just a few feet away.

I walked quietly over to where he slept. Just for a peek.

"Don't you dare wake him," she warned me.

"Of course not," I promised.

I loved that kid. And not in an abstract kind of way. I loved him with a deep affection that I felt for no one in the world other than my sisters. If I ever had a child of my own, I hoped it would be something like Caleb. Of course, if I did have a kid, it almost certainly wouldn't be a boy. The Whitlow women seemed near incapable of producing male heirs. The number of men born into our family over the past three hundred years could be counted on one hand.

Even so, we'd kept the family name because first of all, Whitlow women didn't take much to the idea of marriage, and when a Whitlow woman *did* marry, they never, ever took their husband's name.

My own mother hadn't chosen to marry any of the three men who had fathered her daughters. And it seemed to have become an ingrained sort of bias. I could at times see myself as maybe becoming a mother, but never, ever, did that include a vision of myself as a wife.

The very idea was absurd.

But a child someday? I could see that, especially when I looked at little Caleb.

Gazing at the child right then I wanted nothing more than to sit down beside him, tickle him awake, maybe spend a few minutes swapping Godzilla jokes – he always had a new one for me – but if I did, I knew that Vicki would kill me. Right on the spot.

And who could blame her? You didn't waltz in and wake a sleeping child who'd been put down for the night.

But I almost did it anyway. Caleb was like family. We sisters had sort of adopted the kid. After all, he'd been with us even while in the womb. Vicki had been in the early months of her pregnancy when she started work at the inn, and over that nine month duration, we'd all watched in fascination as her tummy began to grow. I'd even been there for his very first kick. In every way that mattered, both Caleb and Vicki were part of the family.

Minus the magic, of course. Both of them were one hundred percent normals, not an ounce of magic ability between them.

"Okay, Tula, you *promised*." Vicki said, eyes narrowed and shooting 'I dare you' darts in my direction. "Don't you even think about it. If you wake him up that alarm will be the least of your worries."

Vicki, like most everyone who knew me well, had given up on the whole Talullah thing. Way too much of a mouthful. To everyone who mattered I was Tula. I didn't actually mind the name, but when the word started to

19

come out of someone's mouth, I always had this weird certainty that I was about to be called "Tuba", like the instrument. And when I thought of the word tuba, something fat and elephant-like always came to mind. So, though I liked Tula well enough, the fear of Tuba was strong.

Before I could formulate a good reply to Vicki's warning, it occurred to me that the room was silent.

"Looks like you figured out how to turn off the alarm." Though I'd never actually heard that particular alarm go off, I'd always assumed it would be earthshaking in its intensity. Something loud enough to wake the dead – God forbid. "I don't hear anything. What's going on?"

I was whispering. Not so much out of fear of waking Caleb – the kid could sleep through an earthquake – but it just kind of seemed like a whispering sort of moment.

"Well, of course you don't." Vicki was whispering as well. People seemed to do that, whispering is kind of contagious, like yawning, I think. "Maybe if you'd come a little *sooner*, you would have *seen* it though."

"Wait a minute – *see* it?"

After berating my lateness – never mind that I'd gotten there in less than five minutes – Vicki explained to me that the alarm was silent, at least to everyone but my mother. As soon as it went off, my mom had apparently called in with instructions for me to go down to the second basement – yes, we had a basement under the basement – and phone her when I got down there.

"But it put on a hell of a light show," Vicki said. "And next time I need you here, try to hoof it a little more impressively. I can't be responsible for every single

20

thing, you know. You girls act like I live here or something." Vicki smiled when she said the last part because she *did* in fact live at the inn. In her own little apartment in back.

Vicki's room and board was part of what I sometimes thought was an overly impressive salary. Especially at times like this, when she went all bossy-toes on one of us. I sometimes wondered if she was actually an undercover agent for our mother. Maybe getting a little extra cash on the side to sort of keep us in line.

Of course she was.

When it came to our arrangement with Vicki, it was often hard to tell who was actually the boss. Most of the time it sure didn't feel like it was me. But then again, I was about to do a very boss-like thing. Going down to the basement under the basement was huge. No one but a Whitlow could do it at all, and up to now, certainly none of us sisters had ever been allowed.

"Ok. I'm going down."

"Be careful," Vicki said. "I hope you don't run into anything weird."

"Okay, why are you saying that?" I asked her. "Did mom say I might?" As far as I'd been told, there was nothing much down there except, of course, the lodestone. The source of maybe all our power. Certainly the source of the sheltering spell, at the very least. I was a little bit afraid to actually come face to face with the thing, but how scary could a rock actually be? I mean, unless it was falling on your head or something.

"Not exactly," Vicki answered. "But she *did* say that you should be sure and take your bag with you, just in case."

By "my bag" she meant the bag I carried where I kept a wide variety of magical tools. *Emergency* tools.

The bag I always carried with me except when I didn't. Like then. Of course I didn't have it with me. Why would I have needed it for something as ordinary as an evening at Trout's? How was I to know I was going to have to go down into what could possibly be the very pits of hell? Wasn't like that was an everyday occurrence.

In truth, it was perfectly normal that I'd be at least a little bit frightened, should have been more frightened, but the truth was, mostly I just felt excited. I'd never been down to the lodestone. I'd heard about it, of course, again and again, but none of us - myself, Emmery, nor Alafair - had ever been permitted to enter. And now I was finally going to see it - up close and personal. My feckless sisters would be seething. Even if I encountered the devil himself, it would almost be worth it to see their faces when I told them.

The   Lodestone.   Finally.

Chapter 4

Our inn, The Manor House, once our ancestral home, was built on magic - real, actual magic. It sat on what might be one of the largest single lodestones on the planet. Lodestones are essentially magnets, the strongest known to man, and where lodestones are found, so too are fields of magnetite. It grows and flourishes on and around the lodestone, resulting in beautiful black prisms, much like crystals.

What we had in the sub-basement was a literal field of said crystals.

I'd taken the elevator down to the first underground level, which housed what you'd expect to find in the basement of a largish inn. There were rows of industrial sized washers and dryers, dozens of large laundry trolleys, shelving units containing everything from unopened tubes of fluorescent lighting to half-used cans of paint.

Walking toward the rear of the room, I accessed a hidden panel that opened to a set of stairs which led to the subterranean cavern below. At the bottom of the stairs, I came to a stainless steel door with a keypad set into the wall beside it. I keyed in the number that Vicki had written on a small scrap of paper. The door slid open with a near silent hiss.

I stepped through quickly, having an innate mistrust of mechanical doors, almost a phobia, always fearing that halfway through opening, the door would change its mind and decide to just crush me instead.

As the door swooshed shut behind me, I took a few tentative steps forward.

The breadth of the space was overwhelming. I'd expected something along the lines of the upper basement, but this cavern was huge – easily at least the size of four or five Olympic sized swimming pools. And the layout was much like a swimming pool as well. The field was an enormous rectangle, filled with shimmery black rocks, surrounded by a pad of concrete that was probably about eight feet wide.

I walked over to the edge of the concrete lip and stepped onto a long iron walkway, a bridge of sorts that spanned the length of the field.

After taking only a few steps forward, it suddenly felt to me as if the whole world was falling away. For a moment, I was so dizzy that it seemed like I might fall right into that vast sea of brilliant black.

Even without the use of magic, the sheer force of the field was undeniable. The magnetic energy was so strong that it was like a tug inside the air itself. I could only imagine what it must have been like centuries before, when my ancestors had trapped its power.

Once those early Whitlows had brought the lodestone and its energy under control, they'd harnessed it for any number of uses. There were tales of Whitlows training the energy on pirate ships out on the ocean, hundreds of miles away, in order to pull the ship's treasure into the family coffers. The stone would also pull all the nails from said ships, leaving the pirates to whatever fate the waters had in store for them.

24

Whether there was any truth to the legends, I didn't have a clue, but I kind of liked the idea of it. Vanquishing a bunch of greedy pirates and relieving them of their booty seemed like a worthy kind of endeavor to me.

As I gazed out into the field, I was dimly aware that I was on the verge of being mesmerized, and wondered if that was a real risk. Surely my mother would have warned me of that sort of danger. Most people don't know or understand the root of the word mesmerized, but for those who do, the prospect is terrifying.

To my right, on the front of a wide iron column, was "The Phone". Not an ordinary phone to be sure. Though I'd never seen it before, my mother had spoken of it and I knew what it could do. The device required no modern signal, no conduit, no cable. Nevertheless, it could place a call to virtually any locale, in this realm and in others. A call could even be placed to different timelines and alternate realities. I didn't of course know how to do any of those things. But I did know how to call my mother.

Reaching over, I pulled the receiver away from the base and punched in her number. She answered on the first ring.

"So you're down there. You've met the lodestone."

"Yes, it's beautiful," I breathed. The words seemed woefully inadequate, but there really *were* no words for what was spread before me. "I'm dizzy and weak. Is there a reason? Something I should know that you should have *already* told me, Mother?"

"Nothing to worry about. It affects everyone this way the first time. Do you have your almond oil with you? Rub some behind your ears, that will help. I've told you to

25

always keep almond oil in your bag, but very likely you've ignored me."

"No Mother. I have it." I figured there was no point telling her that not only was almond oil not in my bag, but that I didn't even actually have said bag. "Now I'm down here, what exactly am I supposed to do?"

"That depends," she said. "Do you see anything... unusual? Frightening?"

I didn't, but I let my gaze wander all around the huge cavernous space. There was nothing but the sea of shimmering black stone.

"No, it seems to me that everything's as it should be. Nothing but the magnetite."

"You're sure? Have you looked closely? *Very closely?*"

So she was going to insist on an aerial view. She was going to insist on *flying.* Which meant I was going to have to change, to *shift.*

"Do I have to?" The thought of it terrified me. I knew it was important. Probably even more important than I realized. Not much could distract my mother from her new beau and all things Paris, so the fact that she'd taken the time to get involved - even long distance - spoke volumes. "You know I've never done it before," I said, my voice trembling with fear.

"I understand you're worried about the pain. But this close to the lodestone, it won't be so bad. You'll be able to draw from its power. And you just have to. There's no other way for you to truly inspect the field."

"I'll try."

And I did. I tried, even though the pain was enough for me to beg for mercy, for death even. I tried, and I succeeded. Sort of.

I had wings at least. I'd been aiming for an eagle, the fantastic eyesight and all. But wings would have to do. Shifting of any sort wasn't one of my talents and I'd never once managed a full one. Not that I'd tried very often. The pain was just too much.

The wings I'd managed were a ravaged mess. I could feel the blood oozing from the wounds the wings had inflicted as they'd sprouted from my back. Wounds that would quickly heal, but for the moment at least, the pain was excruciating.

I took a deep breath and focused my intent, trying my best to ignore the new feathery appendages sprouting from between my shoulders. In moments I was airborne, and the pure joy of it made me forget about the pain, forget about everything. For the first few minutes of flight, I even forgot why I was flying in the first place, simply allowing my body to rejoice in the pure joy of being airborne. *To hell with the pain.* What I was feeling must be worth at least a thousand deaths.

I swooped down low, so low I could almost touch the magnetite and the lodestone beneath. I flew in a grid pattern until I'd covered every square inch of the massive field. There was nothing. Nothing but that beautiful rock and its vast tidal wave of power.

After a couple more passes, I reluctantly ended my flight and returned to the phone, half expecting my mother to no longer be there. Though it felt as if only moments had passed, my inspection must have taken the better part of an hour, and I wouldn't have been surprised, or even really upset, if she'd have given up and left me to it.

The fact that she hadn't, that she'd stayed with the phone the entire time, was another indication that my mother saw this whole alarm business as very serious indeed.

I wondered if this was one of those shit hitting the fan kind of moments, and if it was, would she be coming home?

"Mother, there's nothing there but rock. Nowhere. It's clean." As I spoke I could feel the wings disappearing, and the huge gaping holes in my back began to close. I was surprised at how sad that made me feel. Maybe Mother was right. I should do it more.

The initial pain I'd felt from the wings tearing open my skin had returned, and was beyond excruciating, not to mention the whole back of my dress was now torn and bloody. Wasn't sure what I was gonna do about that little detail. Especially since I was going to have to walk back to my car amid all the late night revelers that no doubt still crowded the sidewalks. I was bound to attract some unwanted attention.

Emmery will have to pick me up. That's all there is to it.

"Tula. Listen closely to me." My mother's voice held an urgency that was laced with worry, something I'd rarely heard from her. Worrying was something the woman rarely bothered with, even under the worst situations. "Somehow, someway, magic has been performed in the inn, or on the grounds. I don't know how. It shouldn't be possible, but it's happened. There it is. If you'd found something in the field, I thought maybe... Maybe that could have caused the alarm to sound. I'm not sure, but if there's nothing there, then either the spell isn't holding up or something or someone has found a way through it."

"OK. So what now? What am I supposed to do?"

"For the sheltering spell? Nothing. It'll have come from me. But, since I don't know what's caused this impossible situation, I haven't a clue what exactly I *can* do, other than strengthen it. Which I will do immediately. The good news is though, that I can do it from here." I could hear the relief in her voice from the realization that she wouldn't have to return home.

"So, our guests…"

"Do not, and I mean under any circumstances, say a word about this. Whatever happened is over. For now at least, everything is as it should be. So our guests have no reason to be notified."

"Well, if you're sure… Is there anything else you want me to do before I go?" I was certain she'd think of something, but I wasn't remotely prepared for what she then asked of me.

"Yes, you can kiss your sisters for me, and when you leave the basement – I mean, the second basement – I need you to pee in front of the door, if you don't mind."

"Pee… as in urinate?"

"Yes, Tula. I want you to pee, exactly as I said. It brings money to our door, as you should very well know, and also works to strengthen our defenses. You girls, you never study anything, do you?"

After listening to her once more remind me to kiss my sisters for her – this time she remembered to include Vicki and Caleb – my mom rung off and I was left with my final chore.

Peeing in front of the door.

29

Are you really going to do this?

Of course I was.

As I squatted down on the concrete slab in front of the huge metal door, my ankle turned, and suddenly my squat turned into a full on tumble. Panties around my ankles, my bare ass hit the floor, and I could feel the skin on my right elbow split open and begin to bleed.

Shit!

I looked beyond my splayed out legs and feet, and I could see a smallish tangle of vines snaking across the ground in front of the doorway.

Had they been there before? I didn't remember seeing them, but wasn't sure. The question was, *should* they be there? It didn't seem like vines would ordinarily be in a subterranean chamber, but what did I know? I made a mental note to contact Mother and ask her about it.

I stood, jerked up my underwear - *to hell with a bunch of pissing on the floor* - and started out the door. But then my thoughts turned to money, how well I liked having it, how awful it would be to find us all poor, and how I owed it to all the other Whitlows - even those who may yet come. Keeping our fortunes intact meant something. So I turned around, went back through the doorway, dropped my drawers and peed on the floor.

Of course I did.

When I got back upstairs to the lobby, the desk was empty. It was nearly midnight, so Vicki and Caleb had closed down and presumably were in their apartment. Probably both sound asleep. I was more than a little disappointed. I'd been looking forward to telling Vicki about my adventure of pissing in the basement below the basement.

I was happy to see that Vicki had, however, left me a sweet note. It said simply: Goodnight Tula, I hope you're still alive.

It's so nice to be loved.

I phoned Emmery and sat down to wait for her arrival.

By that time I'd completely forgotten about the little green vines and how maybe I should tell someone about them. My brain had already filed the vines away as just more unimportant trivia. Mentally, I was done with them.

As it turned out though, the vines weren't done with me.

Chapter 5

I was dreaming. I knew it was a dream because for one thing, the house was clean. No dishes in the sink, no dirty pots and pans crowding the counter tops, no clothes thrown around the living room floor, no litter boxes overflowing in out of the way corners. But the most obvious - and let me just say it was a wonderful departure from reality - reason that I knew I was dreaming was because there were no sisters. In my lovely dreamworld I'd been gloriously alone, living in an immaculate sister-free home.

Don't get me wrong. I, Talullah Rosamunde Whitlow, also known as Tula, do solemnly swear, that I love my sisters. I love my oldest - Emmery - in spite of her vanity. She never met a mirror she didn't love. And then there was her tendency to overindulge. No matter what Emmery did, from shopping, to boyfriends, to food, it was all about excess.

And she *does* have her good points, such as her love of animals. She'll take in any stray that crosses her path, hence the overflowing litter boxes and the constant reek of cat piss - a scent that Emmery claims to somehow never, ever smell, so of course she never tends to the little beast's filthy boxes.

As for Alafair, the youngest of us three - I love her as well, even though she's rarely sober and when she is, you won't find a lazier human on the planet. Alafair certainly excels in her way, as well. She has elevated the use of profanity to an art form. And she's an incredible cook, which is why our kitchen always looks like a bunch of angry elves have been at it.

Did I mention that Alafair barely stands five feet tall? Mother insists that she's still growing but the kid just turned twenty so I think that's off the table. I've always wanted to be one of those doll-like women, like Alafair. There's something about being petite. It seems to allow you to get away with things that taller people can't. Alafair's foul mouth is one example of that, but there are plenty of others. People just let her do shit. It's amazing.

I do love my sisters though, in fact I love them dearly. I just don't love them in my house.

And therein lies the problem. It isn't really *my* house. It belongs to all of us, at least until such time that I figure out a way to buy them out or run them off. Or maybe I'll get lucky and one or both of them gets married and moves away with some significant other to live happily ever after.

Happily ever after somewhere other than my house, or our house, depending on how you look at it.

But here we are.

If you're wondering how I can have such a conversation with myself while sleeping, let me explain that I have mastered the art of lucid dreaming. It comes in very handy, as I can usually direct my dreams quite easily.

And just as I was about to direct something wonderfully tall, dark, and handsome to knock on the front door of my dream house, another kind of knocking

- pounding really - coming from my *actual* front door pulled me from the dream.

Shit.

I pulled the covers back over my head, determined to ignore the sound until whoever was knocking gave up and went away. Or, even less likely, until one of my useless sisters might see to it.

I really, really wanted to crawl back into that dream. Not only was it sister-free but it had also been a welcome break from the blood and guts that typically met me in the night. And not just in dreams either. In fact, the scariest things I had to deal with were usually in the waking world. I hoped the knocking at my door at this hour of the morning wasn't signaling something along those lines, but it had that frantic kind of urgency that I'd come to dread.

I peeped out from beneath the blanket at the clock on the bedside table. 10 AM. Not as early as I'd expected but still, ridiculously early for anyone to be just showing up on your doorstep, pounding away. Visiting before noon was just downright rude.

Please, whoever you are, just leave!

I wracked my brain for a spell that might chase away whoever was knocking, and came up with a few. I am quite adept at conjuring birds from the sky. I could send down a rain of them on the head of my visitor. That would probably work. But I have some serious limitations with distance, I need to be within four feet of an intended target to make something like that work. If I tried it from bed I'd surely end up with a hallway full of flapping wings, bird shit on the rug, and maybe even an eye poked out.

Or worse. What if I started up some crazy apocalypse like in that Hitchcock movie, *The Birds?* It could happen. I could absolutely muck up that badly.

"I'm coming!" I finally shouted as I climbed from bed, threw on a robe, and ran from my bedroom.

As I went from the hallway to the living room, the sound coming from the front door began to take on even more urgency.

"Hang on!" I shouted. "I'm coming!"

The knocking abruptly ceased. Whoever was out there had heard me, so I mentally gave them Brownie points for a fair level of politeness.

I opened the door and standing in front of me was a very good looking man. Tall, dark, and handsome didn't even come close.

And then it occurred to me that he probably wasn't real.

No, of course he wasn't. Guys like that just didn't show up on your doorstep. Somehow I'd managed to conjure him from my dream.

As I stood there drinking him in, one of Emmery's pet birds flew over my head and out the door.

Mr. Cannot Be Real smiled and then without so much as a 'May I come in please', he walked right past me and into the living room.

Then I remembered that I was standing there in a open robe, t-shirt and panties on plain view. I decided that on the off chance he might be real, it might do for me to throw on a little something more.

"You stay right where you are," I told him as I made a mad dash for my bedroom. "I'll just be a second," I yelled back over my shoulder.

Back in my room, I got a good look at myself in the mirror. My hair looked like a bunch of mice had been playing tag in it, and the mascara that I hadn't entirely washed away the night before had smeared all the way down to my chin. On a good day people told me I looked like a certain very famous Aussie redhead. That would be when my makeup was perfect and I held my head just so. When I didn't smile and show the little gap between my teeth.

This was not one of my good days. No matter how I held my head, I wasn't gonna be able to pull *that* off. And I had no time for makeup. A strange, very good looking man – well *possibly* a man, but maybe a phantom – was waiting in my living room.

I grabbed up a hairbrush and did what I could with my hair, then threw off my robe and pulled a pair of jeans out of the closet and tugged them on over my hips.

Oh shit, my robe. Of course my visitor had gotten a good look at it as I'd run out of the living room.

I'd had it since I was sixteen years old and it featured a giant picture of Keanu Reeves emblazoned on the back. Young Keanu, when he was so gorgeous you could just about die by simply looking at him. But I mean really, at what age wasn't Keanu a god? My sisters had ordered the robe special for me, and it was my absolute favorite piece of clothing in the world.

But if my visitor is a real honest to Pete living, breathing, gorgeous man, what had he thought of a grown ass woman running around in Keanu Reeves fan-clothes?

Resolving not to give a shit, I poked a few fingers into my still semi-tangled mass of hair, swabbed some makeup remover under my eyes, took one last look at myself in the mirror and called it done.

Then I marched into the living room, sat down on the sofa and looked my guest right in the eye.

"So," I asked him, tucking my legs up under my butt and making myself comfortable, "Are you real or what?"

Chapter 6

My guest pondered for a moment, and then said, "Real? No one's ever asked me that particular question. Do you mean in a literal way or metaphorically? I mean, metaphorically, are any of us real? Is the world even real?"

Okay, so this guy, real or otherwise, had decided to be cute. Which was fine. I reckoned I could play that game as well. I could be as cute as anybody.

I was about to launch into some serious Nietzsche – *if you look into the abyss, does the abyss look back* – kind of wisdom when Alafair staggered into the room, clearly still somewhat intoxicated from the night before. She was followed closely by Emmery, who looked like she'd stepped right out of a fashion mag, the high couture kind where all the models looked like they'd just finished up with a night of sex or drugs, or both. But still gorgeous.

The universe is so unfair. I mean really. Just one single morning I'd like to see Emmery looking like crap, or at least poorly dressed. That would probably be enough.

Both my sisters pulled up short when they spotted our guest. Alafair immediately began tugging down her t-shirt, finally managing to cover her underwear, then sat down beside me on the sofa. Emmery glided across the room until she stood right in front of Mr. Tall Dark and

Handsome, then pointed a long, red-lacquered nail right into his face and looked back at me.

"Who is this?" She asked.

"I have no idea." I answered. "Could be he's not even real. I think I might've conjured him." I was only joking. By this point I'd concluded that our guest was nothing less than a living breathing human.

"Can I touch you?" Emmery interrupted, her mouth turned up in a sly grin. "I mean, I need to see. If you're real and all."

Our guest rose from his chair, then politely moved Emmery's finger out of his face. "If you don't mind, I don't want that thing going in my eye," he told her, regarding the spear-like nail with an admirable level of respect. "First of all, I'm very real, and can't imagine why that could even be an issue. Secondly, I'm here to find Talullah Whitlow. Would one of you ladies perhaps be this person?"

I told him that I was indeed Talullah and asked why he was looking for me.

"I'm here because Dale McMahan, from the Marshal's office in Charlotte, suggested that you might be able to help."

Hearing Marshal McMahan's name grabbed my attention in a serious kind of way. He ran the US Marshal's office in Charlotte and was my go-to guy when I needed some extra help. The arrangement was reciprocal. McMahan reached out to me when his office had need of someone with a 'special' kind of skill set. If McMahan had sent this guy, then I needed to hear what he had to say.

"I've found myself in a rather unusual situation," our guest continued. "A very bad situation if you want to know the truth."

"Damn it all!" Alafair spat. "I hate when people say that. No, *of course* we don't want to know the actual truth. Please, *please* tell us a lie instead." Alafair was looking at him with pure disgust. She had a thing about words and hated colloquialisms in particular. Also, I could tell she was more than a little hung over. "I think he must be real," she continued. "No conjured thing would be that fuckin' stupid. I wish I had my pants on so I could get up and get myself something to drink. Tula, go and get me and our guest a beer out of the fridge." And that quickly she'd gone from wanting to pull his eyeballs out to offering him a drink. My dear foul-mouthed sister was nothing if not mercurial.

"Shut up, Alafair." One more F-bomb and I was going to slug her. I needed to hear what this man had to say, preferably without her running off at the mouth like a fool.

McMahan sending the directly to my doorstep meant he thought it was something that needed immediate attention. And the fact that this guy was asking for me, in particular, well, that was because even though all of us sisters had done some work with the Marshal's office, McMahan regarded me as the sane one. Or maybe just the reliable one. Anyway, this man's situation was likely on the dark side if McMahan had recommended me specifically.

I was more than ready for a new case. It had been awhile since I'd had something I could really sink my teeth into. I was anxious to hear what our guest had to say, but I needed to focus. I needed caffeine.

"Emmery, why don't you fix us all some coffee? Could you do that please?"

"I suppose, but only because I want some as well." She turned to our guest, gave him a dazzling smile. "How do you like yours?"

"Black is fine, thank you."

"Beer for me," Alafair chimed in, but Emmery simply ignored her. No one was getting her any alcohol this early in the morning.

With Emmery in the kitchen, that left me with only Alafair to deal with. I wanted her out of the room as well, so suggested she might want to get dressed, to which she answered that I might want to eat shit and die.

Giving up, I turned back to our visitor and inquired if he might give us his name.

"Of course. I'm John Wheaton. I'm from Charlotte –"

"Ah shit. Not another John." Alafair interrupted. Her sensitivity to words extended to include names, and John was one she particularly disliked. "I swear they're under every single rock." She was glaring at our visitor as if she wanted to slap him into next Tuesday.

"Alafair, just let him –"

"Forget it, I'm outta here. My head's killing me and it's way too early for this shit."

As Alafair flounced out of the room, I turned my attention back to our guest.

"I'm sorry," I said. "As you may have noticed, my sister is somewhat..." I searched for a word other than crazy – finally came up with "...delicate. Yes, she's very delicate. But please go on. What is so important that

41

you've barged in and offended my sister and ruined my morning?"

Before answering, he reached into his pocket and pulled out a thin black case, the kind that holds licenses and credit cards, flipped it open and exposed a shiny gold badge. Above it, I could clearly read the letters F.B.I.

"Let's start over," he said. "I'm Special Agent John B. Wheaton. And I've got a body I'd like you to look at."

Of course there was a body.

"People like you come knocking, there's always a body."

"Maybe," he replied. "But this one isn't dead. And this one's my sister."

Chapter 7

An hour later, I was sitting in the passenger seat of John's ridiculously masculine Land Rover while he barreled down the highway.

We'd been on the road for about ten minutes when we came up on Henley Medical Center, but instead of slowing down and pulling into the parking lot, Mr. Tall Dark and Handsome just continued on down Highway 74 as if the devil himself were after us. His driving was erratic, frightening to be honest. It seemed to me that FBI agents should at the very least be able to handle an automobile.

Not this one.

"I thought we were going to the hospital?"

"I never said that."

"But your sister – you said she's in critical condition –"

"No, I said she was gravely ill. Not the same thing. And I never said she was in the hospital."

I thought about asking him where exactly she was then, and where he was taking me, but decided I didn't want to distract him from the road. Wherever we were headed, I wanted to get there with all my pieces still attached.

Better to just wait and see.

I sat quietly and focused my attention on the landscape that was flying by my window. Pines, pines, and more pines, with the occasional oak and maple thrown into the mix. Then, to kill some time, I checked the messages on my phone from that morning. I'd had two, both from Liz Montgomery who wanted me to know that she was sure that cougars had been at her chickens. A couple of weeks ago she'd been sure that it was wolves. Like I could do anything about either of those things. Poor Liz. She'd lost her husband the previous winter and had never quite been the same. And like a lot of the townspeople, she had this misplaced notion that as a Whitlow it was my responsibility to solve most any of their problems, including, but not limited to, those of missing or mangled chickens.

Her latch was likely not catching when she closed her coop. I made a mental note to get out to her place to have a look, then shoved the phone back into my bag.

From the incline of the highway, I could see that we were heading up into the mountains, every spin of the tires taking us further and further from civilization. We weren't yet in the boonies, not the real ones anyway. But almost.

So, she's in a cabin or a chalet.

And we were probably getting close. If his sister was as ill as he claimed, he wouldn't want her too far away from town and the hospital.

A few moments later he proved me right. Leaving the highway, John took a right onto Owl Hollow Road. Another mile and then we ran out of blacktop. The road was mostly dried mud with a thin layer of gravel that didn't do much to improve the surface. We bounced over deep pitted ruts, all the while dodging holes big and deep enough to immediately stall anything other than a four-wheel drive with a lot of clearance.

Which we were in, thankfully. This older model Land Rover Discovery was pretty much invented for rough travel.

I could tell by the way he navigated the road, the way he seemed to know beforehand when the worst sections were coming up, that he'd traveled it more than a few times.

"How did you find this place?" I asked him.

"The same way anyone does," he said, taking his eyes off the road long enough to flash me a smile. "I googled it. Couple of years back. I wanted a place out of the way, isolated, but within an easy drive from Charlotte. Found a cabin out here. The price was right, so I bought it."

His smile was one of those that made you feel good all the way down to your toes. That is, if you let it. I wasn't going to.

"How much longer 'til we get there?" Mostly I was just making conversation. I knew this road, much as I knew every single road and trail in the county. We had to be getting close to his cabin because very shortly this little stretch of dirt and gravel was going to end. Even a Land Rover wouldn't be able to handle the old logging trail that it eventually became.

"We've got a ways yet," he said. Which made me wonder if I'd been mistaken about the road ending, and then suddenly it did, just as I'd expected, right at the head of the old logging trail.

John pulled the keys from the ignition and opened his door.

"We walk from here," he said, looking down at my feet and my ridiculous little strappy sandals. "Sorry. I should have thought to mention there'd be some walking."

"Yes," I told him. "That would have been nice." It wasn't so much that the sandals would hurt my feet. They had good solid soles and were as comfortable as such a piece of footwear could be, but the snakes – rattlesnakes no less – these woods were full of them.

I let my brain bounce around all the possible things I might do to banish the slinky, vile creatures with their mariachi-shaking tails, but nothing came to mind. Nothing I could do with absolute confidence anyway. There were a couple of spells, but with my luck I might get rid of the rattlers only to bring on a pack of wild boars, or even bigger, meaner snakes. Cobras, for instance.

Then I remembered that I had, at least, brought along my bag of tricks.

I took a minute to rummage around until my fingers touched on a small bottle of cologne. Pulling it out, I sprayed a generous amount on my neck, then stooped over and repeated the process on my legs and ankles.

"Want some?" I asked, holding the bottle out toward John, who immediately took a large step back, turning his face away in disgust.

"What on earth is in that thing?" he asked, voice rising on each word.

"What do you think it is?" I asked him. "It's exactly what it smells like."

"It smells like mothballs."

Which was true, though I had no idea why, 'cause no mothballs had gone into it. I'd made the cologne myself, experimenting with various attractants, but what I'd ended up with was an accidental repellant. It seemed to repel lots of small creatures, insects mostly, but hey, it *did* smell a bit like mothballs and snakes typically steered clear of that particular odor. I figured it was worth a try.

"I think I'll pass," John declared.

Which was easy for him to say, him with his ankle boots and heavy jeans. Me in my summer dress and sandals would have to make do with stinky cologne.

"So, who buys a cabin that you can't even drive up to?" I asked. "How did such a thing even get built?"

"That trail used to be a road of sorts, I think. Once upon a time." He gestured toward the sides of the path. "You can see where the bushes are a lot thinner there toward the edges. But since the cabin was vacant for so many years, I guess the woods just took it back. Eventually I'll have it cleared, but in the meantime I've got no complaints. It's one of the reasons I got such a good price on the place."

After about a thirty–minute hike, we came to the cabin. It was pretty ordinary – on the old side, and a little run down, but not to the point of outright neglect. It was one of those cookie cutter versions, really just an ordinary frame house dressed up to look like log and chink. I'd seen hundreds of similar ones scattered all over the North Carolina mountains. In addition to the fake siding, it had a stone chimney running up the south side and a wide front porch that stretched all the way across the front. I knew, even though I couldn't see into the dark recesses, that the porch would have a slatted

47

swing, and at minimum, two wooden rocking chairs. Probably a stack of wood, and more than likely some sort of grill.

They were all basically the same. All of them complete with the trappings that second homers and tourists would deem necessary to complete the whole "hillbilly cabin" experience.

John ushered me up the walkway and onto the porch, where indeed, I saw exactly what I had expected. Same old same old.

He opened the door and we stepped inside, and that's where the sameness ended. The room we were in was no cozy mountain den, and not even a living area at all. It was a hospital room. Complete with a patient – his sister Gwyneth, I presumed, and if the stethoscope hanging around the neck of the old man hovering beside her bed was any indication, an attending physician as well.

The woman lying in the bed was youngish, early twenties I would guess, and in spite of her pallor I could see that she was lovely.

Lovely, but with a body that was partially covered in vines. It looked as if the growths had begun at the ankle, then spread upward, disappearing beneath the thin cotton gown, then emerging again at the neckline. The tiny little tendrils were snaking their way up her face, coming to a stop just above her jaw.

As we moved closer, I see that the vines almost appeared to be *breathing*, or even worse, maybe taking nourishment. They were inflating, then deflating, as if taking monstrous little gulps. I could feel the bile begin to rise in the back of my throat.

I had to look away, look at anything other than the horror unfolding on that bed, so I let my eyes travel the rest of the room.

The space was large, with tall vaulted wood beamed ceilings, but even so, the smell of death was strong. Suffocating even. Not that I needed to smell it to know that death had come to visit. A reaper was right there in the corner of the room, its hooded black cloak cascading down the length of its body and ending in a puddle on the floor. The thing was seated at a small dining room table, dealing itself a game of solitaire.

The creature gave me a dark look, then went back to its game. With reapers it's all about the waiting. What bores the rest of us simply excites the death angels. They love it. Waiting is their only game.

The man who'd been leaning over the young woman straightened up and walked over to join us at the foot of the bed. Both he and John seemed to be blissfully unaware of their card playing guest seated at the little dinette. Which was as it should be.

"How is she?" John asked him.

"She's worse. Her temperature went all the way up to 104, but I've gotten it down some now. But her oxygen is dropping. And her blood pressure." Then he turned to me and held out his hand.

"I assume you're Ms. Whitlow?"

"Please call me Tula," I said, and reached out to shake his hand. I pegged his age at somewhere in the late fifties or early sixties. His grip was firm, yet somehow gentle. Even though his eyes were full of worry and sadness, I could sense that in ordinary circumstances he'd be one of those people who was completely comfortable in his own skin, with a face that spent most of its time smiling.

I instantly liked him. Wanted to ease his terrible burden.

"Ms. Whitlow, this is my dad, Robert Wheaton," John said. "Doctor Robert Wheaton."

I turned to John and told him that things being what they were, he should dispense with the Ms. Whitlow as well. Tula would do. It only seemed the polite thing to do, though I'd determined to keep Agent Wheaton at a distance, I could see that we'd all be on a first name basis before this thing was done. Might as well start now.

It was just going to be that kind of situation. Gwyneth wasn't merely gravely ill. It was clear to me that she was being *invaded.* Relentlessly. I'd never seen or heard of anything like this before, and I had absolutely no idea how to begin to help.

Fortunately, I knew someone who might, but before I went to that someone I needed a piece of the vine and a lock of Gwyneth's hair. A lock cut at the stroke of midnight.

This   was   going   to   take   awhile.

Chapter 8

Over the next several hours, told to me in bits and pieces from both John and his father, I learned what had brought this beautiful young woman to be trussed up in a hospital bed in a cabin out in the middle of nowhere.

With a card-playing reaper patiently waiting inside the room.

If she'd initially phoned anyone other than her brother John, Gwyneth would have been in a real medical facility, rather than the makeshift one inside the cabin. But the young woman had always turned to her brother – he was her rock.

Three days earlier, when she'd phoned him at 2 AM, barely able to speak, begging for his help, telling some crazy story about not being able to find her husband Andrew, and vines growing out of her foot, John had been sure she'd taken some kind of mind-altering drug. It had been in the realm of possibility. He knew that his sister and her husband were fond of the occasional joint, and experimenting with hallucinogens had become a kind of trendy pastime, at least in certain circles. So he'd told his sister to lock the door of her room and wait, that he was on his way. He'd been afraid for her to drive herself to the hospital and was equally fearful of calling an ambulance. If there were any kind of drugs in the room, regardless of how trendy, she could face prison, depending on what it was and how much.

John knew his sister well, and beyond a little recreational weed, he'd never known of her taking any drugs, but try as he might, he couldn't think of any other explanation for Gwyneth's insane babbling. After giving her explicit instructions to stay put, he'd phoned his supervisors at the Charlotte field office and been granted emergency family leave. In less than an hour, he'd packed up the Land Rover and was on the road. Pedal to the metal, determined to make the normally four hour trip in just under three.

John had made only one stop, and that was in Asheville to gas up the Rover. While there he'd phoned his father, something he'd completely forgotten to do before leaving the city. After a few minutes of tongue lashing for not calling before he'd left Charlotte, he was able to convince Dr. Wheaton to stay put until he'd had a chance to find out exactly what was going on.

John arrived at Gwyneth and Andrew's motel room in the tiny town of Henley-on-Hale just after dawn.

At that time only a single tiny vine had been growing, its roots deeply embedded, tiny little leaves peeking out above the skin on top of her foot. Though she'd been near delirious with fever, his sister managed to communicate to him that she'd tried cutting the thing, but within minutes it grew right back. Pulling it from her skin seemed to be impossible as well. No matter how hard she tugged, the roots wouldn't budge. She'd even drenched the thing in RoundUp. Nothing worked. The vine remained and was spreading, getting longer, thicker, with more little leaves sprouting along the fat, bulging stem.

He'd wanted nothing more than to immediately get her to a hospital, but because what he was seeing defied every law of science, a hospital was out of the question. As someone who worked for Uncle Sam, he knew exactly what would happen if they got wind of his sister's condition. And if she was placed in a hospital, the chances her condition would become known to them were high.

The government had facilities reserved for just such things. The kind of places that people entered and very often never came out of. Even if they somehow managed to help her, he knew he'd likely never see her again. Those doctors would consider her always and forever something to be studied. Not a person with a family and hopes and dreams and everything that entailed.

She'd be just another specimen. Nothing more.

He was damned if his sister was going to become a lab rat, an experiment without end. Always and forever beyond the reach of her family.

He already had the cabin sitting and waiting right there, just outside of town, and together with his father, they'd discreetly set up her care.

I tried to imagine what it must have been like for them. The terror they must have felt, the doubts they must have had.

But what had led them to me?

I was about to find out.

"Gwyneth," John said. "She knew her condition wasn't ordinary. Knew it was outside of anything resembling normal. Knew something..." John had trouble saying the word, but it finally found its way to his lips. "She knew something supernatural was going on."

That conclusion obviously hadn't taken any kind of mental acrobatics. Vines don't grow out of people's bodies. Period. Full stop.

"She told me to find you. She'd come across your name online, had been trying to find a way to reach you. Said that you were legit. That you'd worked with law enforcement. I did some checking, found out you'd worked with the Marshal's office. Got your contact info from Dale McMahan."

I told him I wanted the whole story, from beginning to end. Everything that led up to Gwyneth and Andrew being in Henley-on-Hale, and everything that had happened since they'd arrived.

The whole thing had started with a contest. Gwyneth had entered herself and Andrew...

A perfect weekend getaway. A vineyard on the outskirts of Henley-on-Hale was looking for a couple to feature in a photo shoot for a new ad campaign.

Are you a beautiful couple? Would you love to have your picture taken walking the grounds of the majestic Cougar Creek Vineyards? Right in the heart of the mountains surrounding beautiful Henley-on-Hale?

I could see that Gwyneth was indeed quite beautiful and presumed such a beauty very likely had an equally stunning mate. I was sure she'd thought, *why the hell not?*

As he told me the story, John's face was a mask of hopelessness, sorrow, and *shame.* As it happened, he'd seen the flyer advertising the contest while visiting the vineyard on a weekend trip to his cabin.

He'd been the one to tell poor Gwyneth about the contest.

"Maybe if I hadn't none of this would have happened," he whispered. "Can you help us?"

I looked again at the poor feverish young woman.

"I'm sure as hell going to try," I told him. "Now tell me   more..."

Chapter 9

The story of Andrew and Gwyneth was one of love at first sight. The kind of story that millions of romance novels are written about, the ones that made you wish that the whole world could be just like that – all tidy and neat and finished up in one beautiful, tightly knotted bow.

Gorgeous, rich, Stanford grad – but not the snotty entitled kind, the sweet and shy variety – meets super smart but scholarship enabled Harvard man. Early twenties, both of them with futures so bright and shiny they'd be apt to fry your eyeballs.

To say that they were beautiful would be like saying cotton candy is a little bit sticky or that Kilimanjaro is a fairly steep climb.

They were amazing together. Each of them tall and willowy, Gwyneth with the grace of a dancer, Andrew with the kind of tightly toned musculature born of laborious work – he'd put himself through Harvard working summers at a sawmill, stacking logs from daylight til dark. Both of them had reddish brown hair – the lovely chestnut kind. Gwyneth's eyes were as green as emeralds, while Andrew's were lovely dark pools with lashes so thick it was hard to believe they were real.

They made a stunning pair, so when her brother had told her about the contest, she'd thought "Why the hell not?" It wasn't that she was a vain girl, but more a practical kind of realist, and she could look in the mirror, for God's sake, and she could certainly look at Andrew.

They were very good looking. She knew it was a random gift of genes, not a thing either of them had been required to strive for, so she felt no pride in it.

It just was.

So why the hell not indeed?

They'd been planning a trip to the mountains anyway. Though they both loved living in Charlotte – it was close to both their families, and they wouldn't consider living anywhere else – they frequently traveled to the mountainous areas of the state for weekends of hiking and kayaking.

And besides, she'd never been to a vineyard, and who doesn't love wine? An all expense paid trip would be a godsend to their tight but manageable budget.

So Gwyneth had entered them in the contest, and they won. The very next weekend, they'd made the drive from Charlotte to Henley-on-Hale to collect on their prize.

Cougar Creek Vineyards was nestled in a deep hollow, situated on just over forty acres about fifteen miles outside of the town of Henley-on-Hale.

They'd arrived late on a Friday evening and after a delicious country style supper of pan fried rainbow trout, homemade hushpuppies, and hash browns, they'd been installed in a lovely guesthouse right on the grounds.

The photo shoot had been scheduled to take place over that weekend, with most of the pictures being staged on Saturday, and a brief session on Sunday morning, followed by a brunch hosted by the vineyard.

Everything had gone smoothly. The photo sessions had been fun, and there had been plenty of time left over for exploring the grounds and even a couple of excursions into town. On Saturday night, they'd driven into the nearby town of Murphy and spent a couple hours at the casino where each of them promptly lost their twenty-dollar stake of "mad" money - Gwyneth at the slot machines, Andrew at roulette.

After Sunday brunch, Andrew and Gwyneth had packed their bags, piled into their Ford Explorer, and headed back toward the city.

That's when things got weird, when the odd thing happened, though at the time, Gwyneth hadn't attached that much significance to it.

The couple was just about to leave the city limits of Henley-on-Hale when Andrew had pulled the Explorer into the parking lot of a Days Inn and announced that he was simply too tired for the trip, insisting that they stay over in town and continue back to Charlotte the next morning. When Gwyneth had offered to do the driving so that Andrew could nap in the car, he'd refused, claiming that he needed a bed and a pillow, and what did it matter since both of them had arranged to have the following day off work anyway? One day in Henley-on-Hale wasn't going to make a difference.

Andrew assured her that he wasn't actually sick, but merely tired, that he'd barely slept the night before and so she needn't worry about him. He'd suggested that she find something to do to amuse herself, let him sleep for a bit, and then they'd have dinner somewhere in town.

Gwyneth wasn't entirely displeased with this change of plan. They'd passed several antique shops on their way through the town square, and she decided that while Andrew rested she would spend the day browsing the shops. Andrew hated shopping of any sort so she needn't feel guilty leaving him on his own.

She hadn't been worried about her husband at that point. After all, he'd said he was only tired. At worst, she figured he might be coming down with the same bug she'd experienced while they were at the vineyard. While there she'd vomited twice, each time was right after drinking some of their wine. As beautiful as the vineyard had been, their wine had been horrible, at least to her. Andrew had liked it fine.

But that had been the end of it. Thankfully, whatever had plagued her seemed to have passed. There had been some lingering queasiness, but no vomiting or anything else. Probably Andrew would be fine in a few hours as well.

So Gwyneth had spent a carefree day and shopped to her heart's content, thinking to herself what a great idea it had been to stay over in the quaint little town.

When she'd returned to the hotel that evening, she and Andrew had dinner as planned, then had gone straight back to their room and turned in early with a plan to get up at 7 AM to start the drive back to Charlotte.

But the next day, Andrew still refused to leave.

It had taken a flurry of phone calls but Gwyneth had made the necessary arrangements for both of them to get a couple of additional days away from their jobs – hers as a kindergarten teacher, and Andrew's from the law firm where he practiced in downtown Charlotte.

At that point, Andrew still didn't seem ill exactly – merely distracted. Several times when she'd spoken to him she'd had to literally touch him to get his attention.

He was so lost in thought that he barely seemed to acknowledge her existence.

But if he wasn't hearing *her*, he *did* seem to be hearing other things. Several times throughout that second day in the motel, Andrew had cocked his head to the side as if straining to listen.

"Did you hear that?" He'd ask her.

"What Andrew? What did you hear?"

"Music."

By the end of the second day, Andrew's condition was beginning to scare Gwyneth. He seemed even more distracted than he had on Monday, and in addition, he was beginning to *look* unwell. Dark circles under his eyes and a noticeable tremor in his hands were the two main things, and he'd also developed a pallor that was alarming. Also, there was the issue of not eating. As best Gwyneth could recall, her husband hadn't eaten since their first evening at the motel. Sunday night.

Gwyneth determined that the next morning he was seeing a doctor. One way or the other. If she couldn't get an appointment in town, then she'd insist he go to the emergency room.

But when she woke Wednesday morning, Andrew was nowhere to be found.

She'd been surprised, but not alarmed. She figured he'd perhaps just stepped out for a trip to the vending machines or maybe a quick walk. The idea that he felt well enough to leave the room was, in fact, a welcome development.

After about twenty minutes of waiting, when Andrew hadn't returned, she'd called his cell, only to hear it

60

ringing there in the room, from somewhere beneath the bedclothes.

Three hours later Gwyneth was at the county Sheriff's department, where she'd discovered, to her amazement, that they'd already encountered Andrew.

At 3 AM, a deputy had spotted a man stumbling along the ditches beside Gideon Road. It was strange to find someone walking along that particular deserted stretch of blacktop at that hour of the morning, and the deputy figured the guy was drunk, in trouble, or up to no good. All of which gave him reason enough to pull over, ask for an ID, and submit a field sobriety test, which the man had passed with flying colors.

The man's driver's license identified him as Andrew Nathaniel Lindstrom, of 361 Bells Chapel Road, Charlotte, North Carolina. Since Mr. Lindstrom was breaking no laws, and claimed to be simply walking for enjoyment, he'd had no choice but to send him on his way.

He had however, found the whole encounter quite strange so had written it up on his incident report.

That was the last time anyone had seen Andrew, but Gwyneth thought she knew where he must have been headed.

Cougar Creek Vineyards was off Gideon Road.

At her insistence, the Sheriff's office placed a call to the vineyard but they claimed that if Andrew had indeed been heading in their direction, he hadn't shown up, at least as far as they knew, adding that certainly the deputies and Gwyneth herself would be welcome to come and have a look around if they deemed it necessary.

Which they did, but turned up nothing that suggested Andrew had been anywhere near the place.

But Gwyneth wasn't convinced. Where else would he have been going? The deputy had come across Andrew less than a mile away from the entrance to the vineyard.

Andrew had to have been heading there. Nothing else made sense.

Not that any of it made sense.

Over the course of the day paranoia set in. Gwyneth became convinced that not only had Andrew made it to the vineyard, but someone there knew, and for reasons she couldn't fathom, they were hiding it.

That night, under cover of darkness she went there herself.

At this point, Gwyneth's recounting of things became hazy and downright weird.

The young woman was convinced that before she was even able to get past the gates, she'd been bitten.

By   *vines.*

Chapter 10

After listening to John recount what he knew of Andrew's disappearance and Gwyneth's midnight trip to the vineyard, it was clear to me that whatever had caused the young woman to end up in her current situation was directly tied to the place. And I intended to get to the bottom of it.

There were lots of unanswered questions, obviously, but the one I was most concerned with was whether or not whoever was in charge of the vineyard was behind it all, or was it perhaps something else.

There was no doubt that we were dealing with the supernatural, of course, but that didn't mean that it couldn't have originated somewhere outside the vineyard. I knew that whoever had put this in motion was evil, pure and simple, and I wasn't remotely sure that I was up to the task. Not on my own anyway. Very likely I'd need to call in the big guns – aka Aunt Ruby. But first things first.

"We need to go to the vineyard."

"I agree," John said. "Let's go now."

"Wait a minute. When I said we, I didn't mean you and me. First, I want to go on my own. Maybe take Emmery or Alafair."

"Look, I'm willing to step back and admit that whatever is happening to my sister defies science, defies everything I ever thought I knew about anything. And no question I need your help – but if you think I'm going to just take a backseat on this, you're wrong."

Here we go, I thought. Gung ho government guy meets magic. And he just doesn't get it. So what else is new? I was going to have to handle him, spend precious time on handling him, and I couldn't help but resent it.

"You'll have your part to play. But you've already been there. These people know who you are and if they're responsible for this, you'd better believe they'll be ready for you."

I was pretty sure the people at the vineyard would also know me and my sisters, might even guess that we were working to find Andrew, but that was okay. I *wanted* them to know. I had no intention of making a secret of it. But I didn't want John anywhere near the place until I learned more.

At this point I wasn't sure of much, but it was obvious that this was dangerous business and one person with vines growing out of their feet was quite enough for the moment, thank you very much.

"I can't just sit back and do nothing," John said. We were both sitting at the small dinette, the reaper right alongside us, the odor of dying flowers coming off it in waves. Doctor Wheaton was in the bedroom taking a well-deserved rest.

"Then don't," I told him. "Your dad needs your help. Obviously he can't look after your sister day and night. Besides, after a few hours I'll know a little more and if there's a way for you to help, you better believe I'll ask for it."

"It's just – I can accept there are things outside the physical world," he glanced over to the bed where

Gwyneth lay, his eyes clouded with worry. "How can I not? But it doesn't come easy. It's like I thought there were rules that governed everything. I *believed* in those rules. Completely. Now, I'm wondering if it was always just an illusion."

"And you're afraid."

"Hell yes, I'm afraid."

"I understand. But remember, none of this is new to me. I mean, what's happening to your sister – I've never encountered anything exactly like it before, but I can find someone who has."

"There is no new thing under the sun..." he murmured. "I don't know where I've heard that. Maybe the Bible."

Mr. FBI was telling me more than he intended, sharing thoughts that he probably never even dreamed he'd be having, much less discussing with a stranger. But it was that kind of situation, where barriers could dissolve and unlikely kinships might even form. I'd figured out a long time ago that when people are afraid, they usually show their true faces. If I was reading John right, he seemed to be simply lost.

But something was bothering me. He'd gone from FBI to "find me a witch doctor" awfully fast, even considering the situation. Still, his explanation of being afraid of what could happen if his sister went into the system was sound.

You're just being paranoid, as usual.

I looked at the watch on my wrist. It was nearly midnight.

I picked up my bag and pulled a pair of scissors out of the side pocket. I was particularly proud of them. They'd been given to me by my Granny Whitlow and had been

65

blessed by a seventh daughter of a seventh daughter, then dipped in the blood of doves.

"It's time," I told him, moving toward the bed. "I need to cut her hair."

The use of hair in relationship to witchcraft had a history so ancient that no one really knew where it came from. At least as early as the Druids, probably even earlier.

There is no new thing under the sun. John had that much right. In my game, that was something we counted on.

The reaper in the corner of the room looked at me and rasped, its voice papery thin and dead, "It isn't going to make a speck of difference," it said. "This one is mine."

Not yet she isn't, I thought. Not yet.

Chapter 11

The next morning, I rose before 5 a.m., determined to get to the vineyard early. A quick look at their website revealed that they opened for guests between the hours of 11 a.m. through 7 p.m. I thought about going earlier, but wanted this first visit to be as low key as I could make it, and showing up and banging to be let in before they opened would do the opposite.

Okay.

I made coffee, then set about the business of waking my sisters, not a task to be taken lightly. That morning I was taking no prisoners. Emmery got a face full of cold water, and Alafair a tiny little jab with a pin.

"What the hell are you doing? I'm gonna rip your damn eyes out." Alafair obviously didn't appreciate my little pinprick and was ready to do battle. I hurried out of the room and into the hallway before she could make good on that particular threat.

Standing in the doorway of the upstairs bathroom, wiping her face with a towel, Emmery glared at me and spat, "You ever do that to me again I'm gonna jerk you bald. Wait and see."

Yea, yea, yea. I'd heard it all before. Usually once a week at least. Yes, when the need arises, I can be brutal.

Thirty minutes later we were gathered in the living room, coffee in hand, each of my sisters still gleefully enlightening me regarding what I could expect in the form of retaliation for my morning ministrations.

"I'm gonna rip out your liver." This from Alafair. "And the next time I cook? Honey, you better have yourself a taste tester lined up."

I knew she wouldn't actually poison me, but putting something incredibly gross in my food was a distinct possibility.

"Me, I'm not *gonna do* anything," Emmery said. "I've already done it. It'll be a long, long time before you find your Keanu robe. Just sayin'."

"Okay, you're pissed," I told them. "I get it, and maybe I deserve it, so just do your worst. But we have a serious issue, and I didn't have an hour to spare begging y'all to open your eyes and get the hell out of bed."

My sisters were notoriously late risers. In fact, the last time either of them had been up at 6 a.m. would probably date back to some random Christmas morning when we were kids. Though that probably didn't even count because on those mornings, we hadn't actually slept, but stayed up the entire night in hopes of catching someone pretending to be Santa leaving gifts under the tree.

"So," Emmery said, "what is this big, terrible thing that's going on? Has it got anything to do with the alarm going off at the inn? 'Cuz I talked to mom yesterday and she said she'd taken care of that."

"Speaking of," said Alafair. "What was it like? The lodestone? It's so unfair that you were the first one to get to go down there. You should have brought us with you."

I reminded her that she had been falling down drunk, pulling rabbits out of hats, and that I couldn't have taken them even if I'd wanted to. Not without mom's permission.

"Whatever," Alafair sniffed, seeming content to drop the matter. Access to the lodestone was serious business and we all knew it. "So, *anyway*, yet again, what was it like?"

I told them it was black. Black crystal stuff, as far as the eye could see. How could I explain to them the power I'd felt there? The awe? The fear that had leeched all the way down to my bones when that same power had threatened to bring me to my knees?

I couldn't. The lodestone couldn't be put into words.

But flying could.

I told them about flying over the field of black magnetite. How I'd tried to transform into an eagle, but only managed the wings. Told them about the blood and the pain and then the sheer ecstasy of flight, the alien wonder of weightlessness.

"We all need to learn to do that," Emmery said. Even though she was the eldest, at twenty-seven years of age, she'd never before flown. I could tell she was more than a little bit jealous. "If you can do it, I know I can. And without the blood."

And I could see it in the set of her jaw. She'd do it. When Emmery set her mind to something, it was pretty much a done deal.

"What about Mr. FBI man?" Alafair asked. "You were gone with him all day. I assume that's what this whole dragging us out of bed business is about. This better be good."

So I told them. Told them about Gwyneth, the vineyard, Andrew. Told them about the vines and the reaper who'd been lingering in the room.

I laid a plastic bag out on the coffee table. In it was the lock of Gwyneth's hair and a cutting from the vines growing out of her body. Alafair picked it up first, then passed it over to Emmery.

"Grape vines," Emmery said, peering at the bag, running her fingers along the plastic.

"I assume so." I told her.

"No need to assume," she said. "These are muscadine cuttings. Granny used to grow muscadines, don't you remember?"

I remembered Granny used to have two or three grape arbors, but that was about it. I couldn't have told you what kind they were if my life depended on it. But back then, Emmery had been closer to Granny than the rest of us, so I wasn't surprised that she knew.

"I want one of y'all to go to the vineyard with me today," I said.

Alafair raised her hand and waved it in the air like a first grader who had stumbled on an answer to a question. "That would me. If there's wine involved, of course it's me."

"You're just a drunk aren't you?" Emmery said.

"Better a drunk than a bore," Alafair shot back.

My sisters were nothing if not original.

"Okay," I told them. "Alafair is with me. And then after the vineyard, I'm gonna have to see –"

"Aunt Ruby, of course." Emmery interrupted. "I'll let her know to expect you."

Our Aunt Ruby – if she really was our aunt at all, none of us were sure – was also known as The Crone, though no one dared call her that to her face. And The Crone didn't like visitors.

Rumor had it that sometimes said visitors ended up being fed to her pigs if they showed up unannounced. And being family, if indeed we even were, wouldn't make a damn bit of difference. There was the story of one of our distant cousins. As it happened, Aunt Ruby had a pig that she affectionately referred to as *Cousin* Priss. No one knew if she'd fed Cousin Priss to the pig, or if the pig was in fact Priss herself. Or maybe neither. Maybe Ruby just liked the name and had decided to bestow it on one of her sows.

What *was* known was that Cousin Priss hadn't been seen nor heard from in at least twenty years, and the last time she was spotted, she'd been on her way to Ruby's home at The Bluffs.

That much was undisputed fact.

But pigs or not, Aunt Ruby was the only one that I knew who might have an inkling on how to approach the whole vines growing out of your body business. There wasn't much the woman didn't know. If we were a coven, which we weren't, she would without question be our elder. She might be a bit difficult at times, and more than a little eccentric and unpredictable, but Ruby had forgotten more about magic than any of the rest of us would ever know.

And, Cousin Priss or no Cousin Priss, I kind of liked the woman. Admired her even. Aside from being one of the most powerful witches in the world, Ruby was also an award-winning costume designer. As in Academy Award.

She had three of those little gold statues lined up on her mantle.

Ruby split her time between Henley-on-Hale and LA, and as luck would have it, she was in town at the moment.

"Okay. We have a plan," I said.

"What about Mr. FBI?" Emmery asked. "Is he going with you to the vineyard?"

"Not this time. Absolutely not."

Chapter 12

When Alafair and I pulled into the parking lot of Cougar Creek Vineyards, John was already there waiting for us.

Shit. I wasn't used to having my clients look over my shoulder as I worked. I had a feeling with this guy, it was going to be an ongoing problem.

"I thought we agreed that you wouldn't be with us this morning." I was all attitude as I slammed the car door and marched in his direction. John was leaned against his Land Rover, hands shoved in his pockets, a determined set to his jaw. I didn't care how determined he was. If he wanted my help, he was going to have to play by my rules. "I think I was clear on that."

"I changed my mind," he said.

"Alright, I take it your sister's a lot better this morning then."

"No. She's about the same."

"Because it seems to me that if you still need my help, then you'd respect that I have control over how we move forward. The fact that you're standing here right now says to me she must be *much* improved and you've decided my services are no longer needed. Because you won't *have* my services if you continue to ignore me."

"What do you expect me to do? I can't just sit in that room... I can't look at her anymore. I just can't."

There was a bleakness in his tone that made me pause a moment to look past my anger and take in his overall appearance. This was a different man from the one who'd first knocked on my door. He seemed dramatically changed. There was no attempt at charm, none of the playful rancor he'd exhibited that first day. Special Agent Tall Dark and Handsome now seemed more like Little Boy Lost.

And that's exactly what he is, I thought to myself. *Lost, fearful, and borderline unwell.* His eyes were ringed with dark circles, and the scraggly stubble on his face indicated that grooming had taken a backseat to worry.

I decided that at least this once, I could maybe scale back a little on the bossy, and Alafair seemed to be thinking the same thing because she said that she didn't really see what it would hurt for him to come along.

"It's not like we're going in there undercover or anything, for God's sake," she said. "We're gonna be telling them why we're here, right? Just let him come with us."

"And it's not as if I haven't been trained by maybe the best investigative unit in the world or anything." John added. He was at least *trying* for some of the cocky attitude he'd exhibited on our first meeting, had already turned and started walking toward the entrance to the vineyard. "Could be you might even learn a thing or three."

Looking toward the gate, I could see that a small line of visitors had begun to form. Checking my phone, I saw it was about five minutes away from opening.

"Okay, fine, whatever. Let's go." I told them. Alafair kind of had a point. I had no real reason to refuse having

74

him along, and since the man was determined to ignore my wishes anyway, I really had no choice. Other than abandoning the case, and I wasn't about to do that.

Ten minutes later we were inside the gates and being escorted by an exuberant young greeter with a ponytail so tight it looked like it might pull her eyebrows right off of her face. We were headed to the main building where we could sign up for a tour, have a bite to eat at their cafe, or engage in some wine tasting.

Since we were there for none of the above, as soon as we walked through the doors, I headed straight over to the sign-in counter and asked to speak to management. I thought it rather odd that a vineyard would even have a sign-in desk, but I presumed it might have something to do with data collection.

After a little back and forth we were ushered into a large waiting area, furnished with three expensive-looking sofas bracketed by equally expensive marble-topped tables. The room had tasteful artwork hanging on the oyster colored walls, with recessed lighting, everything all soft and low-key. It was a study in the minimalist type elegance that's weirdly most often found in the homes and offices of those who have too much of every damn thing.

It was all very chichi Feng Shui stuff, obviously arranged by someone who knew a little something about interior design. If the room was supposed to invite relaxation and comfort, it was having the opposite effect on Alafair and I. Ours was a family that wasn't above drinking out of jelly glasses, and we arranged our furniture for the sole purpose of giving every single seat the best possible view of a TV screen. Never mind all that silly tranquility nonsense. Tranquility was overrated. If a person wasn't careful, they could tranquil themselves right out of existence. Tranquil got you snuck up on, maybe even killed.

Rooms like the one we were now in would instantly put a Whitlow on edge. Rooms like this meant somebody was trying to put on some airs. Trying to make those who entered feel a little bit *less than*. That's what this kind of shit was really all about, and my sister and I both knew it.

"I think we might be dealing with a bunch of uppity assholes," Alafair whispered as she looked about the beautiful waiting room. I nodded in agreement.

Very soon we were joined by a gentleman who introduced himself as Gregory Moncrieffe, who it turned out was not only the manager but part owner of the vineyard.

He looked exactly like what you'd think of when conjuring an image of a vineyard owner. Very sleek, with an air about him of someone quite cosmopolitan, probably a world traveler, definitely a wealthy man. Most certainly the kind of man who'd have signed off on their ridiculous waiting room.

Impeccable manners were on display as he nodded to each one of us in turn, getting our names, shaking our hands, smiling warmly throughout it all.

I instantly disliked him.

"What can I do to help you folks?" he asked, sitting down on one of the sofas, then indicating with a wave of his well manicured fingers that we should do the same. "Since I've already been told about your earlier visit, Agent Wheaton – I believe you spoke to my uncle Roger –

I assume this has something to do with Andrew Lindstrom. Has he been found?"

"No, he hasn't." John answered. "And you're right. That's why we're here."

"I'm so sorry to hear that. Andrew and your sister – Gwyneth, wasn't it – seemed like such a nice couple. And very much in love. But then you never know, do you? The local police seem to think he's probably just taken off. People do these things sometimes. Unhappiness can manifest in such strange ways it seems."

Okay. Lie number one, Gregory Moncrieffe was not sorry to hear that Andrew was still missing. Lie number two, I knew for a fact that no local cop had told him that Andrew had just simply *taken off*.

I had a bit of an "in" with the local cops. Even though none of them had any kind of supernatural powers, they were pretty good at their jobs, good enough to know a lie when they heard one anyway. And according to Sheriff Blaylock, the folks at the vineyard couldn't open their mouths without lying. He'd warned me that the Moncrieffes were hiding something, and not to expect a word of truth out of the bunch.

Well, when it came to lying, I could play with the best of them.

"Actually, we know he came back here. In the early hours of Wednesday morning, in fact." I knew no such thing, of course. "We tracked his cell phone to the gates." Also never happened. Andrew had left his cell phone in the motel room when he'd vanished.

I was on a roll.

I could see Moncrieffe's little brain working behind his beady black eyes. The man knew I was lying and was

77

busting a gut to call me on it. Since I was pretty sure that Moncrieffe had, for whatever reason, obviously taken Andrew, he'd know of course that Andrew hadn't had his phone with him. But he couldn't say that, because he couldn't admit that Andrew had come back to the vineyard at all. I thought about making the lie more believable, maybe tell him we'd found Andrew's phone in the grass by the gates. Something he couldn't be sure was a lie.

But I liked it better this way. Better if he thinks I'll lie at the drop of hat, even a lie that I have no hope of passing off as the truth, which I actually often do. Better for him to believe that I might just do or say any old thing, also a pretty valid concern.

The last thing I wanted was for this idiot to trust me. Better that he's unsure. Keep these assholes off balance. In games of strategy, and detective work often was just that, this type of double deception was usually a good play.

I could see him gathering his thoughts. Trying to decide where to go with this new realization that he was dealing with a woman who was at least as slippery as he was.

"Well, he might have come here, but he couldn't have made it onto the grounds," Moncrieffe finally said, a small smile of satisfaction playing across lips.

"How can you be so sure?" John asked. "You told me when I was here earlier that you have no security cameras, so maybe he did and you just aren't aware of it."

"No. Out of the question, because if he had, we'd have found a dead man, or at least bits and pieces of one."

78

Gregory Moncrieffe smiled, then rose from the sofa and headed toward the outer door. "Come on, it's better I just show you."

I was about to be introduced to the Fila Brasileiro. A dozen of them.

Chapter 13

I am a dog person – I dearly love them. Eventually I knew I'd own at least a couple. A dog is said to be man's best friend, although I kind of hate that sexist way of phrasing it. Dogs are of course's woman's best friend as well, maybe even more so. Anyway, dogs rock, and I've never seen a single one that I didn't instantly love, or that I was even a little bit afraid of.

End of story. Or so I thought.

But that was before I knew that such a thing as a Fila Brasileiro, sometimes called the Spanish Mastiff, existed.

They were huge beasts with super wide chests – kind of like baby rhinos – and long flopping ears, whip-like tails, and a way of looking at strangers like they were waiting patiently for one good reason to start ripping out throats, or maybe not. Seemed like the Filas might not wait for a reason. Maybe they'd rip your throat out just for fun.

I immediately knew I had to have one.

The dogs were in a large fenced area that bordered the woods at the back of the vineyard. I counted a dozen of them, ranging in color from light fawn to dark brown, with a couple of brindles thrown into the mix. Even with the six foot tall heavy duty chain link between us, I felt the need to keep my distance.

Their silence was particularly unusual and intimidating. I'd have almost felt better if they'd been barking or snarling. That, at least, I could have understood. They were guard dogs after all, and we were strangers. But they never uttered a sound, just watched, pacing us, mirroring our movements step for step on their side of the enclosure.

One brown and black brindle female in particular seemed to have focused her attention on me – if I moved just a little to the left, she immediately did the same, while also moving forward, getting closer and closer to the fence until her large black nose was pressed up against the steel mesh barrier. When Moncrieffe opened the gate and walked into the enclosure, all the other dogs rushed to his side, but not her. She lingered at the fence, her huge liquid brown eyes fixed on mine.

And then something seemed to pass between us, and I could almost feel her peering into the depths of my soul,making a judgement, then marking me just as surely as if she'd placed her brand on my forehead. For whatever reason, this dog had measured me, and found me acceptable.

Without even realizing I was going to do it, I reached out my hand and placed it against the fence. Underneath my palm I could feel her nose, then the long wet tongue licking my skin.

"Daisy! Here, dammit!" Moncrieffe yelled. But even after her owner's harsh command, the dog lingered for a moment more, then finally, with a deep whine and a wag of her tail, she left me, reluctantly joining the others.

"Looks like you made a friend," Alafair said. "I have to question that dog's taste."

"She's not like the others," I replied. "Can't you tell? She's not a killer."

"That's something I sure as hell wouldn't want to put the test," she said, turning back in the direction of the main building. "I've seen enough. When you guys are done, come get me. I'm off to do a little wine tasting."

"Okay. But keep it to a minimum. We've still got Aunt Ruby today and I don't want to drag you with me if you're gonna be sloshed."

"Yes boss. You got it." Though Alafair's tone was dismissive, I knew she understood the danger associated with the upcoming visit to our aunt. Even though we'd be expected, the woman was given to extreme mood swings. She might be in the pits of depression, or burning with anger, or maybe, if we were lucky, in love with the whole damn world and everybody in it. With Ruby there was no cruise speed.

I watched my sister hobble along the grass toward the main building – why on earth she'd worn four-inch heels was beyond me – then turned my attention back to John and Moncrieffe, who were carrying on a conversation through the fence.

"I can see why you don't require much else in the way of security." I told Moncrieffe as I stepped up beside John. "How long have you had these dogs?"

"Ever since we've had the vineyard – that'd be four years now. Of course, we got them as puppies, so for the first half year or so they weren't much use. And during that time they were being professionally trained."

"To kill?" John asked.

Moncrieffe laughed and shook his head. "Of course not. When I said there'd be a body if someone came on the grounds after hours I was only being dramatic. The dogs are trained to alert and detain. Never kill."

"I don't know about that." John looked pointedly at the dogs gathered at Moncrieffe's feet. "If I were you I'd make sure to keep my insurance policy paid in full."

I noticed that Daisy was holding herself apart from the other Filas, and as I watched, one of the larger males made a slight move in her direction and growled. This captured the attention of the other dogs and for a minute I thought they were all going to go after her, but thankfully, that didn't happen. It was obvious the poor thing was an outcast. I felt bad for her, but also somewhat pleased, being something of an outcast myself.

It took a bit of effort, but I managed to drag my attention away from sweet Daisy and back to the business at hand.

"So, after the weekend photo shoot, no one saw either Andrew or Gwyneth again?" I already knew this was what he'd told John and the local cops, was pretty sure it was a lie, but still – the question had to be asked. Again.

"That's correct. I'd say to go ahead and question the staff if you like, but I know the police have already done that. Twice. I think we've told you everything we can." To John he said, "That includes you as well, Agent Wheaton. I completely sympathize with your situation, but there is only so much disruption that I can allow. We're in the middle of our season here, you understand."

"A man is missing," John said. "A man who was last seen only a couple hundred feet from this vineyard. A man who'd just spent the weekend here. It's only logical to assume this could very well be where he was headed."

"And as I've already told you, if he was, he didn't make it." Moncrieffe stepped out of the kennel and spent a moment padlocking the gate, then looked up at John. I wasn't sure if the look in his eyes signaled a threat or a dare. Maybe a little bit of both. "I'm afraid I have to insist that this be the end of any further questioning of either myself or the vineyard staff. If you need anything more, you'll need to speak to our lawyer in Charlotte." Moncrieffe reached into his back pocket and pulled out a card.

"Here are his details. Feel free to contact him any time."

John took the card and tucked it into his shirt pocket. Though he didn't say a word, I could see the tension in his neck, the set of his jaw. I was pretty sure he wanted to take a fist and shove it into Moncrieffe's face.

"Well, thank you for your time, Mr. Moncrieffe," I said. The three of us were walking back toward the main building, and I could feel the dog's eyes boring into our backs. I looked over my shoulder, and there was Daisy, still well away from the others. She sat on her haunches, watching us go. I knew it was silly, dogs don't understand a hand wave of course, but even so, I held up my hand and gave my fingers a little wiggle in her direction. To my surprise, she answered with a sad little thump of her tail.

We were about halfway back to the main building when John stopped and pointed in the direction of a section of tall fence that separated the grounds from the forest beyond. The fencing was at least ten feet tall with a double gate set into its center.

"I thought you said you didn't have security cameras," he said to Moncrieffe.

At first I didn't see them. They were very small, set at about six foot intervals, running along the top of the fence line, pointing in the direction of the woods.

Moncrieffe shrugged dismissively. "I said we didn't have any security cameras monitoring the vineyards. Those cameras monitor the woods."

"Why would you want to watch the woods?" I asked.

"I guess you both weren't listening when I said no more questions, but I'll let you have this one." Moncrieffe was clearly irritated. It was easy to see he was done with us, but he went ahead and answered. "We're doing a study on the various types of wildlife in the area. My uncle is convinced there are still cougars out there. Ridiculous – I know – but even so. He has high hopes that they'll eventually make an appearance. You might be interested to know that he has cameras placed in various locations throughout the woods there as well. Stupid really, but there you go."

"A lot of people think they're out there," I said. "Mountain lions, cougars, whatever you want to call them, and plenty of people claim to have seen them. So maybe your uncle will get lucky." I thought about Liz Montgomery and her insistence that cougars were getting at her chickens. Maybe she was right.

"We need to see what those cameras have recorded," John said quietly. "Right now. Going back to the day that Andrew disappeared."

"So you think he walked through those woods, then climbed that ten-foot fence? Then braved the dogs?"

"I think I want to see those tapes."

"Get a warrant then. This is ridiculous. I'm done." Moncrieffe turned to me and said, "Ms. Whitlow, I'm

85

sorry if I've appeared rude. I haven't meant to, and I do hope you and your sisters, hopefully your mother when she returns, will consider taking us up on our invitation to join our community outreach program. We'd love to have you."

I had no idea what he was talking about. Knew nothing about any such invitation. Likely he'd extended it to my mother at some point. I wasn't surprised that she hadn't passed it along to any of the rest of us. Mother wasn't a joiner. That wasn't the Whitlow way.

I told him we'd give it some thought, though I didn't think I'd be able to overcome my dislike of the man enough to join him in any capacity, even one with a worthy cause. I'd pass the information along to Emmery and Alafair though, and they could do with it what they chose. I wondered how he knew my mother was away, but it wasn't a secret or anything. Still, it showed me that our family, for whatever reason, had come to be on his radar. I wasn't sure I liked that much. In fact, I was pretty sure I didn't like anything about the man. And it wasn't just that he'd seemed less than willing to help, I had a pretty good sense of people, and the guy was setting off alarm bells. I wasn't sure he was responsible for Gwyneth's condition, but I *was* sure something about him was off. I'd already put him well and truly in the bad guy column.

Alafair was waiting for us when we got back to the main building. She was a little bit tipsy, barely holding onto what appeared to be a large crate of wine.

"They gave us this! Just as a gift! Can you believe it?"

Someone had clearly discovered the way to my sister's heart.

86

Chapter 14

John and I arrived back at the parking lot first, with Alafair falling behind us as she was lugging the crate of wine – John had offered to carry it for her but she wasn't about to part with her new found bounty. I think we were all feeling a little bit soiled by our encounter with Moncrieffe. The man gave new meaning to the term oily. I was happy to be out of his presence, but knew I'd be back. Probably soon, and hopefully with reinforcements.

Because not only had I found him to be a distasteful individual, I was pretty certain he was dangerous as well. In particular, I hadn't liked the way he behaved with the dogs. I could kind of understand that the animals weren't pets, but even so, he'd seemed especially aloof. I believe you can tell a lot about a person by how they interacted with animals, and this man was cold.

It took all of my powers of persuasion – not my strong point I admit – but before we left the parking lot of the vineyard I was able to convince John that he needed to go on his merry way and leave me to do my work on my own, at least for the day. Taking him with me to Aunt Ruby's was out of the question. As an outsider, and an unannounced one at that, he'd be about as welcome as the flu.

I was thinking that surely a Special Agent with the FBI could find a better use of his talents than tagging along after me. Like maybe conjure up an illegal wiretap or

87

something? Lay up on the hillside with some binoculars, maybe apply some old-fashioned spycraft?

I'd have given a lot to know who Gregory Moncrieffe made contact with after our visit.

I was just about to tell him as much when he pulled out his cell phone. As soon as it came out of his pocket I could hear the faint buzzing of a text message hitting his inbox.

After a moment, he looked up at me, a grin of satisfaction lighting his face. I couldn't help noticing how nice that grin went with the blue of his eyes.

"It's receiving," he said. "Already. The guy didn't waste any time."

"Receiving?"

"Yea. I planted a bug in Moncrieffe's office."

"Don't you need a warrant for something like that?" Alafair asked him. "Right to privacy and all that shit?" Which was super funny, coming from her, because I knew that while she'd been exploring the vineyard, she'd been busy sprinkling frequency dust all around the place. I imagined she'd pretty well saturated it.

Frequency dust was our version of wiretapping. It didn't always work and was hugely dependent on a variety of different factors - weather for one. Though it could withstand a fair amount of rainfall, a downpour would kill it, as would several hours of very high humidity. And even when it worked well, often it wasn't clear enough, or there would be so much overlap that it would be hard to figure out who was saying what and to whom.

Still, you could cover a very large area at once, rather than a single office or telephone. Without anyone being the wiser. Overall it was a good thing to have in place.

John ignored Alafair's question. "I gotta go," he said as he turned on his heel and began walking toward the Land Rover. His movements were determined, eager even. Just like any Fed I'd even encountered, he was clearly excited by the prospect of a little domestic voyeurism. I'd always thought most law enforcement types were all master spy wannabes, and it looked like Mr. Tall, Dark, and Handsome was no exception.

But maybe I was being too hard on him. With what was going on with his sister, I guess it was no surprise that any amount of forward progress was worth celebrating.

Gwyneth. What was happening to her was sad and mystifying to me, but for him it must surely be a nightmare. To see something so alien and horrifying happening to a loved one was something I could only imagine. But John and his father were living it.

I reminded myself to be more generous, less judgmental. To keep my bitch–wolf inner self on a leash. At least for a while. Unless he really pissed me off, I'd save that side of myself for Gregory Moncrieffe and whoever else got in my way.

And they would. That was one thing I was dead certain about. I had no idea what Moncrieffe and his bunch were up to, but it was nothing good. And as sure as the sun was gonna rise, he was going to get in my way. No doubt about it.

But that was okay. Moncrieffe wasn't the first and wouldn't be the last.

He was hiding something, and it was all connected to the vineyard. I didn't believe his story about those security cameras on the back fence.

Something was in those woods. Whether it was something they feared or something they treasured – I wasn't sure. But was gonna find out. I'd be exploring that strip of forest soon.

But first I had to survive my visit with Aunt Ruby. Always an iffy proposition.

Chapter 15

I dropped Alafair at home – she was much too tipsy to visit Aunt Ruby, and besides that, I was super pissed at her. Turns out she hadn't sprinkled even a speck of frequency dust. Her four-inch heels had caused her to stumble in the vineyard's restroom and she'd dropped the entire packet in the toilet. I asked her why the hell she was even trying to sprinkle it in a *restroom* of all places. "Shit Tula! People tell all kinds of secrets in the john. Everybody knows that. Remember high school?" she'd said. "It was frequency dust in the girl's restroom that told us two-faced Jenny Frazier was screwing your boyfriend. You were happy enough to have it in the toilet *then*, I reckon."

She was right about that, but still. I was done with her for the day.

Finally rid of my troublesome little sister, I phoned my equally troublesome older sister who was working at the inn to make sure that the arrangements were in place for me to drop in on our aunt.

"She's expecting you," Emmery said. "And don't dawdle. Get up there as soon as you can. She was none too happy that I couldn't give her a specific time."

I told her I was going to run by Liz Montgomery's place first. It was on my way, and I'd had two more texts from the woman. I would've loved to pass the chore off to one of my sisters, but Alafair was probably still tipsy, and Emmery couldn't leave the inn until Vicki came in at four. So it was going to be me.

And seeing Liz would be nice. It had been awhile. So I really didn't mind, though I was a little worried about squeezing it in before my visit to Aunt Ruby. Being late for Ruby would be unthinkable.

So I ended the call with instructions – a plea really, no one instructed Emmery about anything – to call Ruby and let her know I'd be there in about an hour.

Then I burned a little rubber, something I normally wouldn't do, but at least it had me turning into the rutted driveway of the old Montgomery place in less than ten minutes. I pulled the Subaru up in front of Liz's tiny house and got out of the car.

The old place had definitely seen better days. The paint was blistered and peeling, the front porch had a dip in the middle that was deep enough for one of Ruby's sows to wallow in, and one of the windows was covered in plywood. If I didn't know different, I'd have thought it was abandoned.

I was walking toward the house, making my way carefully through the knee high grass when I heard the creak of a screen door opening and Liz Montgomery stepped out. She was a small woman, dressed in worn jeans and a loose fitting chambray shirt, her snow white hair cropped short against her skull.

"Don't step up on the porch Tula," she cautioned. "It might not hold you."

I watched as the old woman carefully made her way around the rotted wood then down the steps and into the yard.

"I was about to give up on you young lady," she admonished, then pulled me into a surprisingly fierce hug. Liz might be small and stooped and pushing ninety, but she was still strong as an ox. "You never texted me back."

"Sorry, I was driving. When did you learn to text anyway?" I teased her.

"Good lord a mercy! You can't get through this world without it now, can you? But of course I learned the same way you learn anything, didn't I? I saw it on YouTube. I reckon a body can learn just about anything on there."

I told her I was well acquainted with the wonders of YouTube instruction. That I'd managed to figure out how to operate our new dishwasher with just such a video. Then, though I knew she'd refuse, I offered to send somebody down to fix her porch and window. Liz Montgomery had helped our grandmother raise me and my sisters, and I loved her dearly. I was more than a little ashamed when it hit me that I hadn't been by even once since the death of her husband last year. I made up my mind that I was going to arrange for somebody to start work on her house before the day was done. I didn't care what she had to say about it.

"Tula you know I'm not one for handouts," she said. "I feel like a thief every time I cash the monthly check your grandmother's estate sends me."

"That's your retirement, Liz. You earned it. Thirty years working for Granny I'm sure you deserve every cent." I was joking. Most days my grandmother had made sure that Liz never broke a sweat. She fussed and worried over the woman something awful. Their relationship had been more than just an employee-employer situation. The two women had become like sisters.

I could remember the two of them on Granny's deep veranda, butts on each end of the porch swing, a bushel of green beans on the floor between their feet. Granny and Liz would be stringing while all us girls sat on the porch floor, waiting for the beans to be tossed down so that we could snap them and then sling the pieces into a gigantic metal tub. After that would come a week of Granny's pressure cooker going day and night, and then the root cellar would magically be full of gleaming glass jars of white half-runner beans.

For a minute I fantasized about having a big pot of those simmering on the stove, waiting for me when I got home. I couldn't even remember the last time I'd had any.

"What you thinkin' about?" Liz asked me. "You got that dreamy look in your eyes. Always dreaming. That's you Tula."

"Stringing beans." I answered. "How I used to love to help you and Granny when I was little. How I'd love to have a pot of them to lay into when I get home."

"Oh hell yes, I remember stringing beans," she laughed. "Nothing better than a pot of white half-runners, I reckon. Wish I had a dollar for every bean I strung with your granny. I could run off to Florida."

"I would love to send you on a trip to Florida. Will you let me? I'll even go with you."

To which she answered that I must have surely lost my mind. What in the world would she do in Florida? And besides she might end up like all the other old folks who went south and just never came back. She was of a mind that all that sunshine could addle the brain.

"And besides maybe going crazy from the sun, you know they all just go down there to die, don't you? Me, I'll just stay in Carolina. I reckon I'm doing just fine. Well, I would be if I could figure out what's killin' my chickens."

"Let's go have a look," I said, and we both started walking down the little dirt trail that led to the chicken coops. When we got there we were greeted by the squawking of a few fat hens pecking around in the feed scattered in the dirt.

"A couple of weeks ago I had more than a dozen hens and two roosters," she said. "Now, these'uns are all that's left."

I counted four – all hens, no roosters. Liz hadn't been exaggerating when she'd said something was getting at her chickens. Not much chance that in a couple weeks' time so many would've just run off.

"At first I thought it was coyotes, or maybe a wolf. But looky here," she said, walking around to the side of the coop. "Them's cat prints, ain't they?"

No sooner had I squatted down to get a closer look at the prints when the smell hit me. It was powerful enough to rise above the overall stink of chicken shit, and it was coming from just inside the woods behind the coops.

I looked at Liz and could see that she smelled it too.

"Oh lord a mercy..." she whispered. "Somethin's dead in there. Somethin' big.

"You stay right here," I said, then proceeded to follow the horrible scent into the woods. The odor seemed to swell around me with every step, and it was all I could do to keep from turning around and running back in the opposite direction. I was about ten feet in when I saw that Liz was right. Spread out on the forest floor right in front of me was all that was left of a big wild boar. And whatever had brought it down had chewed the thing right to the bone.

I turned away, but not before I could feel the bile rising into the back of my throat. This was bad. This boar hadn't just been killed. It'd been eaten.

I reached deep inside myself and sent my intent out into the forest. Searching, listening, trying to get a bead on what could have done this. But nothing unusual came back. There were squirrels, and birds, and toads, and I even picked up on a bobcat off in the distance. But that was it. And none of those things could have done something this savage to an animal the size of that boar. Even a bear would have some trouble taking one of those down.

But a cougar? Maybe. I wasn't sure. A bear would outweight a cougar, but they were clumsy fighters. And the black bears that populated our area weren't much for bloodshed of any kind. Unless they were starving or their cubs were under threat, they tended to be extremely timid creatures.

Whatever had done this was the opposite of timid.

When I stepped out of the treeline Liz was right there waiting for me.

"I was right wasn't I?" she asked me. "What was it?"

"It's a boar. Something's ripped it to pieces. Eaten most of it from what I can tell."

"Well, is what killed it still out there?" she asked me.

"Not right now, no."

If I'd been expecting the woman to be worried, I was dead wrong. That might come later, but right that minute, Liz Montgomery was simply enraged. She walked over and stabbed a finger down at the tracks in the dirt. "Those sons-a-bitches! It's a damn bunch of panthers, I know it." I was about to tell her that if it was indeed a panther or cougar or whatever you chose to call it, that it wouldn't be in a pack, but more likely a single animal, when she walked to the edge of the woods and screamed, "I'll be in there with my shotgun and then we'll see what you do! We'll see how you measure up against a damn bullet!"

It took a few minutes but I finally got her promise that she would do no such thing. The last thing I wanted to worry about was her off in the woods looking for some wild animals that had just killed a boar that probably outweighed her by eighty pounds.

"And don't you try to bury the carcass, Liz. I don't want you in those woods at all. Not until I figure this out."

"Well, I sure as hell ain't gonna try to bury a wild boar. Let the buzzards have it."

I assured her that I'd be sending someone down to check on her and replace the chicken wire that had been shredded.

"Whatever's out there'll be back, Tula."

"I know it will. Which is why I'm going to have your chickens taken over to the Millsap's place until we figure this out." The Millsap's farm was about a mile away and already had about a hundred chickens. Four more wouldn't make a difference and they owed me a favor or two. Jerry and Gemma Millsap were city people from

Charlotte, both of them retired dentists, who'd come to Henley-on-Hale with the idea of becoming farmers in their golden years. They were both good as gold, but about the worst farmers I'd ever seen. I'd used my intent to find a flock of sheep they'd somehow managed to lose. If I'm being honest, any idiot could've found them, but I'd done it quickly and hadn't charged them a dime. They'd be more than happy to help in a situation like this.

Before leaving, I tried to convince Liz to pack a bag and come with me back into town.

"You can stay with us," I told her. "It would be like old times. Emmery and Alafair would be tickled to death." I desperately wanted her to come with me. I had one of those really bad feelings that over the years I'd learned not to ignore

But she refused, as I'd known she would. So I did the only other thing I knew that might help. I cast a protection spell. It would take a dozen witches working together, under perfect conditions to cast one strong enough to really make much difference, but I thought I'd probably done enough to maybe cover the house. For a day or two at least. And I'd make sure Blaylock sent a deputy out to keep an eye on things as well.

I could see Liz watching as I drove away, standing on the edge of the awful rotted porch, a hand on her forehead shielding her eyes against the noonday sun. I thought of the acres of acres of forbidding forest that surrounded her property, the awful condition of wild boar's corpse.

98

And the prints. And the cameras in the woods behind the vineyard. Whether it was all somehow connected and if so, how?

One thing I knew for certain. The forest behind the Montgomery place was essentially the same stretch of acreage that backed the vineyard.

Finally I rounded a bend and Liz disappeared from view, but that bad feeling stayed right there with me.

Chapter 16

After I left Liz I headed out in the direction of Ruby's place, a sprawling estate she'd named "Willowbrook" in an area referred to as The Bluffs. Once upon a time The Bluffs were nothing more than a dozen or so old homesteads scattered over a series of flattened cliffs edging the river on the southern end of the county. Now it was home to the very, very rich. There weren't a lot of those in Henley-on-Hale, but most of them lived alongside my Aunt Ruby.

I couldn't even imagine what a building lot, much less a home, on The Bluffs would cost a person – more than a lot of people could earn in a lifetime.

But most people weren't Aunt Ruby. She'd freely used magic, brains, and beauty to secure for herself not only wealth, but pretty much anything else her heart desired. Unlike the rest of the family, she didn't buy into the whole idea of blending in, discretion, or anything that might limit her own appetites.

In a way I admired her for it, but then none of the rest of us had her skills, so even if I'd wanted to create for myself the same kind of lavish lifestyle that Ruby enjoyed, I'd probably only succeed in burning down our house, or the inn, or some equally devastating outcome.

I drove up the long winding drive, up and up, passing under willows and oaks and more willows – she hadn't named it Willowbrook for nothing. The trees were everywhere. I didn't know much about landscaping or trees, but even I knew that willows, weeping willows at any rate, were usually found along riverbanks, not growing along the side of bluffs. I wasn't sure that even Aunt Ruby's remarkable powers could be the reason these had somehow flourished. The willows of The Bluffs were kind of a mystery, even to Ruby herself.

When I finally reached the end of her drive, the land that lay in front of me was perfectly flat, kind of like a towering hillhad been sheared neatly off at the top, leaving an endless sea of emerald green grass stretching out to a backdrop of stunning mountain range.

Which was why this land was owned only by those with serious wealth. On the one side you had an uninterrupted view of the legendary rapids of the Hale River, and then to the back, a steep slice of the Appalachian mountains shadowed the entire vista.

I knew from experience that in the autumn the view was so breathtaking it could almost make you cry.

And if the view didn't do it, Aunt Ruby might. She was very good at getting people to cry – or laugh, or disappear, or any damn thing she pleased.

For about the tenth time since I'd decided on the visit, I wondered if I'd get out of there in one piece. The woman liked me well enough, but depending on her mood, basically anything was possible.

I got out of the Subaru and started up the cobblestone path to the short flight of steps leading up to the porch. The house was enormous. It was a low and sprawling structure, constructed of stone with huge swaths of beveled glass windows. Ivy was growing wild everywhere, its green spidery fingers spreading up to and over the gray slate roof. The sun hung like a bright golden orb above it all, surrounded by white fluffy clouds in a sky so blue it hurt your eyes to look at it.

Some people might have called it enchanting, but the idea of the pigs at the edge of the twelve acre property, one of whom may or may not be Cousin Priss, made it seem more like something Hansel and Gretel might have stumbled on while lost in the woods.

Before I'd even stepped onto the porch, the door opened and Aunt Ruby appeared, a big smile on her face, a fluted glass of champagne in each hand. God, the woman was beautiful. Hair the warmest color of blonde that money could buy, eyes that weird shade of amber, a color that wanted to be green but couldn't get past gold, lashes black as night, and smooth unblemished skin the color of fresh cream. And as if that weren't enough, the woman had been blessed with a captivating Mae West style beauty mark just beside her full red lips.

Even though she was more than twice my age – or even older, no one really knew –Aunt Ruby looked younger. Could have easily passed for one of my sisters, rather than an aunt. Which of course, she actually wasn't. None of us Whitlows knew exactly how Aunt Ruby figured into the family tree.

"Honey, I heard that old car of yours comin' up the drive and got these poured for us." She slammed one of the champagne glasses into my hand then pulled me into a fierce hug. "Look at you! I swear you've grown two inches since I saw you last!"

At twenty-five years of age, it had been more than ten years since I'd added even a fraction of an inch – well, not counting my butt of course – and I'd visited Aunt

Ruby just last month, but I certainly wasn't going to correct her. She also knew very well that I didn't drink. Not for the first time it occurred to me that my sister Emmery was a whole lot like Aunt Ruby – bossy, controlling, and more or less unwilling to entertain the idea that everything wasn't already exactly as it should be.

After she'd hugged me so hard I feared she'd rearranged every bone in my body, Ruby let me go, held me at arm's length and looked me up and down with those amber, cat-like eyes.

"Something is different..." she mused.

"Well, I've trimmed my hair a bit since I last saw you."

"Oh dear! I do hope you remembered to bury the trimmings. Please tell me you did? You wouldn't want some asshole to get hold of them. I've *told* you what can happen."

"Yes, of course I did." I well understood what people in the know could do with a bit of hair, were they so inclined. I thought about the bag I had in my purse, with Gwyneth's hair and the pieces of vine. Though my intentions were good, there was no getting around the fact that I was about to allow Aunt Ruby to violate the young woman, peek into memories and emotions that the she would never normally share with a stranger. Even though I knew it had to be done, I couldn't help but feel a tad bit sleazy for doing it without her permission.

Ruby was still looking me over. I couldn't tell if she was suspicious or just plain interested, but I was hoping for the latter, when suddenly her eyes widened in surprise and then comprehension.

"You've been to the lodestone," she said. "My oh my. Little Tula. So you were chosen. I always figured it would be one of the other two."

"Well, yes, I was down there. But I don't exactly think mom *chose* me. It was more like I was the only one available at the time."

"No. You were chosen. I can smell it on you." Aunt Ruby had taken me by the hand and was leading me through to her den, where we both sat down on an overstuffed corduroy sofa situated right in front of a huge creek stone fireplace. The thing was so big I could have easily stood inside it if the urge happened to strike.

Even though the day was warm, a fire was lit, as was always the case at Ruby's. Much of her power was concentrated in smoke, so you'd seldom see her without a fire in the hearth and a cigarette or pipe clenched in her fingers. As she made herself comfortable in the deep cushions of the sofa, she picked up a slim gold case off the side table, drew out an impossibly long cigarillo, lit the end, and continued the conversation.

"Your mother would have known you were the one. I'm surprised she hasn't already told you."

"I don't understand," I said. "My mother wouldn't choose me for anything. You know Emmery's her favorite. She doesn't make a secret of that."

"Your mother didn't choose you dear, though as I said, she'd have known of course. The *lodestone* chose you. Just as it chose her once upon a time."

"But what does that mean anyway?" The workings of the lodestone had always been a mystery to all of us sisters. We knew that Mother's famous sheltering spell depended on it, and that we'd been forbidden to go anywhere near the thing. But that was pretty much it.

"Why do you think your mother has power over the lodestone?"

"Well, I haven't really considered the question." And that was true. My mother's relationship with the lodestone simply *was*. I guess I'd assumed that she'd inherited the control when she inherited the inn, but other than that, it just wasn't something I'd even wondered about.

"Had she not been chosen, she could have brought a spell from the Earth Mother herself and the lodestone would have rejected it. She harnessed the power because it *let* her. She became the lodestone made flesh."

"So..." I was having some trouble wrapping my head around what Aunt Ruby was telling me. "Chosen by the lodestone? Wouldn't I have known it somehow? Felt something?"

"You will. And then there will be the handover. It's all really quite simple."

"Aunt Ruby, I know absolutely nothing about any of this. What kind of handover? Is it some sort of ceremony?"

"Well, it could be. That's up to your mother. If she doesn't hand it over formally, the power will simply leave her on its own and pass to you. But no ceremony is necessary, though it would be kind of fun! I haven't had my robes out in ages." I could see her eyes light up at the thought of a witch's ball or maybe a ritual feast. I'd only been to a couple in my entire life, so I knew they were rare occurrences.

"She hasn't said a word to me. Not a word," I told her.

105

"Hmmm. Well, I'm sure she isn't entirely pleased to pass the power on. Especially to you. You're right in thinking she'd have rather it been either of the other girls."

Hearing someone else voice what I'd felt my entire life was somewhat shocking. And sad. I'd always known that my mother had singled me out for indifference. I hadn't realized that others saw it as well. Knowing that they did made it hurt all the more.

"Oh, don't look so sad girl," Ruby said. "Your mother loves you, I'm sure of it. She just can't forgive your father for being the only man with sense enough to leave her. Other than him, she was always the one doing the leaving, and I'm afraid that's always colored the way she looks at you. It's not fair, but it is what it is."

"I didn't know my father left her." I hadn't known my father. I was pretty sure he'd been out of the picture even before I was born, but the circumstances surrounding his leaving had never been discussed. That wasn't unusual, none of us girls had known our fathers and my mother never spoke of any of them.

"Well, when he left it devastated her. I think he was the only man she ever truly loved. He was a handsome devil, your father, and a Scotsman. A laird as it happens." I wasn't sure exactly what that was, but I liked the sound of it. I'd always wondered about my father, but asking about dads wasn't tolerated. As far as our mother let on, they'd all been little more than sperm donors, which in truth wasn't unusual with Whitlow women.

"As far as the lodestone goes," Aunt Ruby continued, "don't worry. Your mother will be speaking to you soon. She'll have no choice."

Knowing my mother as I did, it wouldn't surprise me at all if she never said a word. Just sat back and let it happen without giving me even a hint it was coming. Then another idea occurred to me.

"Are you sure she knows?"

"Oh yes," Ruby answered. "She knew the minute the lodestone made its choice. I'll bet she was furious."

So, I would have the power of the lodestone. That was even bigger news than what little bit I'd just learned about my paternity. I barely even knew what that power meant. But I was now determined to find out and right in front of me sat one of the most knowledgeable witches on the entire continent. Also one of the most dangerous. I suddenly knew that I wanted her to prepare me, even if it meant having to spend hours with the woman – putting myself in absolute peril given her mental state – I had to do it.

"Aunt Ruby, can you teach me more?" I didn't want to be like my mother. Never taking anything seriously, only focused on the next manicure, the next boyfriend, the next shopping trip. She'd had the power of the lodestone as far back as I could remember, and beyond the sheltering spell, had never used it for anything. *That* would not be me. "Please? It would mean everything to me. I know almost nothing."

"Well, I don't know..." I could see her mind working, thinking about the hours she'd have to spend away from her garden, her books, her designs, and worst of all, having to endure a regular visitor.

"Please. You must." I told her, then, remembering the ongoing feud between her and my mother, I added, "Just think how it will infuriate Mother when she finds out you've taken me under your wing."

"Ah, now I'm tempted." Placing a long red fingernail at the tip of her chin, Ruby gazed out through the open window, and very gradually I could see her lips lift into a satisfied little smile. "I'll do it," she said. "Of course I will. It will be tons of fun. But you'll not disappoint me, will you? I seem to recall that you can have a very disagreeable side, Tula. It's the Taurus in you I guess, though I don't normally hold with all that astrology rubbish. But with you I have to wonder. Just know that I'll have none of your bull-headed nonsense. Not a spec of it."

"Of course not. I'll be perfect. I'll be so agreeable you won't even know it's me."

"You'd better." Aunt Ruby narrowed her eyes at me as if daring me in advance to even think about stepping out of line. "Okay. We'll work out the details before you leave. But now tell me. What brings you here today? Your sister - such a lovely girl that Emmery, agreeable too, might I add - insisted you were on a life or death mission. I rather think she was probably exaggerating. Am I right?"

"No exaggeration. I've never even heard of anything like this." I went on to tell her all about being contacted by John Wheaton, about Andrew's disappearance, the horrible affliction Gwyneth was now suffering, and their visit to the vineyard that I believed might have started it all. I didn't mention the fact that John was with the FBI, as Aunt Ruby, like most of us Whitlows, had a particular dislike of any type of law enforcement, and the higher up the 'cop' chain they were, the more that dislike increased. I figured even the mention of the Feds would send her into absolute orbit.

When I was done, I fished the bag containing Gwyneth's hair and the vine cutting out of my purse, then handed it over to her.

"I wish you'd gotten some nail clippings too," she said as she ran her fingers over the plastic, examining the contents. "This will get me something though. Even through the bag I can feel the energy. Something monstrous is at work here."

Ruby rose from the sofa, walked over to the massive fireplace and pulled down on an iron lever that was built into the side of the mantle. As she did, a large, shallow, cast iron tray lowered and came to rest about a foot above the flames. Then she stepped back, picked up a carpenter's level from a table next to the fireplace, and carefully checked the balance of the tray.

I knew of course that she was preparing to read the ashes, but had no idea there was any great importance placed on the receptacle being perfectly level. It occurred to me that I really knew next to nothing about magic, which made all this lodestone business even more confusing. Perhaps, unbeknownst to me, I actually had some crazy mad talent. Maybe I was a witch that could someday rival Aunt Ruby. I almost laughed out loud at the thought. It was that ridiculous.

Still. Maybe I was *something.* Something kind of *way* cool. Something that would make Alafair and Emmery steam with jealousy. I couldn't wait to tell them. I imagined the look on both their faces, imagined Alafair blasting me with a truly epic stream of profanity, and Emmery blasting me with – well, whatever heavy, deadly object she could lay her hands on. Imagined myself sitting back, reveling in their envy, all smug and happy.

It was a pretty picture, no doubt about it. I let myself fantasize for a minute or two about how that would all go down, then turned my attention back to what was happening at the fireplace.

Little wisps of smoke were starting to appear above the cast iron tray, which now held bits of the vine and strands of Gwyneth's hair. Aunt Ruby was standing by, mumbling something I could barely hear, her body swaying every so slightly, but in an ordered, *intentional* kind of way. Like some practiced dance to music only she could hear.

For some reason, seeing her like that, so wrapped in the magic, stirred in me a great loneliness. I was on the outside looking into something I very much wanted to be a part of, and that was like a shot in the heart.

I did want to belong. For the first time in my life, I realized I wanted this. I wanted this world of magic and everything it entailed. I wanted what Ruby had. All the years wasted, looking at the whole thing as if it were some kind of a joke, only half real, I regretted every minute I'd spent that way. I wanted it all.

And maybe I could have it.

The idea of what was possible brought a smile to my lips, and without even realizing I was doing it, I stood, walked over to the fireplace and joined Aunt Ruby.

And then I heard the music too. Finally, the music was mine.

Chapter 17

We danced for what felt like hours, but in truth was only minutes, and when it was done, I felt as if I'd run a marathon. Not in the exhausted kind of way, but more like every nerve ending in my body was jazzed, tingling with excitement.

It was energy. Pure energy. And for the first time in my life I felt what it was like to drink my fill of it. And I wanted more, I wanted to drink it in until my body was full to bursting.

Aunt Ruby was now taking a tiny brush, collecting the ash from Gwyneth's hair and the vine, carefully transferring it into a small copper plate. When she was done, she carried the plate back over to the sofa, laid it down on the coffee table and began to study the contents. Without turning away from the ashes, she said, "You heard the music, Tula. You know you'll never be the same. It's an enormous responsibility, you understand."

"I know," I whispered, wondering how I could have spent my life not knowing. The realization that magic was more than spells and incantations and simple craft. It was the earth and the moon and the stars and the ocean and... life itself. The burden of knowing was both heavy and weightless all at once. A piss poor description really, as any such attempt to describe it would be.

There were simply no words.

I tried to bring myself back to what was happening in the room. Aunt Ruby was speaking, and it wouldn't do to ask her to repeat herself.

"This young woman, Gwyneth you said?" I nodded that was correct and then she continued. "She's being invaded, obviously, and she's very near death. Her spirit is floating somewhere between the here and the afterlife, but at the same time being pulled into an entirely different plane. A terrible place. If that pull is successful, the poor girl will be a captive forever. I see..." Aunt Ruby, put her finger into the ashes, stirred them around a bit, then put a tiny bit of ash on the tip of her tongue. "Oh, no, no, no..."she moaned. The look of fear and disgust on her face was enough to take my breath away.

When she finally spoke again, her voice was little more than a whisper.

"I can hear her screaming. If we don't stop this - this abomination - she'll scream for a thousand years. She'll be lost until there's nothing left but the screams."

"It's the vineyard, right? It's the Moncrieffes. We have to stop them."

Aunt Ruby took a long time to answer. I could see the wheels turning over in her mind, see her trying to come to some sort of a conclusion. Finally, she pushed the ashes away and leaned toward me, her eyes as intense as the red-hot embers glowing within the dying fire.

"It started in the vineyard," she said. "I could feel it when the vines wrapped around her foot, feel it when they bit. It went deep. And yes, the Moncrieffes are behind it all. Their presence is strong in those vine cuttings, and I sense an insatiable greed."

"But how can we stop it?"

"Her husband," Ruby answered. "You have to kill him."

"Andrew? But..."

"You have to kill him, Tula. Andrew *is* the vine. Then you have to burn the whole place to the ground."

Chapter 18

I left Ruby's with a draught she'd concocted for Gwyneth. Then I had John meet me at the turnoff to The Bluffs and handed it over to him, making sure he understood that it probably wouldn't cure the poor girl, but hopefully would at least slow down the invasion. At this point, any kind of help seemed huge.

I watched from the roadside as he sped away in the Land Rover, then when he was out of sight I nosed the Subaru out onto the highway.

The trip back to the inn was an adventure. I was alternately driving too fast and then too slow, my mind was just everywhere at once, but decidedly *not* on the road. A few times I even let the wheels drift off the roadway onto the grassy shoulder.

The euphoria and power I'd briefly felt when Aunt Ruby told me about the lodestone, then the sheer purpose and joy when I heard the sacred music – all of it had disappeared.

Ruby had just told me I would actually have to kill a human being. To save Gwyneth, Andrew would have to die. Knowing that he might no longer be himself, might now be some sort of monster or demon, helped some. But was it going to be enough? Would I be able to bring myself to do it?

The idea of it was enough to make me sick.

Somehow I made it to the inn without crashing, where I still had the sheriff to deal with. Emmery had called right before I'd left Willowbrook to let me know he was waiting for me there.

"And hurry up if you would," she'd begged me. "The man's going to eat through every damn scrap of food in the place if I don't get him out of here soon, plus I'm sick and tired of him trying to look up my dress." Sheriff Blaylock was known for his hearty appetites, for food, women, and drink. In fact, he was one of the few people I knew who could out drink Alafair, or at the very least hold his own against her. The two of them had kind of a running competition whenever they ran across each other at Trout's.Right now, I was pretty sure Alafair still had the edge, but the man was giving her a good run for her money.

I had so much to do, between contacting Mother, dealing with Gwyneth, and now the sheriff, for a minute I felt like just backing out of the parking lot, going home, crawling into bed and pulling the covers over my head.

And then there was the issue of John. Eventually I'd have to tell him about Andrew. That was a conversation I wasn't looking forward to having... "Oh by the way, Mr. FBI agent, my crazy aunt says the only way to save your sister is to kill your brother-in-law. Post haste."

That was really going to go down well, and anyway,I had about as much killer instinct as a puppy dog. And now I was supposed to somehow just be okay with murdering Andrew?

The whole thing just seemed utterly hopeless. Being a naturally optimistic type of person, it was unusual for me to feel this kind of despair. And I didn't like it. Not one little bit. Of course I'd never really been face to face with a life and death situation like this before. Never even dreamed I'd be faced with these kinds of choices.

After a while, I was beginning to bore myself. My little pity party had gone on long enough.

I got out of the car and walked toward the entrance to the inn. Maybe seeing the sheriff was just what I needed. Whatever else Sheriff Blaylock might be, boring wasn't going to be in the mix.

As soon as I walked into the inn I spotted him. He was standing over Emmery, clearly having decided that trying to look down her blouse might even be more fun and likely easier than trying to stare up her dress. Especially since Emmery's blouse was already showing more than it covered. At least the first four buttons were undone and I wondered if she'd done that just to spite old Blaylock.

"I'm here," I trilled, putting on my very best fake 'good to see you' grin. I watched in amusement as Sheriff Blaylock reluctantly pulled his gaze away from Emmery's impressive cleavage.

My bosom isn't bad, I mean, I can hold my own, but I don't have the *goods*. Not like Emmery anyway. I could see Blaylock giving me the once over and I could also pinpoint the very second that he decided I might just do. In a pinch.

He strolled across the lobby to meet me at the door.

"Tallulah honey. It's good to see you," he said. "I hear you've been up at Ruby's. Brave girl, you."

"Yeah. Thankfully she seemed actually happy to see me, so it wasn't so bad."

Blaylock gave a little shudder and shook his head. "Better you than me, girl. Better you than me."

"Let's go sit down," I told him. "Inside or out?"

"Oh I'd love to go out on that fancy deck of yours for a bit." The deck at the inn *was* pretty spectacular. It overlooked a section where the Hale River formed a small waterfall, then fell away over large black boulders before it rolled on beyond a huge bend and finally disappeared out of sight.

"Me too," I told him. "C'mon, we'll round up a table." I asked Emmery to send out some coffee – to which she answered by rolling her eyes and shaking her head – and led him out the back door. The coffee, I knew, may or may not arrive. Maybe better if it didn't. Blaylock would probably linger till he'd drunk the whole damn pot.

The deck was mostly empty – lunch time was well past and only a few guests were still lingering. I saw one of the shapeshifters sitting alone, toying with her dessert. Looked like it had been strawberry shortcake. I was thinking to myself that I hoped there might be a bit left for me. I was suddenly starving, and no wonder. I hadn't eaten anything since the night before. At another table sat Mr. Gibbons, some sort of dark magician, and across from him was Joe Canary, an invisible man whose specialty was bank robbery, though as often as he had to take shelter, I had to assume he wasn't much good at it.

I steered Sheriff Blaylock to a nice table at the easterly corner, well away from the others. When we both were seated, I asked what I could do for him.

"Thing is Tallulah, something weird is going on with the grass."

"The grass? Our grass here at the inn?" I thought about it and as far as I could tell nothing was going on with the grass except what was always going on with it.

117

It grew, it got cut. Every two weeks, like clockwork. "If someone is complaining about our landscaping Sheriff, they can kiss my ass."

"Good Lord no, nothing like that. Your grass is fine, I reckon. Well, except for the strip out back that's dying. But it's not just your place, it's all your neighbors too. It's like somebody painted a line or something."

"I don't understand." I tried to picture what he was describing, but couldn't.

"Listen. It's hard to explain. Ok, imagine that a giant hand took a brush and just painted a line all the way across the county, and in those painted areas, everything died. That's what we got here." He sat back, folded his hands in his lap and began nodding his head up and down as if satisfied he'd offered up a good explanation.

"I don't get it. Are you saying you think we have a giant somewhere in Henley-on-Hale? Running around with a magic paintbrush?"

"Holy hell, Miss Tula!" The Sheriff never called me by anything other than my full name, so I reckoned that he must be pretty frustrated. I wasn't sure if it was from the situation or myself. "I know we don't have a damn giant. At least I hope to hell we don't. That would be a first. But that's for you to figure out."

"Me? Why me?" I could feel my anger rising. With everything else I had on my plate the last thing I needed was some stupid issue with dying grass. Though there was something about his story that tickled something in the back of my mind.

But what the hell did I know about grass anyway?

Which is exactly what I tried to explain to him. I'd gotten control of my temper, knowing it wouldn't do any good to lose my shit. And Blaylock wasn't doing anything unusual. He came to me for pretty much every damn thing so why should now be any different. Still, I told him I wasn't the kind of expert he needed. I advised him to call someone at the university.

"That's what their agriculture departments are for," I said. "One of those professor types would be foaming at the mouth to come down here and solve some kind of grass emergency."

"Well, there's a little more to it than *just* dying grass. Whatever's causing the grass to die seems to be killin' anything it runs up on. Small animals – we've found dead field mice, a opossum or two, and you know old lady Crenshaw? It got her little yorkie the other day."

I told him I agreed it sounded terrible, but still didn't see how it was something I could help with, or even needed to worry about. It was obviously some kind of poison, but probably nothing supernatural. I did however make a mental note to walk the grounds of the inn. I wanted to see this weird strip of dead grass for myself. Again, the little tickling at the back of mind. Something I needed to remember, something important.

"I think this *does* concern you," he said as he took a long drink from his mug of coffee. "It concerns you a lot. You see, the dead grass stops right here at the inn. Comes right up to the foundation out back and that's the end of it."

"Okay..." That was a bit concerning, but still.

"But that's not all. A little bird told me you've developed an interest in Cougar Creek Vineyards."

"So?" I wasn't entirely surprised that Blaylock knew that I'd been nosing around the place. Everyone in

Henley-on-Hale seemed to instantly know everyone's business. Trying to keep a secret around this place was a fool's errand.

"So... this crazy strip of dead grass. Guess where it starts?" He asked me.

"The vineyard?"

"Yep." Blaylock took another swallow of his coffee, then stood to leave. "Starts at the vineyard and ends right here at the Whitlow backdoor. I'd say that's a little concerning, wouldn't you?"

"Shit." I didn't believe in coincidence. It had to be connected.

"Shit indeed," the sheriff answered, standing up and readying himself to leave. "Tell Alafair I look forward to seeing her tomorrow night at Trout's. I'm gonna beat that little she-devil this time. They're gonna be having two for one shooters so she doesn't have a prayer. Tequila shooters. Nobody can match me with king Cuervo."

I knew Alafair wasn't going to be drinking Cuervo at Trout's the next night, or any other night in the foreseeable future. We had way too much on our plates right now for that kind of bullshit. I was gonna need all hands on deck.

Then a thought occurred to me and I shouted after Blaylock, who was already heading through the door.

"Wait a minute, sheriff. When did this start? The grass dying?"

He thought about it for a second, then said, "Best I can tell, three days back."

I considered a moment. As soon as the Sheriff had started to explain the whole dead grass issue an idea had begun to form in the back of my mind that it could be connected to my involvement in this case. But if it had begun three days ago, that was before John even showed up at my door. And right about the same time that Andrew disappeared.

So, it might have plenty to do with what was happening to Gwyneth. Vines, grass dying, I mean it was all agriculture more or less.

Then that little tickle at the back of my brain became a full-blown memory.

The basement under the basement. Vines. Growing out of the base of the rock, and running across the threshold. Vines that I'd ignored, even though Mother had asked me if I'd seen anything unusual. I'd meant to call her back and tell her about them, but hadn't. Maybe because finding vines in a basement didn't seem that out of the ordinary- I'd figured it was just growth from some little crack that I couldn't see, had thought there were probably plenty of them – so I'd let it completely slip my mind.

I hadn't even considered the precious lodestone right there, beyond the vines. Just thinking of the mere possibility that it might be under some sort of attack almost brought me to my knees.

A week ago if someone had told me that vines were dangerous, I'd have laughed in their face, but that was before I'd seen Gwyneth. And obviously those weren't ordinary run of the mill trailing little green creepers. What if the ones in the basement weren't as well?

Five minutes later Blaylock was out of my way and I was in the lower basement, standing on the walkway over the field of magnetite and the lodestone below.

One day earlier there had only been a few fingers of vine. Now there was a green twisted sea of the things. They'd sprouted all along the sides of the basement walls and were growing right toward the field of magnetite.

Almost there.

Almost to the lodestone.

Time to bring out the big guns.

Time   to   call   up   the   dead.

Chapter 19

Calling up the dead probably brings to mind some huge weird ass ceremony underneath a waxing moon – or maybe a waning one. Since I'd never done any kind of ceremony at all, much less one to summon the dead, I wasn't sure how the whole thing worked. And luckily for me, I wasn't going to have to figure it all out.

We had some dead right under our own roof.

At least three of our guests would qualify and I knew just the one I was going to start with. Not only was he dead as a doornail, but he was smart as hell, and gave the lie to what my mother thought about vampires – that they were all hideous, bloodthirsty monsters. This particular vamp was easy on the eyes, and if I wasn't badly mistaken, he kind of had a thing for me.

And even if he didn't, he was a vampire that could be bought. I knew that from past experience. He'd worked for me a few times before. So the next major item on my agenda was a visit with Victor, the only vampire ever allowed to shelter at our inn.

But first things first. I had some catching up to do.

I placed a call to John, who told me that Gwyneth had improved somewhat since they'd given her the draught. The vines weren't dying or anything as dramatic as that, but her temperature had fallen some and she was beginning to get a little bit of color back. Which meant it might be doing more good than Aunt Ruby had assumed.

Maybe it was going a little further than just halting the growth.

I spent a few minutes bringing him up to date on my visit with Ruby - when I'd met him earlier, there hadn't been time. He'd just taken the draught and immediately headed out to make sure Gwyneth got it as soon as possible. I told him that there was no doubt that his brother-in-law was somewhere on site at the vineyard, and that my first order of business would be to find where they were keeping him.

As for the rest of what I'd learned from Ruby, I told John just enough to let him know that Andrew was at the bottom of it all, just not the 'maybe having to kill him' part. But then, John wasn't a stupid man, and he wasn't about to let me keep him out of this investigation, so I was going to have to break it to him eventually. Assuming Aunt Ruby was right, and that Andrew was now some kind of evil thing, directly responsible for his wife's condition.

When I was finished with John, I gave Emmery the rundown on my visit with Aunt Ruby, Sheriff Blaylock's news, and the vines making their way toward the lodestone.

When I was finished updating Emmery, I left the lobby and started up the staircase that led to the second floor. The scent of lemons was heavy in the air, which meant someone had been polishing the wood railings, a job my mother had made us kids do just about as soon as we were tall enough to reach them.

At the top of the stairs I walked down to the end of the long hallway, stopping in front of the very last room.

There was a big number six painted on the door. Victor's room. I gave the wood a few sharp knocks.

After a moment, the door swung inward and there he was, all six feet four inches of him. Dark wavy hair falling down into his violet colored eyes. He was shirtless and wearing a pair of black leather pants that hugged his body like a second skin.

Victor called out my name, and then with great enthusiasm, pulled me into a freezing cold embrace. Handsome though he might be, vibrant though he might look, there was no mistaking that cold. Victor was about as dead as dead could be.

Finally letting me go, he gestured for me to come on into the room. I took a seat next to the window, as far away from the big brass bed as I could get.

"I'm so glad to see you love."

"And I you," I told him. "Been meaning to pop in and say hi. Has everything been okay with you?"

"Right as rain. Always is here at the inn." He made himself comfortable on the unmade bed, leaned his back against a huge stack of pillows, stretched his long leather clad legs out and crossed his feet at the ankles. I noticed that he had beautiful feet, long and narrow, with perfectly formed toes and what looked to be a very recent pedicure.

"Speaking of," I said, "what brings you to us this time around?"

"Oh, you know. Same old same old."

"With you there's always a woman involved. Was this one living or dead?"

"Now Tula, you know I don't break those rules. Only the dead ones for me." Then his mouth spread into a grin

125

that I'd have called sweet if he hadn't chosen that moment to give me a little peek at his fangs. I knew he was teasing me, showing off just a bit. "Though with you I'd be more than happy to make an exception. Whenever you're ready."

"Oh hush, Victor. You know as well as I do that can't happen. Not in this life anyway." Truth was, I really didn't want him to hush at all. I loved listening to Victor speak. He had one of those beautiful lilting Irish accents that seemed to be full of sweet damp earth and soft rainfall, endless fields of wildflowers and bumblebees.

"I don't see why not," he replied. "If I'm not mistaken, it almost did last time I was here."

He was right about that. I'd allowed him to kiss me even. Or at least I was pretty sure I had. The whole episode was kind of hazy, almost like a dream. I wondered if he'd somehow managed to glamour me that evening, though I was supposed to be immune to such nonsense. I was attracted to Victor, there was no denying that, but then any woman would be. Being near him was much like sharing space with some kind of Nordic god. Very hard to resist even without the glamouring business. But then, there was that *cold*. I was pretty sure I'd never be able to get past that.

I straightened my body in the chair, let the smile on my face change into my very best 'this is all business' kind of look, and told him I needed his help. I explained to him about Gwyneth, Andrew, the vineyard, and even a little bit about the Moncrieffe's maybe waging some sort of sneak attack on the inn. I outlined what I wanted him to do, and what I'd be willing to pay. When I was done, he dug his long white fingers into the pocket of his leather jeans and pulled out an ancient old timepiece on a fine gold chain.

"Sounds interesting," Victor said as he peered down at the watch. "As of now I'm on the clock. Presuming that we can come to an agreeable payment arrangement, that is. What you've offered is generous, but not quite what I'd say it's worth. I mean, it could be dangerous."

Leave it to a vampire to try and squeeze you. Be it blood or money, they'd go for every last drop, every single time.

"Okay, name your price."

Which he did. His price was nearly double what I'd offered plus dinner with him when the whole thing was done. Which I was pretty much okay with as long as I wouldn't be on the menu.

After agreeing to his terms, I gave him instructions for the evening. As Victor listened, he was rummaging through the closet, pulling out various garments, holding them up for inspection, and then tossing them on the bed. I couldn't help noticing that all of them were somewhat gaudy, bordering on flamboyant even.

"Where is my damn paisley shirt," he mumbled. "I know it's in here somewhere."

"It doesn't matter what you wear," I told him. "You can go bare ass naked if you want to – you're going to be *vapor*, remember? No one's going to see you."

"You never can tell, Tula. And you know me. I always want to look my best, even if I'm invisible."

Then he turned and gave me a wink and added, "But you're right, you know. My absolute very, very best is, as it happens, bare arsed naked."

"Just get out there as soon as you can, please. This is life or death here." I reached into the closet that was filled to bursting. Victor had so many garments hanging there that it was no wonder he couldn't lay his hands on any one particular item. My intent was to pull out any old thing, but suddenly I could feel an odd sort of pulsing, almost like some invisible thread tugging my fingers. Magic was coursing through me, unbidden, unexpected, but there it was. I let that tug lead me toward the middle of the hanging garments and my hand, almost of its own accord, latched onto a piece of fabric. It was the paisley shirt, wedged between a pair of velvet jeans and a ridiculous faux fur blazer. I pulled it from the closet and tossed it, hanger and all, in his general direction. "Here. Get dressed," I snapped. "Go. I'm not paying you to dig in your closet."

"Ah, Tula. Nothing I love better than a resourceful witch. Especially one as lovely as you."

I hoped his assessment of me was right. On both counts. But especially the resourceful part. I was going to have to be to come out on top of the shit-pile I was currently under.

Chapter 20

After leaving the inn, I went home to grab a sandwich and then changed into my creepy crawling costume – camo all the way. Loose jeans with plenty of pockets and a tight fitting t-shirt underneath a hooded fleece jacket. Even during summer, nights in the mountains could be cold as a witch's tit (no pun intended), and besides, the heavy sleeves would help with the dozens of thorn bushes and the blood-thirsty bastards that spent the summer pretending to be mosquitos. They probably *were* just plain old mosquitos but the little beasts were so vicious I sometimes had to wonder.

I had just finished filling the deep side pockets of my jeans with an improbable assortment of goodies – perfume (yeah I know, but you never can tell when perfume might come in handy), switchblade, lip gloss, hunting knife, high-powered lightweight flashlight, matches, compass, Hershey's kisses, and then after a second's hesitation, I shoved my Glock down into the bag as well. I'd just zipped everything up when I heard a car pull up outside in the drive, followed by heavy footsteps crossing the porch.

I had the door open before John even had a chance to knock. Like me, he was decked out head to toe in camouflage.

"I feel a little ridiculous dressed up like GI Joe," he said. "I hope we don't stop anywhere on the way. I don't know how I'd explain this. Maybe say I'm hunting?"

"God no. It's not hunting season. People around here take that shit seriously. They might knock you on the head or something if they got the idea you were hunting out of season. Anyway, nobody's gonna look twice. You're in camo heaven. In case you hadn't noticed, plenty of folks around here wear this shit to church."

"I feel like an idiot."

"It suits you anyway," I told him. And it did. I could just see him on the front of a U.S. Army recruitment poster. Strong square jaw, about a million shiny white teeth, short hair, lots of muscle. Maybe a bit on the lean side of Rambo, but he'd do.

"Do you think this is all really necessary? The camo and everything?" He asked.

"Well, you heard Moncrieffe. He says they have cameras scattered out all over the woods. We need to find out why, unless you buy his whole thing about scopin' for wildlife."

"Yea, you're right, and no I don't buy his explanation. But you know, this get-up isn't gonna hide us from cameras."

"Duh." I reached into my pocket and pulled out a small black electronic device. "I have something a little extra."

"What's that?"

"It's a jammer. Once I activate this bad boy, it's gonna murder any wi-fi signal within 50 yards." I put the little box back into my pocket. "I'd have figured an FBI type like you would've already thought to bring one of these along."

"Well, I *did* think of bringing *these*, so maybe I'm not hopeless." He held out a bag, pulled it open and inside were two pairs of night vision goggles. I had some in my bag too, but didn't have the heart to tell him. *Let Special Agent Wheaton have his little moment.* Tucked right up next to the goggles I saw the glint shiny black metal of a pistol. Not sure how I felt about him being armed, I decided not to mention it. I had, after all, brought my own, so I really had no room to argue.

"Anyway," John continued. "I think I already mentioned that my work primarily deals with analytics."

"So you haven't spent a lot of time in the field with the bad guys?" I asked him.

"I'm up for it," he said, raising his chin a bit, kind of daring me to say otherwise.

"Okay then, 007, let's go."

Then we piled into the Land Rover and were on the road. John suggested I drive since I knew where we were going. Most of the ride passed in silence. John seemed to be lost in thought. I got the feeling he was stewing over something he might or might not end up telling me.

I had plenty on my mind as well. Victor, for instance. I was wondering if he'd gotten to the vineyard yet, hoping he had. I was also worried about the vines trying to gobble up the lodestone, about being chosen by the lodestone and what the hell that even meant. Not to mention worrying about the little adventure John and I were about to undertake. A lot could go wrong and though I knew next to nothing about Moncrieffe and his motives, I knew he could possibly be dangerous. You could see the meanness in him. It literally came off the man in waves.

And then there were the dogs. The big Filas that were Moncrieffe's security force. That was one big whopper of a worry. I just hoped the things didn't have access to the woods. I was glad I'd stuck the Glock down in my bag. Shooting a dog wasn't my idea of a good time, but I would. I'd do it before I let them turn me into their next chew toy.

Not the one called Daisy though. I was pretty sure she was a sweetheart.

Regardless of my various worries, I was really getting a kick out of driving the Land Rover. It had a kind of masculine power that I wished more actual men possessed. I had it pointed east, heading out of town.

My destination was an old logging road, barely worthy of the name. It was really more akin to a trail, but it backed up against the vineyard woods, so it was perfect. With a little luck we'd be able to sneak right in, ending up in the exact little piece of forest where Moncrieffe claimed all the video cameras were located. Cameras for tracking the movement of mountain lions, something I probably should be worried about, but wasn't. Not about the cameras *or* the big cats.

The cameras I'd already figured out how to deal with – my little jammer thingy – and the cats, well odds were they didn't exist. Most people around our part of the country loved to believe they did, but even the most die hard believers would admit, if pushed, that they were likely just a piece of local legend. Nobody reliable would ever swear to have actually *seen* one.

But then again, maybe the cats *were* there. I knew for a fact that plenty of things existed that were never actually seen, so if there were some big cats in those woods, it wouldn't exactly shock the pants off me. And seeing as how we were gonna be ditching the car and taking about a half mile on foot, I was sure planning on keeping that in mind. And anyway, mountain lions or no mountain lions, just my fear of snakes was enough to make me want to turn around and go back home. This whole little piece of business was nothing I was looking forward to. Especially in the dead of night. But there was really no other choice.

I didn't believe for a minute those cameras were there so that Moncrieffe and his uncle could go all Peeping Tom on a bunch of wild cats.

No, those cameras were meant to keep watch on something else. And I intended to find out what that something else was.

I had just turned off the highway onto the gravel road that led to the logging trail when John finally decided to speak.

"Look, I need to tell you something I've found out, though it really isn't mine to tell," he said, eyes cast down as if he were ashamed, or maybe just worried. He was a hard guy to read. "Dad says that Gwyneth is pregnant." He looked over at me and I could see that he was terrified. So, not shame, but worry. "Probably three months along."

I didn't answer for a minute, trying to wrap my head around the fact that the need to hurry the hell up had now increased by about a million.

In the end I just said, "Oh."

A baby. Damn. And I had almost no idea at all what was going on at the vineyard, much less how to stop it. I thought about Ruby and what she'd said about the possibility that Andrew would have to be destroyed in order to save Gwyneth. Andrew, who was about to become a father. I wondered if he knew.

I was probably going to have to let John in on Ruby's assessment, and I wasn't looking forward to it. FBI dude that he was, killing civilians was gonna be even more out of his wheelhouse than it was mine, especially now that said civilian was his soon to be his niece or nephew's father.

God what a mess.

I felt like jumping for joy when we finally got to the end of the logging trail, and the entrance to the woods beyond. Give me an ocean full of sharks or a hundred acres of the meanest wild cats in North America. I'd take either of them any day over having to deal with a bunch of human drama. I put the Rover in park and pulled up the emergency brake.

"Ready to rock and roll?" I asked.

"Why not. Let's hammer." John had finally managed what looked like a genuine grin, and I was surprised to find myself grinning back.

Let's hammer. That expression was new to me. Maybe some kind of FBI talk. I'd never heard it before. But it made me think I should have brought one, or even two. A hammer, especially if you had two of them, one for each hand. When you stop and think about it, a hammer is a damn fine weapon.

I resolved to add a couple to my trick bag next time out, and then, John following close behind me, we headed into the woods.

Chapter 21

Fifty yards into the woods, I smelled it. The odor was hanging there, somewhere under the pine needles, dead leaves, and gray slimy moss. Strong and ugly. Like our cat box at home on steroids. A very large, very effective dose of steroids.

This was kitty-cat major league stuff here.

"You smell that?" John whispered. He was looking around like he expected most any second for something to jump out from behind a tree, claws outstretched, ready to take his face off.

Could be he was right.

"Of course I smell it." How could I not? I also smelled a little bit of cucumber. Copperheads. Give me a saber-tooth tiger over a copperhead or rattlesnake and I'd take it. Always. At least you'd likely see it coming.

"Maybe Moncrieffe wasn't just making stuff up," John declared.

"You think?" I was being sarcastic, unduly so, but that's what I do when I get nervous. Mountain lions and copperheads will do that to me every time. And a cat smell this strong would only come from something big. Really big.

"We have to keep going." He said it in his best 'I'm the FBI and you'll do as I say' kind of voice, as if he thought I might be ready to turn around and head back to the car. And he was one hundred percent correctemundo. I was ready, alright. Didn't mean I was gonna do it.

I thought of Gwyneth with the vines eating her up, and the baby she carried inside her.

"Of course we keep going. Just keep your eyes open, hand on your gun." I told him. "If it's a cougar it'll probably just stay away from us. That's what they usually do."

Like I even knew. What I knew about cougars, mountain lions, panthers, whatever you wanted to call them, you could put inside a thimble. A very small thimble. But I knew a bit about bears and was hoping that a big cat's behavior in the wild would be comparable. Which was kind of like assuming that dogs and elephants were pretty much twins.

Clearly I was at a complete loss. Out of my depth didn't even cover it.

We continued on, stepping a little more softly now, a little more slowly. I'd already activated the jammer, so I wasn't overly worried about Moncrieffe having sounded the alarm and sending goons out to meet us. Could be he'd stationed some of his guys out here though. Assuming we were right, and the cameras were for more than just spotting cougars, anything worthy of surveillance might be important enough to have sentries as well.

We'd gone maybe another fifty yards when we hit the edge of Dead Buck Creek. Though us locals called it a creek, it was probably technically a river. Dead Buck was about eighty feet across, bubbling with rapids. Not the big ones like you see people kayaking on, but the smaller, gentler ones that were good for tubing. I'd tubed this creek myself about a hundred times, though never this particular section.

I'd warned John before we even set out that we might have to cross Dead Buck, and luckily, fording it here wasn't going to be any big deal. The deepest part wasn't even two feet, but it was gonna be cold. Not to mention slippery. And there were lots of big bad boulders to crack open your skull if you fell the wrong way.

I hoped he'd taken my advice and worn shoes with decent soles. Waders would've been good to have, but I hadn't thought of it in time for either of us to run out and buy some. And that wasn't the type of thing I had on hand. Also, I'd always heard that waders sometimes made things worse. Might keep you a little less cold, a little less wet, but they were clumsy as hell.

I saw the prints before we stepped into the water. Dozens of them, right there in the mud on the creek bank. I knew nothing about tracking wildlife, but it looked like a cat to me. Judging from the size and depth, I figured a momma cat and her babies. A big momma. And not so little babies at that.

The largest of the tracks was about four inches at its widest, and as best I could tell maybe a half inch deep. I wasn't Daniel Boone or Davy Crockett, but even I knew that meant the tracks were left by something big and heavy. For a cat anyway.

I wasn't an expert, but Emmery's cats typically left about a hundred prints on the hood of our cars each and every day, so I had *some* authority at least. And the ones on the mud by the creek looked like those same prints, only magnified. About a hundred times over.

Exactly like the prints outside Liz Montgomery's chicken coop. If this was the same animals, they'd already killed a large sized dog. Wouldn't be much of a stretch to think they'd be dangerous to humans as well.

John had spotted them as well, and was bent over, peering at them intently through his goggles. He reached down and put a finger inside one.

"Deep," he said. "Whatever made these, it's heavy. I'd say maybe even a hundred pounds."

"Well, let's get our asses across as quick as we can. Maybe they're only on this side of the creek." My experience with house cats led me to think felines weren't happy splashing around in water. I'd seen Emmery trying to bathe a few and it hadn't been pretty. No telling though, if this water aversion was shared by their big bad cousins.

If I was right, and they too didn't like getting soaked, maybe this little family hadn't crossed. Course, this might not be the *only* kitty-cat family out here roaming the woods. But I wasn't going to worry about that just now. One thing at a time.

We both stepped into the water. John leading the way, me following close behind.

We were a little more than halfway to the other side when the cougars showed up and decided to join us for a swim. A momma cat and two cubs. Not little tiny baby cubs, but big ones, each of them probably weighing at least fifty pounds.

The momma was into water up to her neck so I didn't know for sure how big she was, but big enough. The two cubs were more or less still on dry land, standing at the very edge of the creek, with only their paws covered in water. They were just watching as the whole thing played out. Maybe they were holding back, waiting for mom to make the kill or maybe the little shits just didn't want to get their feet wet. Either way, I was happy they were staying put.

Sharing the creek with one of these monstrous beasts was bad enough. Three would probably be the end of us.

"This isn't good," John said. "I don't suppose you know what to do here? Mountain girl that you are and all." He was trying to be cute, but I could tell he was at least as scared as me. Maybe more.

"Okay, first of all I'm not a mountain girl. Second, I don't have the slightest idea. Maybe throw rocks at them?" I'd already reached down into the creek bed and gotten myself two handfuls. The little stones felt puny and useless. I doubted they'd scare away a house cat, much less something like this monster coming toward us. She was advancing at a moderate speed. Not as fast as we could walk, though. The current was slowing her down more than it was us.

"Maybe we can get across before she does." I said.

"Ok, and then what? We're not gonna outrun her on the other side. You realize that I hope?"

And then he shoved me out of the way, stepping in front, shielding me. I was about to come out with something like, 'Dude, just because I'm a girl, don't think I can't fight a mountain lion as well as you,' but that kind of died on my lips.I mean hey, if they guy wants to take one for the team. So be it.

I have to admit though, he did go up in my estimation. Just a bit.

I was still thinking about this when John made a sudden lunge for the cougar. By that time it was only about three feet from closing in on us and he just went for it.

I was frozen in place, useless little pebbles still clutched in my hands, my mind searching for something – anything – that I could do to even the odds. Man against beast, in a situation like this one, the beast has a mighty advantage. I mean shooting it was an option, but all I could see was blurred bodies behind a wall of spraying water. I could easily kill John and then I'd be the next thing on the menu.

I thought about everything I had with me. Throwing Hershey Kisses sure as hell wasn't going to stop it, and it likely had no need for lip gloss. I thought I might be able to get in close enough to use the hunting knife. It had a wicked long blade, and that's what it was for, after all. But in the seconds that all of this was flying around in my head, underneath it all I realized I didn't want to kill the cougar. Just get it the hell off John and out of the way. But how? Maybe the knife was the only option. I knew I couldn't conjure a kitty-love spell and just waltz up and scratch it behind the ears, give it a nice little pat on the head. I didn't have that kind of magic in me. And even if I did, I couldn't imagine a scenario where the cougar didn't take off my hand. Magic was fast but in my experience, cats were faster.

I was just about ready to give up and try my luck with the hunting knife, just kill the thing, when I thought of the perfume. It was zipped up in the left side pocket of my camos. I reached down under the water, found the zipper with my fingers, pulled out the bottle and started moving toward the writhing mass in the middle of the creek bed.

I knew there was a good reason to bring perfume!

When I'd made the stuff, I'd put some kind of magic into it, I couldn't even remember what. Mostly I'd just wanted to smell good. Being a witch and all, I wasn't gonna go to the trouble to make a thing unless I could put a little bit of magic in there somewhere. Maybe I'd used something calming, possibly attracting, but that didn't matter because what I'd remembered about the perfume, what had me literally running over the slippery rocks to get to the damn beast, was the effect it had on Emmery's cats. Anytime I was wearing the stuff, they avoided me like the clap.

Could it repel this giant kitty-cat from hell? I was about to find out.

I was almost on them. If I'd leaned over I could have put my hand on the cougar's fur. I was close enough to notice that most of her left ear was gone, and what was left was covered in a thick knob of scar tissue, so she was a fighter, for sure.

I couldn't get a good look at John but I saw enough to tell he was injured. I could see blood, and I could also see that he was losing. A few more seconds and the cat would have him, either by ripping out his throat or drowning him. At that very moment it had its teeth sunk into his shoulder. Deep, all the way to the gums.

I put my free hand on the whistle that was hanging from a chain around my neck, said a little prayer to anything that was listening, and blew into it as long and as hard as I could.

And something out there in the great beyond must have been paying attention. Or maybe cougars just hated whistles.

The cougar let go. Just for a second, but that was all I needed.

I pressed down on the nozzle and released a huge cloud of *parfume de la Tula* right into its face, filling eyes, nose and yes, even its bloody mouth with the stuff. And I kept spraying. And blowing the whistle. I don't know how long it took, time was passing in slow motion, but of course it could only have been seconds, maybe even milliseconds.

Suddenly there was an ear splitting howl and the cat was moving away, swimming as fast as it could to the other bank. Back to the cubs.

When it reached dry land, both it and the cubs disappeared into the forest, long tails twitching in either excitement or fear. I didn't know or care which.

They never looked back.

Now all I had to do was save John, and it looked to me like he might be dying.

Chapter 22

John was conscious. Maybe bleeding out, certainly at least clawed to pieces, but fully awake for it. Under the circumstances, I wasn't sure if that was a blessing or a curse. Of course, I wasn't a doctor, didn't even have an ounce of medical training, so was hoping it looked worse than it really was.

To be honest, I was amazed that the cougar hadn't just killed him. If it had gotten him in the throat instead of the shoulder, that would have been the end of special agent John Wheaton. He'd been incredibly lucky.

"How bad is it?" He asked me, his voice thin with pain, gasping almost.

"Bad enough," I said. "I'm pretty sure I can stop the bleeding, but you're going to need a doctor. Sooner rather than later. Do you think you can make it back to the car?"

"I'm not leaving these woods." He was thrashing around, trying to raise himself up on elbows that were bleeding and raw. The cat had done a real number on both his shoulder and arms. Finally he gave up and fell back onto the muddy creek bank, and whispered, "Remember why we're here. We don't have time for this shit."

"Well, a mountain lion attack wasn't something we planned for. I can get you to the hospital and come back by myself."

"Hell, no. Dammit Tula. Isn't there something you can do? Rub some frog spit on me or something? Go on. Do your thing. Whatever it is."

If the circumstance had been different, I'd have gotten a good bit of satisfaction out of hearing him, for the very first time, referencing magic as if it was something more than just a complete load of bullshit. But at the moment, all I could feel or see was a desperate man. Desperate but determined. He wasn't going to give up. At least not yet.

And the frog spit actually wasn't such a bad idea.

The moon was high and nearly full, lighting the sky and the forest below with a fierce kind of white. Like it was damning the darkness but not all the way. I was glad of the moonlight. In the struggle with the cougar I'd lost my night vision goggles, and so had John.

"Lay still and let me look at you," I told him.

As I was examining his wounds, which were many, it occurred to me that I hadn't brought along anything in the way of first aid, not even a band-aid. I wasn't the nature-girl type, but even a townie like me should have known better. John, being the ready for everything FBI man that he was, would have certainly brought a first aid kit. I'd have bet money on it. But his pack was even now floating its way to town, and the Hale River, pulled along by Dead Buck Creek and its not insignificant currents.

I didn't dwell on it. I wished I'd thought of it. But wishing wouldn't make it so. Wishing wouldn't make a satchel full medical type shit appear on the creek bank. It wasn't like I could conjure such a thing.

But maybe I could conjure *something.* What could I do? Granny Whitlow could stop bleeding, and I'd seen and heard her do it plenty of times. Knew the verse she'd

145

used. Didn't I? Something out of the Bible. Granny hadn't been much for organized religion, but the woman would give credit where it was due. A lot of what she practiced came out of that book. And other books like it. Religion, she'd always told us, was a powerful tool. Regardless of which one it was.

I unbuttoned John's shirt, which was already ripped to shreds, and laid my hands, palms flat, down on his chest. Underneath my fingers I could feel his beating heart, galloping away, like it wanted to bust through his ribcage and rip right through the skin.

I mumbled the words that Granny had used, twice, for good measure, then took the edge of his shirt, and wiped away the blood on the worst of his wounds, where the big cat had sunk its teeth into his shoulder.

To my utter astonishment, no new blood rose to the skin.

Thank you Granny Whitlow. At least he wouldn't bleed to death. Maybe. Now, I needed to do something for the pain. Lucky for me, but even luckier for him, John was now out cold. *Thank you for that too, Granny.* Maybe. If an unconscious John was her doing, and it probably was. Cause right then I could feel her with me, all around, just like she was peeking over my shoulder, and a better healer had never existed. Alive or dead.

But I couldn't just count on the ghost of my dead grandmother.

There were things here, things right in these woods that I could call. That was my gift, if you could call it that. I had a way with small creatures: birds, bats, mice, toads, snakes - yes, they terrified me, populated my nightmares, but most reptiles were part of my domain.

But it was toads I needed now. I needed their venom. I'd settle for any old kind that came my way, but was hoping for a bullfrog or two. Most people don't know that toads and frogs are different. Not that it matters, the Average Joe or Jane won't ever find themselves on a muddy creek bank with a ripped up man maybe dying at their feet. And if they did, frogs and toads probably wouldn't be on their mind right about then.

Ideally, I'd have time to wait for some of the more exotic species that were native to Africa, but time was a luxury I didn't have. And magic summoning was weird. If distance was involved there seemed to be no guarantees. Sometimes it would take only seconds for one of my creatures to travel thousands of miles, but I'd also seen it take days. This time, I'd settle for size. The larger the toad the more venom I'd get. So a good ole American bullfrog would do just fine. And since bullfrogs secreted their venom from behind their ears, I wouldn't have to listen to a bunch of frogs spitting. Which was a plus. Frog spitting was a sound that tended to set my teeth on edge. I just couldn't abide it.

Truth is, if I'm being honest, I have a fear of frogs. They light me up with the same kind of fear that snakes do. I mean, I'm not afraid they'll bite me, I'm afraid they'll *touch* me. To me, being touched by a toad is about the worst thing I can think of. Plump, pulsing bodies, sudden movements, hopping any old damn place. Maybe hopping on your head, down your shirt. I just can't handle the uncertainty that frogs bring to the table. But I was gonna have to handle it this time.

I reached out into the darkness, letting my energy mix with that of the night, willing that greedy moon to carry it. Willing the wind rushing through the trees to carry it too, willing myself to push and then push more.

Come on, you gross little buggars. Come to momma.

I sure hoped John appreciated this crap.

It was taking way too much of my energy, way more than it should have. As I felt myself near to fainting, I cursed my laziness. Magic was a muscle, and like my mother and my sisters, and pretty much all of us Whitlows, Granny and Aunt Ruby excepted, I never gave it the work out it required.

I thought about the music that had filled me while I danced with Ruby. Was it lost to me? Would I ever feel that kind of power again?

I felt nothing. If my energy was touching anything, I couldn't tell. I was thinking about giving up, and then it was as if I could hear Granny in my head. *"Dammit Tula! You stopped the bleedin' didn't you? You can do this. Do it or you're no kin of mine."* Was she really here or was it just my imagination? With Granny Whitlow one never knew. I could feel her presence, but maybe that was just wishful thinking.

Anyway, the voice in my head was right. I *had* stopped the bleeding. I could do this. With renewed vigor, I called to them...

And then they came. I could feel the movement. Tiny amphibious feet, heading in my direction from all around the forest. They were coming.

The first ones to show were tiny, and knowing it would take dozens of them, I shooed them away, continued calling, harder this time, louder, until in the woods behind me, I heard a chorus of chirps, raspy and deep, climbing up to a pitch so high it sounded like the peal of tiny bells.

There were dozens of them, and they knew what I wanted. Single file, they climbed onto John's naked chest, then spread, softly, gently, until they created something like a green, vibrating shield of amphibious skin all over his body.

And then, one by one, they began to spit.

What the hell? Bullfrogs don't spit. What kind of frogs had I summoned? Very slowly, I leaned forward and put my face up close to one of the things. I didn't want to; it was like putting my face next to an open flame – I was that terrified, but I had to get a better look.

And when I did, it was obvious. I was no frog expert, but I knew what a bullfrog looked like and these bad boys weren't them. I had no idea what kind of frogs they were.

What if you're poisoning him? What if you've called up one of those South American or Asian toads that are like puffer fish or something? The ones that can flat out kill you?

No. Magic can go haywire, but not by that kind of margin. My intent had been there. I wouldn't have summoned up murder toads.

Hopefully.

I watched as the frogs writhed around all over the unconscious man. Their squirming, fat little bodies made me want to scream and rip my own skin, but somehow I stayed quiet and still.

I hoped the frogs knew when to stop because I sure as hell didn't. I'd never heard of someone being poisoned by external use of frog venom, but I wasn't sure. Once again, I reminded myself that my intent had been clear in the calling. The frogs were there to stop John's pain. They weren't going to cause harm.

And then as suddenly as the spitting began, it stopped. As if someone had turned off a switch. One by one, the frogs left his body. Most disappeared back into the forest, but a few made for the creek, bodies making a fat, noisy splash as they jumped from the bank into the water.

My work wasn't yet done.

I put my hands into the glistening venom and began to massage it into the skin on John's chest, arms, and neck. Once again, I had a flash of worry about the mysterious frogs, possibly murder toads. But I pushed it down. It was done, and there was nothing to do but trust in the magic. Trust my intent.

His pants were ripped right around the calf. Pulling back the torn fabric I could see a deep gash, about six inches long, but other than that his lower body seemed to be unharmed. I rubbed more of the venom into the injured leg.

Hopefully I'd now stopped both the bleeding and the pain, though I knew it would only be temporary. Maybe a few hours if we were lucky. A better witch could have done more.

The truth was, even though it was hard for me to admit, I felt ashamed. For the first time ever, I'd been put in a life and death situation, where my magic could have made a real difference, and the best I could do was call up a bunch of frogs.

Well, there was the whole blood stopping thing, but I was pretty sure that had been Granny Whitlow's doing, rather than my own.

Sitting on that creek bank, alongside a man who could easily have died - may yet die, truth be told - I was ashamed that I'd had to take such a ridiculously roundabout way of helping him. *If* I'd helped him. That remained to be seen.

What had I been thinking? What had we all been thinking? If *I'd* been dismissive of our magic, Emmery and Alafair had been even worse. Instead of doing the work, putting in the time to hone our skills, we'd simply ignored it. Performing half-assed magic for our own amusement. It was a wonder we could even tap into it at all.

I felt like a kid who's been given a toy and just thrown it in the dirt. A toy that any child in the world would treasure, just tossed aside as if it were nothing. I could rationalize it, of course I could. You never knew the value of a thing until you needed it and didn't have it. And us three girls, we were the definition of privileged. No doubt about that. It was surprising we knew the value of anything at all. We'd never wanted for a single thing our entire lives, and until this night, I'd never really *needed* the magic. Not in a life or death serious kind of way.

And the best I could do was toads. Maybe even murderous ones.

I looked down at John and was surprised to see him staring up at me, smiling a little.

"I don't know what the hell you did, Tula. I think, wait... the trees are purple."

"Purple? The trees aren't purple, John. How do you feel?"

"I feel... I feel pretty damn good. But yeah... you're beautiful, you know that?" He was looking at me with

151

something like wonder, then his eyes widened in surprise. "Woah. Yeah. Two Tula's. How did you get another *you* out here? Shit, you really are a witch."

I started laughing. I laughed until tears were streaming down my face, till I was on the verge of peeing myself. Of course I hadn't gotten just plain old North Carolina bullfrogs, that would have been too damn perfect for the likes of me. But I hadn't gotten murder toads, either. No, I'd summoned up some weird LSD kind of frogs. Stoner stuff.

Mr. FBI was high as a kite. Good to go, maybe, but tripping like nobody's business.

Chapter 23

The cougar attack had effectively put an end to our little adventure. Finding out why Moncrieffe had the woods under surveillance would have to keep. Right now my biggest concern was how to get a severely injured six foot three, two hundred pound man – that was just a guess, but I'm pretty good at that kind of thing – across 80 feet of rushing creek. Even without the rough currents and slippery rocks, I simply wasn't strong enough. If I had to bear his weight, he'd just fall on his ass. Could even drown, especially considering the shape he was in.

Because said injured man was also stoned out of his gourd. In a very serious kind of way.

John was on his hands and knees, crawling around, sniffing the dirt, pulling up ferns and vines, peering into them as if he'd never ever seen such amazing things, like they'd been dropped onto the forest floor by some alien wanderers. Their colors he seemed to find particularly wondrous, which was actually starting to irritate me just a little.

The only thing worse than being stuck on a creek bank, possibly surrounded by mountain lions, one of them a seriously pissed off momma, and maybe things even worse, was being stuck there with someone who was obviously having a blast.

I knew he was hallucinating; I mean ferns don't fart, and if they did it wouldn't smell like apple blossoms, but tripping or not, Mr. FBI was right about one thing–

The bushes *were* moving.

At first I'd thought it was all part of his crazy trip, but then I'd seen it myself. Just a tiny bit, a foot here, a foot there, but some of the foliage was, in fact, shifting around. Six or seven large leafy humps – I figured bushes that were covered in vines – weren't in the same place they'd been when we first crossed the creek. Granted, I hadn't been paying that much attention, what with a chewed up man at my feet, but I knew that this section of the creek bank had been nothing but a mud slick with a fringe of ferns before the woods took over again.

There had been plenty of bushes, but they were *beyond* the treeline. Now they were right behind the ferns, forming a near perfect semi circle well in front of the trees. Where they had no damn business being and damn sure weren't before.

I was starting to feel kind of surrounded. And more than a little bit afraid. That little voice that tells us *no, dumbass, don't help the strange man look for his puppy, don't open that door, and no no no, don't go down into the basement,* that little whisper had blown up into a screaming banshee inside my head.

And it was telling me to get the hell across that creek.

"John, can you stand up?" I bent down and took him by the arm, tugging, just a little, not wanting to break open his wounds. Once we crossed the creek, if we made it, that is, there was still a long walk ahead of us to get back to the Land Rover, and it wouldn't do to have him start bleeding again.

If John heard me speak, he gave no indication of it. Just continued his examination of the brand new world of mud. He'd managed to dig up some earthworms and was absolutely convinced the squirmy little things were cobras. But nice ones.

By this time I was really starting to get pissed at my little army of toad EMT's. Really wishing I'd just let Mr. FBI suffer the pain. At least he'd have been sane. Maybe even sane enough to cross that creek. Now it was going to be like trying to convince drunk Alafair not to dance on the bar, or some other nonsense she'd regret come morning. Only this was worse, 'cause drunk Alafair, despite all her flaws, was at least smaller than me, and I could kick her ass with one hand tied behind my back. I didn't have to *convince* drunk Alafair of any damn thing. When it came down to it I could force her ass.

What I needed was some kind of antipsychotic treatment, but I hadn't a clue what that might be. Nothing like this had ever come up. I had some spells that would calm him, but if he got any calmer he'd be asleep. I also had ways to stimulate, to bring clarity, but under the circumstance, since that was a bit like an amphetamine, I was pretty sure such a spell would only send him into an even worse orbit. I'd probably end up with stoner dude John, down in the mud but chattering like a magpie.

The wind was picking up, bringing with it the smell of fresh rainfall and ozone. Somewhere nearby it was storming, and if my nose was right, and it usually was, the storm was heading our way.

Also the moving bushes had inched a little bit closer. And their shape had changed. They were lower now, and

155

wider. Like they'd hunkered down even more, but spread out.

They looked like reclining bodies.

And then I saw something like a hand separate from the bottom of one of them. And then the hand became an arm, and then the thing *sat up*.

My terror level went up by about a thousand percent.

I thought about Gwyneth, back at the cabin, stretched out on the makeshift hospital bed, the vines growing from her body, invading every cell in her body, probably invading her baby as well.

One of the bush-things seemed to roll over on its side, prop itself up on an elbow. And then I saw it all with absolute clarity. This was what Gwyneth was becoming. If I didn't figure out a way to stop it, that poor woman would soon be just like whatever lived inside these clumps of vine and bramble.

Is this what had happened to Andrew? Was he even now, inside one of the things surrounding us?

"John! Get your ass up. Right this minute!" I was literally yelling at him now. We had to get to the other side. I knew the cougars were over there. Maybe hiding inside the trees, watching, waiting. But I didn't care. I had the gun. And this time I wouldn't hesitate to use it.

As I finally got John into a standing position, I looked back over my shoulder at the humps of vine. I had the distinct feeling the things were watching me, and if they were, there wasn't much I could do about it. I felt certain that my gun would be utterly useless against whatever lurked inside, that whatever kind of abomination these things were would be immune to guns and bullets.

Whatever they were, I knew I needed to get us the hell away from them.

I slung John's good arm over my shoulder, then gripped him around his waist. We took a step toward the water, then another, and another. I knew that I wasn't going to make it. I was fairly strong, but the dead weight of his body was quickly dragging me down. Another step, almost to the water, and I could feel my legs buckling, feel the weight of the man beside me pulling me toward the dirt.

Then we were falling, both of us about to hit the ground, when suddenly the weight beside me was lifted. I thought for a minute that John had regained his sense, his strength, and had simply stood, but then I heard laughing, and the hand I had wrapped around John's waist was touched by another.

Another much *colder* hand was now clasping my own and shouldering the bulk of John's weight.

Victor.

"Just let go of him, Tula," Victor was pulling John out of my grasp, lifting him up, cradling the man in his arms like he weighed no more than a bundle of sticks.

"Victor... where did you... how did you..."

"Later," he shouted, already in the water, heading for the other side. "If you don't want those things taking a nibble out of your backside, you need to get your lovely ass across that creek."

I looked back at the viney monsters who were now only an arm's length away. Then I turned and ran into the creek.

I didn't look back until I'd reached the other side. As soon as my feet hit dry land, I dropped to the ground.

During my mad dash across the water, I'd turned my ankle and the pain was almost crippling.

"What are they?" I asked Victor. When we'd gone into the water, I'd been right on Victor's heels. But even with John in his arms, I was no match for the vampire. He'd reached the other side well ahead of me. John seemed to be sleeping, which I thought was damn near a miracle. And then I had a terrible thought. What if the hallucinogenic had actually ended up killing the man? Or, even more likely, what if Victor had done something to him? Murdered him even. I mean Victor was pretty okay, for a vampire, but everybody knew that deep down vampires, no matter how nice they seemed, were just about the nastiest creatures on earth. Or anywhere else. Apt to do any manner of awful thing when you least expected it.

"Is John OK? Did you do something to him?" I had my hand on the Glock. Not that it would do a damn bit of good. It was as useless against Victor as it would have been against those vine creatures. Where was a good stake when you needed one?

"I glamoured him, Tula, relax. Your boyfriend here has just gone beddy-bye. That's all."

"He is most certainly *not* my boyfriend."

"Good. You can do much better. I sense that his blood is very red. You know – red blooded American kind of red. Mixed up with every damn kind of thing. Mutt blood is what I call it. You'd do better with a somewhat more complex vintage, a bit more... European, maybe. A bit more Irish, I think."

"Oh come on, Victor. You're an ass. We're about to be eaten up by cougars or vine people or maybe even something worse and you want to hit on me? Are you for real?" Victor was cute, but not that cute. And the pain in my ankle was making me more than a little pissy. "Let's get out of here," I told him.

Somehow I managed to get to my feet. I was covered from head to toe in mud, and all I wanted to do was get home, change out of my soaked clothes, fix myself a cup of tea and start all over the next day. Dry, and rested, and hopefully free of both John and Victor.

Then it hit me.

How the hell had Victor come to be there? He was supposed to be down at the vineyard. I'd paid good money for him to be there. So why had he been skulking around in the woods?

I asked him as much and he suggested we walk and talk at the same time, what with maybe us being about to be attacked and all. As we made our way up the trail in the general direction of the Land Rover, he told me what he'd discovered at the vineyard, which wasn't much and kind of light on details.

Victor told me that Moncrieffe and his bunch had launched some kind of an attack on the inn. This I'd already figured out for myself – the vines making their way to the lodestone. But what he told me next was a surprise. The sneak attack on the inn predated Andrew going missing. So they'd been after us Whitlows even before we got involved with Gwyneth. That was something I hadn't even considered.

It was troubling to say the least.

"And the reason I came to your rescue dear Tula, is because I can *sense* you. When you gave me money today, you gave me a piece of you. Now I'm connected to you."

"Forever?" Please no. Don't let it be so.

"Sadly, no. Just until I spend all the money you gave me. Unless of course you'd like to give me something a little more intimate?"

I wouldn't look at him, but even so, I could hear the smile in his voice.

"You're not getting anything else from me Victor, intimate or otherwise."

"Ah, but think about it. I did save you and your friend tonight, didn't I? Seems to me it might be a good idea to keep me handy til you've wrapped up this ugly piece of business. And it is ugly. The Moncrieffes, they're basically beasts."

"C'mon, I might not be a vampire, might just be a lowly little witch, but even I can tell they're one hundred percent human."

"Oh yes, they're human alright. But they've captured a god. A Green Man. Or maybe the Green Man has captured them. Could be either way."

A Green Man. I knew a little bit about the legend. The Druids had worshipped what they called The Green Men. Gods of the forest, gods of harvest. It was said it took the skulls of a thousand dead to summon one. And the skulls had to be nearby. If Victor was right, somewhere on this property, maybe in the vineyard itself, a thousand skulls were screaming.

Legend said that if you destroyed the skulls, you destroyed their god.

Skulls were bone, and bone wasn't quite so easily done away with. Would crushing them do it? There would still be fragments of bone, but maybe the skulls only had power when they were intact. I didn't know, but how the hell would a person go about crushing a thousand skulls? How long would that take? And you'd have to have a bunch of people doing an awful lot of bashing.

Didn't seem practical.

Maybe burning? Sure, if you had a mobile crematorium. Just roll one of those bad boys through the woods or down to the vineyard. Piece of cake. Then there was the good old wise-guy method of using barrels of acid. I tried to picture myself going all *Don Corleone* on a thousand skulls. That would take maybe hundreds of barrels full of acid.

How many skulls could fit into a fifty-gallon drum?

I hoped I wasn't gonna have to find out.

Twenty minutes later I was still thinking about my problem with the skulls and how to destroy them when we got to the logging trail and the Land Rover. And then through the darkness, I could see what else was waiting for us there, and suddenly a thousand skulls were very much the least of my problems.

Chapter 24

Moncrieffe and three of his goons were waiting for us. Standing in front of them, guarding them it seemed, were four large cougars and two cubs. One of the big felines was the cougar that attacked us in the creek. I recognized the white blaze that ran down the middle of her face and the mangled left ear. Also, she was wet, as were the two cubs that were crouched down on either side of her.

Same cat, no question about it. Could have been my imagination, but it seemed that the amber eyes of the beast were regarding me with a hint of satisfaction and a heaping dose of malice. Those eyes should have been expressionless, at least that had been my experience with felines, but not this one. This one seemed like it had a score to settle.

With me.

At that moment, all I could think was that maybe I should have killed the beast when I had the chance, and even as I had that thought, my fingers were itching to grab the Glock out of the back of my pants and start firing. Which was a very strange urge for me. Though felines of any kind were not on my favorites list, I loved animals, commanded many of them, and before I'd met this particular cougar, had never seen one I actually *wanted* to kill.

There was just something about this cat that was wrong. I couldn't put my finger on where that sense of wrongness came from, but it was there. I could feel it all the way down to my bones.

But there were more important things to worry about than cougars. However menacing they might appear, they didn't have guns, and Moncrieffe and his goons *did*. And those guns were pointing straight at me, John, and Victor.

Moncrieffe stepped out in front of the group, leveled his gun, and spoke.

"I believe you three are trespassing, but oddly enough, I'm actually glad you decided to come visit us tonight. Even if uninvited. Saves me a bit of trouble, as it happens." Moncrieffe gestured toward Victor and asked, "Who is this gentleman? I don't believe I've had the pleasure."

Victor was regarding the man with a slow kind of insolence, pretty much his go-to look in any situation. Like most vampires, he tended to carry a chip on his shoulder the size of Mount Everest.

"You should be glad you haven't made my acquaintance," Victor told him. "But come a little closer and I'll show you who I am. If you dare."

"I'm sensing you're maybe something a little more than human? Maybe you're considering some type of heroic attack, perhaps? No matter. I think when all of you see what I've brought with me you'll find yourselves to be, well, I think agreeable would be the term I'd use." Moncrieffe turned away from us and spoke into the darkness. He was looking toward a section of thin pines just to the left of where the Rover was parked.

163

Someone was coming. At first I could only hear the muffled sound of footsteps crunching against loose gravel, but after a few moments the moonlight captured two figures moving from behind the vehicle, making their way forward, past the goons and cougars, until finally they were standing just behind Moncrieffe and his gun.

I couldn't make any sense of what I was seeing. Standing with Moncrieffe was a man, another one of his goons, I presumed, and he had his arm locked around a little boy, a wicked looking hunting knife held against the kid's throat.

"Go ahead, Frank, move a little closer, I don't believe Ms. Whitlow can see who's come to visit."

The goon, nudging the boy along, moved forward, and then it was as if all the air left my body, as if time itself had become a vacuum that was sucking me down into some horrible nightmare. What I was seeing had no place in the world.

They had little Caleb.

I didn't know how they'd done it. Certainly not at the inn – both he and Vicki would have been under the protection spell there. The shield of safety it provided didn't just guard against supernatural threats but also everyday assholes like Moncrieffe and his bunch. They must have gotten to the kid while he and his mother were out and about. Very quickly my disbelief transformed into epic rage.

This would *not* stand.

Thankfully, Caleb appeared to be unhurt, and I could tell from his vacant expression and drooping eyelids that they'd likely given the kid a sedative. The kind of evil that could do this to an innocent child was an evil that I'd never before encountered.

Moncrieffe would pay for this. Moncrieffe and all his little helpers that were gathered here this night. I took a moment to memorize every face. One way or the other, I knew I'd see every single one of them pay. The hatred I felt in that moment almost matched the terror I was feeling at the idea of little Caleb being at their mercy.

"You've just made a huge mistake, Moncrieffe." Somehow I kept my voice level, managed to hide the fear that lay in my gut like lead. "You mess with my people, you'll pay a price. A big one. You need to hand the kid over to me, right now."

I was trying to determine if the three of us could take on Moncrieffe and his merry men – not to mention a half dozen cougars thrown into the mix. Beside me, John was waking, but when I looked at his face, I could see that he was still high as a kite. So it would be me and Victor alone. I thought we could maybe do it. Victor, possessing the phenomenal speed that vampires were known for, could probably have most of them on the ground before they knew what hit them, but the odds of Caleb being hurt during the melee were just too great.

"Tsk. Tsk. Now Ms. Whitlow, I think I know what you're studying on. You really don't want to make any sudden moves here. That would be very dangerous for everyone, most especially little Caleb here." As he spoke, he threw his arm around the child, a fatherly like gesture that under the circumstance was beyond obscene.

"Tell me what you want." I knew he'd taken the kid for a reason, and that reason was leverage. I wasn't sure how he'd figured out that he even *needed* leverage where

165

I was concerned. I'd hoped that he'd taken my visit to the vineyard as nothing other than following up on Andrew's last known location, but somehow he'd known it was more than that.

"What I want is a simple exchange, nothing more. Gwyneth for Caleb. Bring her to me, and you can take the kid home to your safe little inn and the arms of his mother."

At the sound of his sister's name, John seemed to regain some of his senses. He stood up straight, then took a couple of faltering steps forward before Victor pulled him back.

"It's no good," Victor hissed. "This asshole's gonna get his, but not tonight man. Not tonight." Then he shot Moncrieffe a look that should have had the man crying like a little baby – a look like that one, coming from a vampire, should have scared the shit out of the arrogant asshole, but the idiot thought he had the upper hand, and I guessed he did. For the moment anyway. But it was clear that Victor had marked Moncrieffe, and being marked by a vampire was dangerous business.

I could see that Victor had tightened his hold on John, which meant Mr. FBI wasn't about to get loose. When a vampire has hold of you, you're well and truly stuck. Which, under the circumstances, was a very good thing. I didn't need John showing his ass, going all Rambo or something – moves like that could get Caleb killed for sure.

"Why do you want Gwyneth?" I didn't think he'd actually tell me, but the question had to be asked.

"I want Gwyneth because she's my wife, and she belongs at my side." The words came from behind us, out of the darkness, the voice deep and full of power. Then the figure that owned the voice stepped into the moonlight.

Andrew.

Chapter 25

I hadn't met Andrew, but I'd seen several pictures, so knew him on sight. However, this wasn't the same man I'd seen in the photographs. That man's face had literally beamed with sincere good will - even through the lens of a camera. But this man... *was he even a man at all?* This man exuded no goodness, only dark, fierce, unyielding intent.

And the physical differences couldn't be denied. He was much larger than I expected, really, everything about him seemed just larger than life, as if someone had taken regular old Andrew and just kind of *bolded* him. The weirdest thing though... and in the darkness, I had to wonder if my eyes were deceiving me, but... I could swear the man's skin was green. And not just green, but green and mottled, sort of like the camouflage John and I were wearing.

And now this bold, greenish, evil Andrew was addressing me. Telling me that if I wanted Gwyneth to live, I'd bring her to him, and quickly, that only he could save her.

"Here, with me, she'll reach her full potential. She'd be here already, of her own accord, if it hadn't been for the vomiting. She drank, just as I did, but it didn't sit well, so she must have thrown so much of it up that she literally purged herself." As he spoke, Andrew's face was vacant, staring off into the distance. I wasn't sure he was even speaking to me at all. It was almost like he was making a point to himself alone. Reasoning out why he'd been drawn to the place, but Gwyneth had not.

"I don't understand," I told him. What did drinking have to do with any of this?

"It was in the wine, you see. The evening we left the vineyard. The god poured his essence into it. He did it for us – Gwyneth and I – we were chosen." Moving over to Caleb, Andrew reached down and gathered the listless child into his arms, picked him up off the ground, and held the boy out as a sort of offering.

"Bring Gwyneth and I will give you this boy. Refuse, and his skull will join the others."

And then Andrew's body began to glow, rays of green light shooting off his skin, the glow expanding, amplifying, until the whole forest seemed to be pulsing with a sickly green brilliance.

I was afraid, trembling, but I was also strangely entranced. I could feel myself becoming one with the earth in a way I'd never experienced, like every particle of my being was in the woods and in the red clay beneath my feet. I was the leaves trembling in the wind, and the spiders scurrying up and down the rough bark of the trees, and I was in the vineyard too. In the vines and the grapes. I was in everything. I felt joy and power, but underneath it all, I also felt something ugly. Something twisted and raw and poisonous. The thing I sensed there was an abomination, but I didn't care. Not in that moment. A foreign, down deep part of me was ready to embrace it all, even as I was repelled.

In spite of my revulsion, I felt myself being drawn to Andrew. Wanted to step forward, give myself to his light.

Become one with it. I took a single step, was on the verge of taking another, then Victor was shouting.

"Tula! Look at me. Right now!"

His voice sounded like it was coming from a million miles away, but I heard it. I looked at Victor, and his lips weren't moving, yet he was still speaking, urging me, begging me, then commanding me. He was in my *head*.

"Look away from him!"

And then I did, and slowly, very slowly, the spell was broken. I stepped back, fatigue and dizziness almost knocking me into the dirt. I could feel bile rising into my throat.

I turned my eyes away from Victor. I couldn't look at him. Not now. My shame was just too great. I had almost been mesmerized by the Andrew thing. Had almost gone to him. I took a deep breath. *You will not vomit. You will not show weakness. You are a Whitlow, by god, and that's not what Whitlows do.*

Whitlows don't cower, they kick ass.

I walked over to where Andrew held Caleb aloft, and placed my hands upon the boy's body, ran my fingers through his damp, curling hair. No one made a move to stop me, knowing that any kind of sudden snatch and grab was a danger that I wouldn't risk.

"Caleb, I'm getting you out of here. I promise. You're coming home."

Then I looked at Andrew, Moncrieffe, and the rest of the bunch.

"I'll do it. I'll bring Gwyneth, but I have a condition. I want Caleb's mother here with him."

It was risky, I knew. They'd have two hostages rather than just one. But Vicki would want it. And the thought of

Caleb stuck with these strangers, alone and terrified, needing his mother, was more than I could bear. I could only imagine what Vicki herself must be going through.

If I could get this much out of them, Caleb wouldn't be alone. Then I'd figure out what to do next. I wasn't sure whether that would include actually giving them Gwyneth. I hoped it wouldn't come to that, but I knew deep inside that if it came down to Gwyneth or Caleb – now probably Caleb *and* Vicki – I knew what my choice would be.

Again, I resolved to myself that every last one of them would pay for this. And pay hard.

"Well, what's your answer, Moncrieffe? Can the kid have his mother or not?" I asked him.

Moncrieffe nodded. "Why not? You can send the mother. The more the merrier. I seem to recall that she's quite easy on the eyes. Could be fun."

"It goes without saying that you don't lay a single finger on her, on either of them," I snarled. "If you do, all bets are off. And it won't just be me, and it won't just be the Whitlows. The whole damn town will be here and I don't care how many green men you've got on the place. We'll burn this god-forsaken place to the ground. Your green god-thing there can't mesmerize every single one of us."

I looked behind me at Victor and John. Victor's eyes were burning with rage, and John, thank goodness, still seemed to be completely out of it.

"Let's go," I told them.

"You have until midnight tomorrow," Andrew said. "One minute later, and I'll have little Caleb for a midnight snack."

He smiled, a big wide smile, a smile wider than any human could ever manage, showing teeth that were long and pointed, in a mouth reeking of putrid rot. Then with an audible click, the Andrew-thing dislocated its jaw bone and the smile turned into a yawning chasm that was easily half the size of it's entire face.

As I watched, there came the stuff of nightmares – hundreds of long black shiny roaches skittered out, crawling down onto his chin, and then his neck, then falling onto the forest floor.

I froze that horrid image in my mind, for there was nothing left of what had once been Andrew. Only evil wore that skin now. *It was something I knew I'd do well to remember.*

Leaving Caleb in the grip of that monster was the hardest thing I'd ever had to do.

Chapter 26

We manhandled John into the backseat where he immediately curled up and fell asleep. Victor was driving the Rover, and I was busy on the phone.

First, arrangements were made to get Vicki to the vineyard. As I'd expected, it was the only place she wanted to be. I felt humbled by her absolute faith that I'd be able to find a way to put things right. It was a huge responsibility and I only hoped her faith in me was warranted.

Emmery and Sheriff Blaylock would drive her there, and the Sheriff would escort her onto the premises. I figured having him on board would do two things. First it would show Moncrieffe that I did in fact have some control over the township, and if it came to it, its people, and second, that I wasn't afraid to flex some muscle.

Once the business with Vicki was taken care of, I called John's father to get an update on Gwyneth and also to let him know what had happened to his son. I had no intention of telling him about Andrew, the kidnapping of Caleb, or their demand to have Gwyneth brought to them. That would wait until I knew exactly what I was going to do about the situation. Hopefully, Dr. Wheaton would never even have to know any of it. I didn't want to be the one to tell him; I was sure the man would hear it in my voice – he'd know – that if it came down to his daughter or Caleb, his daughter was as good as dead. Or transformed, or whatever insane thing Moncrieffe and Andrew had planned for her.

It took some doing but I finally convinced the doctor that John was fine, just incapable of driving, and that I was going to have him stay either at my house or the inn. I could tell he didn't like it, would have much preferred that I bring John back to the cabin in order to look him over personally, but I just didn't have the time to drive the distance and then make the not insignificant trek through the woods just to get to the cabin. Especially seeing as how Victor and I would have to drag John along that narrow little snake infested trail. I was far from sure he'd be able to walk on his own.

No. John would be staying in town.

In spite of the obvious aggravation Dr. Wheaton had regarding John not being brought to him, the good doctor did, in fact, give me the only good news of the day.

Gwyneth was still showing signs of improvement. Not only had Aunt Ruby's potion halted the growth, but the young woman had continued to steadily improve. Very good news, indeed.

When I was finally able to end the call, Victor looked over at me.

"Are you done?"

"Yes, for the moment anyway."

"If we can find those skulls, we can end this shit," he said.

He sounded very sure of that. I hoped he was right. "So, your visit to the vineyard was fruitful? No pun intended."

"Somewhat." His voice had gotten a bit softer, and I could hear his attitude notching down just a hair. "Like I was telling you earlier, these guys, these *maniacs*, I don't know how they've done it, but they've figured out how to command a god. Or... I don't know... maybe the god's commanding them. To be honest, that seems far more likely. I don't really understand how some scumbag like Moncrieffe could manage something this big."

"Moncrieffe's not really the one in charge. From what I gather, that would be his uncle. Desmond is his name. Desmond Moncrieffe. I think he's got one of those thirds, or fourths or some such shit after his name. From what I've been able to find out, he's kind of a big deal. Richer than Midas with brains to match."

"But you've never met him?"

"No. I'm not even sure he's here. Word is he stays mostly in California. The family has a couple of vineyards out there too."

"Hmmm. Well, at any rate, whoever's in charge, this god they've conjured is something like The Green Men the Druids worshipped. Only the bad version. The Green Men were gods that supposedly made the harvests bountiful, bringing plenty to the earth, fruitful crops and fertile women, all that mother nature stuff. That's the good version."

"And the bad one?" I asked him.

"Ah darlin', as us Irish would say, the bad 'un is a whole 'nother kettle of fish," Victor answered. "You see, many depictions of The Green Man show vegetation coming out of his eyes and mouth. Now, those who believe this god to be good and benevolent will tell you that this represents all the bounty pouring *out* of The Green Man and *into* the earth. But there's another interpretation... Some, including certain sects of Druids and Celts, believed the stuff was going in, not coming out; that the god was basically swallowing up the entire world."

"Did you learn all this just tonight?" It seemed like a lot to take in during a fairly short surveillance operation.

Victor laughed. "Hardly. I go back a ways, you know."

"Not that far, surely."

"To the Druids? No. But far enough back that I remember a time when there wasn't a tavern in London that didn't have an etching of this god hanging over their door. In Europe, Britain especially, the Green Men are kind of a big deal. There are ancient carvings of them everywhere. Usually depicting a face or sometimes a skull, but always surrounded by leaves and vines. Sometimes the faces look kind and cheerful, big smiles and all that. Sometimes they look angry and demonic. And even the historians are split on whether these deities represented good or evil."

"I think in this case we can hazard a wild assed guess that whatever Moncrieffe's mixed up with at the vineyard is nothing benevolent." I thought of Gwyneth's body all eaten up with vines, and Andrew. I didn't know what had happened to him, but certainly nothing good. "I mean, they've kidnapped a child. How much more evil can you get."

"Killing one, I would think. That would be worse."

"And that's what they'll do, Victor. If we don't handle this perfectly. That's exactly what they'll do. And not just Caleb, and now his mom. It'll be all of us as well."

"I told you. If we destroy the skulls we end this. But there's another problem. Very likely destroying the skulls will kill Andrew as well."

I thought about that for all of two seconds before I answered. "I guess Andrew may be a dead man walking then." Where Caleb was concerned, Andrew dying wouldn't even make me hesitate.

I'd noted Victor's use of the word *we*, asked him if that meant he was signing on to help, and if so, how much that was going to cost me.

"As much as I hate to charge a fee for something I'd happily do for free, it goes against my principles to pass up a chance to get paid. So, how 'bout you agree to dinner? When this whole thing is over. You and me, dinner and drinks."

"Okay, but only because I'm feeling generous. I think between you, me, and John back there, there's going to be a line of people waiting to take that asshole down."

Victor pointed out to me that we had only hours to figure out a plan, put it in motion, and execute it, and he didn't think John would be up for that kind of thing anytime soon.

"It was only frogs." I said.

"Yeah. I know a little bit about those frogs. That guy is gonna be gaga for days. Take my word for it."

We were traveling well above the speed limit, the landscape outside my window flying past in a moonlit blur. I knew we were coming up on the cutoff to the River Road and The Bluffs. I thought about Aunt Ruby. If she wasn't still in town I wasn't sure what I'd do. Her help would be essential.

It was tempting to have Victor go by there. I really wanted to talk to the woman, *had* to talk to her soon. But more than anything I hoped to get to the inn before Vicki left to join little Caleb. I didn't want it bad enough to ask them to wait for me, not that Vicki would let anything delay her joining her son, and I felt exactly the same. Any words I might have for Vicki were secondary to getting her on the way as soon as possible.

But so many things *needed* to be said. Somehow I'd taken my eye off the ball to the extent that someone outside our family was now at risk. As Whitlows, we lived in a perpetual state of peril. We were so accustomed to threat that it almost didn't even register. Our family was old and powerful and that didn't happen, especially in the world of magic, without making equally powerful enemies. But thanks to my mother, Aunt Ruby, and many of our astute forebears, for centuries, we Whitlows had managed to protect ourselves with an astonishing degree of success.

I thought about Moncrieffe and his little sneak attack on the lodestone. He certainly wasn't the first one to come after our family, but I'd never heard of anyone going after the lodestone itself. I might have even given him the thing if I'd known that Caleb might be put at risk.

It would be easy to tell myself that there was no way I could have ever foreseen such a thing as Caleb's kidnapping, so I couldn't possibly have prevented it.

But that would be a lie. It was a lie I'd love to tell myself, but that would only make it the worst kind of lie.

The truth was, I should never have allowed a mortal to live and work at the inn. Should never have allowed a mortal inside the heart of our family. Because that's what had happened. Vicki and Caleb hadn't just become close to us, they were as much a part of our family as they would have been had they been blood. I'd allowed that to happen, and now the two of them were paying the price.

I wanted to look Vicki in the eye and own this thing.

I owed her that much. At least.

"What are the odds we figure out where these damn skulls are and how to destroy them before we run out of time?" I asked him.

And then he surprised me by stating the obvious.

"It's just gonna take some luck, I reckon," he answered. "That's pretty much our only hope, best I can tell. Everything ultimately comes down to luck. As an Irishman, I know that better than most."

He was right, of course. The odds were certainly against us. But maybe we could pull it off. That is, if the stars aligned perfectly and I held my mouth just right. And pigs flew and donkeys started singing lullabies and my sisters suddenly developed brains.

Yep,   we   could   do   this.   Maybe...

Chapter 27

At my urging, Victor had been driving like a bat out of hell, and we made the distance between the vineyard and the town proper in record time. We were traveling so fast that more than once I'd felt the wheels leave the pavement as we took the curves at breakneck speed. I was a little worried we wouldn't get back to town in one piece, but I wasn't about to ask him to slow down.

When we pulled into the parking lot outside the inn, I was glad to see both Sheriff Blaylock's cruiser and Emmery's sleek black Jag.

They're still here. I can speak to Vicki.

I left Victor to deal with getting John over to the county hospital's emergency room, then hurried to the back of the inn where the entrance to Vicki's apartment was located.

Emmery came to the door and let me inside. I could tell she didn't want to; could tell she wanted to claw my eyes out on the spot.

"We were just about to leave," she hissed. My sister was furious. The rage was pouring off of her in waves.

Good. Better fury than fear. That she lay the blame for this squarely at my feet was no surprise, and I had no argument.

"Where's Vicki?"

"She's back in the bedroom." I started to head toward the back of the tiny apartment where the two bedrooms were located, but Emmery stopped me.

"This is your fault," she spat. "How could you let this shit get so out of control?"

Normally Emmery laying hands on me like she was now doing, holding my arm in a vice like grip, then squeezing, hurting, would have resulted in a knock down drag out fight. At that moment though, I welcomed it. Really wished she'd just go ahead and slap my face. I hadn't seen the Moncrieffes as a serious threat, hadn't even been absolutely sure until that very day that they were behind what was happening to Gwyneth even.

And the vines in the basement... I'd known about them for several days, but if Sheriff Blaylock's visit hadn't jogged my dumb ass into going back down there, I might not have ever made the connection on that score. Might have just sat back on my big stupid ass while Moncrieffe and his green creepy monster took over the inn and then the whole damn town.

I'd been behind the curve from the beginning, but that was about to change. I'd rip that vineyard up by the roots, burn it to the ground if I had to.

I reached up and peeled Emmery's fingers from my shoulder, but didn't say a word, because I had none.

Sheriff Blaylock was sitting on the edge of the sofa, watching the two of us. The look on his face told me that getting between me and Emmery was not something he was in a hurry to do. Which was smart of him. Stepping between two angry witches was dangerous business.

"Go on back, Talullah," he finally said. "But make it quick, we need to get on the road."

I was about to continue to the bedroom when it hit me that Alafair was missing. She should have been there too. No way she'd let Vicki go without seeing her off.

"Where's Alafair?" I asked.

"She's out making herself useful," Emmery said. "You should give it a try sometime."

I didn't like the sound of that. Not only was it literally impossible – Alafair hadn't seen a useful day her entire life – but it was downright scary. I hoped that someone had sent her on a very specific errand, otherwise Alafair's idea of useful could mean just about anything.

I could tell that Emmery was winding up to throw some more verbal abuse my way and even though I knew I deserved it, we didn't have time for any more finger pointing.

"Enough!" I shouted. "There'll be plenty of time for this shit later, okay? Right now it isn't helping anybody, least of all Caleb. So, somebody please tell me, where the hell is Alafair?"

"She's upstairs knocking on every single door, trying to round up some help for your ass. You may have forgotten, but we've got some very powerful guests with us right now. Guests that owe a favor or two. She's up there calling in those favors."

But I could tell something wasn't right. Emmery was looking just about everywhere but at me, and Sheriff Blaylock was shifting nervously on the sofa, like something was squirming around under his ass.

"Okay, what the hell's wrong? What aren't you telling me?"

"Tell her, Emmery," Sheriff Blaylock said.

Emmery folded her arms across her chest and looked directly at me. "I'm sure it's nothing," she said. "Just, Alafair should have been back by now, and I sent the Sheriff upstairs to look for her and she wasn't there."

"What are you saying? She's missing?"

"Of course not," Emmery said. "I mean, why would she be? And she'd been to all the rooms. The sheriff checked on that."

"Yep, everyone registered told me she'd been by," Blaylock added. "And by the way, everyone is willing to help. You've got yourself an army there if you need it."

I was just about to ask Emmery if anyone was out looking for Alafair, when the phone in my back pocket started buzzing.

It was Moncrieffe. I swiped to answer and said, "They're about to leave. Going out the door in ten minutes."

"Oh! So I take it Miss Vicki is still coming?" Moncrieffe asked me.

"What? Are you nuts? Of course she's coming. Why wouldn't she be?"

"Because your lovely sister Alafair showed up ten minutes ago and offered herself as a replacement."

"Alafair is there? Let me speak to her. Right now."

"No, I don't think so. She's kind of busy at the moment. I will tell you though, little Caleb was very happy to see her. Bring the mother or don't, that's up to you."

Moncrieffe ended the call. I immediately tried him back but it went straight to voicemail. I looked up at Emmery.

"Alafair's at the vineyard. She went in Vicki's place."

183

"Oh, no." Emmery whispered.

Vicki walked into the living room, and I couldn't help but think that this Vicki was a far cry from the competent, put together young mother that I had come to know. She looked like a survivor of some death camp, or like she'd been in a war. Her eyes were red and swollen, her hair a matted mess stringing about her face. Held loosely in her hand she carried a small bag and I could see that it held some of Caleb's favorite toys.

"I don't give a shit who's there," she announced, eyes glinting like steel. "I'm going. Don't even think about trying to stop me."

"Vicki, I'm so sorry-" I began, but she held up her hand and cut me off.

"Tula honey, I don't blame you. This is *not* your fault."

"But -" I tried again, and again she stopped me.

"No, I don't want to hear it. All I want to hear from you is that you have a plan to get my kid back. And one more thing..."

"Of course," I told her. "Anything."

"Kill every single one of those bastards." Then she looked at Emmery and Blaylock. "Let's get the hell on the road. I want to see my boy."

Chapter 28

Once Vicki, Emmery, and the Sheriff were gone, I left Vicki's apartment, walked around the side of the inn and entered the wide double doors at the front. I was alternating between being pissed off beyond measure at Alafair and proud as hell.

The kid was made of stronger stuff than I'd realized. She had put her life on the line for Caleb and Vicki. All of us, really. Even Gwyneth, a woman she'd never even met.

I sent a silent shout out into the darkness, to whoever was listening, to please keep them all safe and strong. And to give me the wisdom to help get us through the whole thing. I guess it was a prayer, an entreaty, a wish. It was all of those things at once. I just hoped it would be answered.

I'd had it on my mind that I needed to call Ruby. I knew having her help might make the difference in getting my loved ones out of the vineyard alive. I was counting on her to help us figure out where the Moncrieffes might have stashed those skulls. When I entered the lobby, I saw that a call wasn't going to be necessary.

She was already there, curled up on the sofa, flipping through a magazine, a long slender cigarette curling smoke between two fingers of her right hand.

The first thing that hit me was the way she was dressed. I was used to seeing Ruby decked out to the nines. Even when she was up at Willowbrook, she typically kept up the whole couture designer vibe thing, but tonight she was dressed exactly the same as me. Camos and boots. Better labels I was pretty sure, but still. I'd never seen her dressed in such a fashion.

When she saw me, Ruby put down the magazine. Lifting her gaze to mine, I could see that her eyes were filled with anger and worry. And something else...

Resolve.

"Emmery called and filled me in on everything that's going on." As Ruby spoke, she was taking in my appearance, clothes covered in dried blood and streaks of dirt and mud caking my pants and boots. "It looks like you got into something while you were out there. Fill me in."

So I did. When she found out that Alafair, Caleb, and Vicki all three were now being held by Moncrieffe, her eyes filled with anger.

"Having the boy there was bad enough. Who's bright idea was it to add two more innocents to the mix?"

"If you'd seen the kid, you'd understand why I wanted his mother out there with him."

"Okay, I'll give you that one," Ruby said. "But Alafair? What on earth was she thinking? Surely she'd have realized that trading herself for Vicki wasn't going to work. She must have known the woman would go to her son come hell or high water once Moncrieffe agreed to allow it."

"She wasn't thinking, Ruby. She was just trying to help."

"Well, we've got a royal mess now, that's for sure. Now that they've got Alafair, they may not even want this Gwyneth anymore, which means they might just kill Vicki and Caleb."

"But why wouldn't they? Andrew, or this thing that used to be Andrew... he was pretty clear. He told me in no uncertain terms that he wanted his wife," I told her.

"I know why they wanted Gwyneth. And it has nothing to do with her being Andrew's wife. I think that is more a matter of convenience than anything else. Andrew was the one they really wanted, but of course they need a woman, any woman really, to complete the ceremony. I'm sure the prospect of having that woman be one of the Whitlows, a born witch, is kind of like a cherry on top. The power of a true witch sacrifice would be phenomenal."

I had no idea what kind of ceremony Aunt Ruby was referring to. Things had moved so quickly that I hadn't had time to really put everything together. I knew the Moncrieffes were behind it all, of course, and tonight I'd figured out that they hadn't simply killed Andrew, as I'd originally suspected, but had used the man, transformed him into a physical representation of some deity. I knew Gwyneth had somehow been infected by this same evil presence. But the *why* of it all was still a complete mystery. Now, if Aunt Ruby was right, Alafair...

"Are you saying they may kill Alafair? Or turn her into some kind of evil forest creature thing like Andrew?" Both outcomes made my blood run cold.

"They could do either. It depends on what kind of end result they're after. There are so many ceremonies associated with the Green Man, some require blood sacrifice; others, a kind of a joining, like you've seen with this Andrew fellow. And based on what they've done to the poor man, my guess is the latter."

"Aunt Ruby, as bad as all this is, there's more." I went on to tell her about the vines in the basement, how they were on the verge of covering the lodestone. That Victor had discovered that the Moncrieffes had initiated this assault even before they'd gone after Andrew and Gwyneth. They'd targeted us very specifically.

Ruby rubbed her chin thoughtfully, taking a few moments before responding.

"Have you told your mother?" She finally asked.

"I only just found out tonight."

"Well, call her and let her know. But later. There's not much she can do from Paris. Not about something like this. I don't know why in the world that woman can't keep her ass at home. I've always said she'd be the downfall of this family." Aunt Ruby sighed, then rose from the sofa, tucking a loose strand of hair behind her ear. She clapped her hands together and started heading toward the door that led to the basement.

"Well, come on, Tula," she said. "We've got work to do."

"Right now? I think we need to..."

Ruby stopped and turned back to look at me. I was still seated on the sofa. I wasn't about to head down to the basement and do any damn thing. My mind was on formulating a plan to get my people back, and even though I realized that the threat of the vines down there was a real one, I wasn't going to take the time for a midnight jaunt down to the basement to worry over a bunch of vines.

"If those vines cover the lodestone..." Ruby began.

"I know, I know. The protection spell will be broken..."

"Whoa, girl," Aunt Ruby took a couple of steps in my direction, then stopped, put her hands on her hips, and looked at me as if I were about the most annoyingly stupid thing she'd ever encountered. "Has your damn mother told you nothing? Really? You have no clue do you?"

"I don't know what you're talking about."

"Obviously." Ruby shook her head and let out a long sigh of exasperation. "Tula honey. If those vines completely cover the lodestone, it'll be the death of us. Anyone with Whitlow blood, they'll simply die."

"What? That can't be right..."

"It's right. Of course it's right. Do you honestly believe that I wouldn't know a thing or two about this?"

Of course she would. There was nothing about the Whitlows and our magic that Aunt Ruby didn't know. It was hard to fathom, but I believed her. If she said we'd die, then we'd die. Time was running out. In more ways than one. We had to come up with a plan for Moncrieffe, and quickly, but if we were dead, then obviously any such plan would be moot.

I got up from the sofa.

Time   to   do   some   midnight   pruning.

Chapter 29

As we descended to the bowels of the old inn, Ruby asked me if I knew anything at all about the inn's history and its relationship to our family. I told her I didn't know much beyond that it had once been our ancestral home. I'd always found that pretty amazing, that a place this huge would be anyone's home. As a country inn, it was already large, but as a residence it was obscenely massive.

"This place was built in the late seventeen hundreds," Ruby began, "shortly after the birth of our nation. Built by a Whitlow, of course. Virginia Whitlow – who at the time was married to Captain Verland Smith. Like all the Whitlow husbands, he took her name of course."

"Was that even allowed in those days?"

"Well, of course it was pretty unusual, but yes it was allowed. And since Captain Smith was a renowned hero of the Revolutionary War, and from all accounts a man who suffered no fools, no one would have dared to raise an objection. Not publicly, at any rate."

Maybe not, but from what I understood of history, in those days, women weren't even allowed to vote, were considered to be not much above farm animals, so I imagined that a husband assuming the surname of a wife, war hero or not, would have certainly raised a few eyebrows. I figured he'd caught a fair amount of shit for it, regardless of what Aunt Ruby had to say. The simple fact that Captain Smith had been up for such a thing made him rise in my estimation. By a lot.

"I wonder why he built such a large home?" I asked her. "In those days it must have seemed like a palace."

"Well, it didn't start out quite as big as it is today. I believe the original building was only about half this size. Still huge by the standards of the day, and then over the years various Whitlows added to the place."

When we reached the bottom level, I stepped forward and keyed in the code on the security panel. With a barely audible hiss, the door slid open and we stepped through.

Immediately I could see that the vines had spread even further. Ruby stepped up to the edge of the concrete lip that surrounded the field of black, shimmering rock. For a few moments she just stood there, silent and tense – the kind of silent that makes you think when someone finally speaks whatever comes out of their mouth isn't going to be anything good. Probably going to be something along the lines of a tongue lashing. And with Ruby, well, you had to figure she might decide to skip over the tongue lashing part and just kill you outright. But when she finally spoke, she didn't seem angry, the opposite really.

The woman was excited.

"Oh, this is going to be *fun*," she said. "The audacity of those people. To think they could succeed in such a thing. It's almost admirable."

"So you can stop it?" I asked, keenly aware that every second we spent down in the basement dealing with this problem was time I needed to be spending on getting Caleb, Vicki, and Alafair back home. And destroying the Moncrieffes and the Andrew thing while we were at it.

Then there was the matter of finding maybe a thousand skulls and figuring out a way to get rid of them all. My plate was beyond full. And I said as much to Ruby.

"Well honey, like we discussed upstairs, you have to be alive to do anything at all. And if these vines cover the whole field, you won't be alive anymore. Nor will I, or Emmery or Alafair, nor half the county. Maybe more. Most everyone in town carries a drop or two of Whitlow blood. These little vines could kill every single one of us."

"Whatever we do, we have to hurry. So let's do this fast."

To this, Ruby laughed. "It's going to take days to fix this. Maybe weeks. Of course, if we're successful tonight at the vineyard, that alone will put a stop to this nonsense. But we can't depend on that. These vines are moving *fast*. I can see and hear them spreading. Could be they get to the lodestone before we even get back to the vineyard."

"So what? You're saying we all might die within the next few hours?"

"Well, yes, except I have a plan, of course."

And then she told me. While stopping the growth of the vines was something she couldn't do, not quickly anyway, that would require her going back and forth to the vineyard at least a couple of times, and waiting for a full moon if she wanted to ensure success. Naturally though, being Ruby, she still had an ace up her sleeve.

"Okay," I said. "What are you going to do?"

"I need to get into your mother's office."

"Mom doesn't have an office."

"Of course she does," Ruby said. "Come with me."

She started walking toward the corner of the basement which was a good fifty yards from where we stood. I followed, keenly aware of every second passing, my worry level now turned up to about a hundred. All I could think about was getting this behind me. Even though I understood on some level that what was happening in the basement posed the greater overall risk, wrapping my head around that wasn't easy. I'd never been known for my multi-tasking skills and this was no exception. I had people at the vineyard at risk, and for the moment that's where my energy demanded to be focused.

I felt like a dog who'd just had their favorite bone snatched away.

When we finally made it to the corner, Ruby stood before a smooth section of concrete wall, and spoke an incantation in what sounded to me like a strange and foreign language.

As if on cue, a section of the wall slid aside and revealed a room that was so extraordinary I could never have even imagined it.

"What the hell is this?" I was standing in the doorway, rooted to the spot by something somewhere between shock and awe. How could such a room exist, right here inside our inn, and no one had ever spoken of it?

"This is the office of the keeper of the lodestone, but we just call it The Library. It'll be yours one day soon, so you may as well go on in and make yourself at home."

"But how... why..."

"Your mother didn't tell you about it because, well... because she's a twat. A twat who prefers to spend most of her time pretending to herself and others that she isn't a witch. Cluing you girls in on the lodestone, and The Library, or anything remotely witchy means she has to acknowledge her own roots. I'll never know why the lodestone chose her in the first place. Maybe just as a stepping stone to you. Or maybe just because your mother has always been blessed with things she doesn't deserve. Sometimes I think that's her true power. Who knows?"

Finally, I was able to get my feet to move and stepped into the room. The Library. If Ruby was right, soon to be *mine*.

The room was about forty feet deep and half again as wide, every inch of wall space taken up by floor to ceiling bookshelves and glass cabinets full of curiosities the likes of which I'd never even dreamt. I stopped in front of one such cabinet that showcased an animal that looked very much like an owl, and though it did have a smattering of feathers, the lower part of its body was decidedly reptilian.

"What is this thing?" I asked. "Is it alive or stuffed or what?" It seemed to be neither alive nor dead, but somewhere in between. Something akin to what I understood suspended animation to be. Yet, there was something in its eyes that made me feel like I was being watched, as if there was a glimmer of life or a kind of awareness lurking deep inside it.

"Oh, Nelson there is very much alive." She moved over to the cabinet and put her hand onto the glass. I couldn't be sure, but it seemed to me that the creature responded ever so slightly.

"He's just resting until he's needed. I don't imagine your mother has needed him in a very long while. If ever. You'll find dozens more creatures like Nelson, though probably none quite as cute and cuddly. And sweet Nelson there is very special to me."

I didn't want to ask, wanted with every fiber of my being, despite this amazing room, to get back to my problem of the vineyard. But I couldn't help myself. I had to know. If something was "special" to Ruby, it was a thing I'd likely want to avoid. Like her pigs. They were damned special to the woman, and she'd like as not feed you to them if you were dumb enough to cross her.

"Why does this thing mean so much to you?" I asked.

"Well, Nelson has the blood of my first love flowing through his veins. He didn't make much of a love, or even a man, for that matter. Broke my heart, actually. He works quite well as a Nelson, though. Don't you think?"

Okay, so this... thing in the cabinet had either eaten an old boyfriend of Ruby's, or had previously been said boyfriend. Either thought was pretty petrifying. I didn't blame my mother for leaving Nelson locked up in a cabinet.

I wanted to explore every inch of this place, and I had questions – lots of them. If this space was meant primarily for one person's use, why were there at least a dozen library tables set up in the middle of the room, each of them with a half dozen or so individual reading lamps? I wanted to know how many books were actually here, surely a thousand or more, wanted to know if that was a real mummy on the far left wall. I had at least as many questions as this room had books.

But they would have to wait.

195

"What are we here for Ruby? What do you need?"

"Oh, I've already grabbed it, see?" In the hand that wasn't pressed lovingly against Nelson's cabinet, she held an old hourglass.

"What are you going to do with that?" I asked her.

"Well, as I mentioned, I can't kill the vines, not quickly, not in time for you to do what you must tonight." Ruby was running her hands up and down the hourglass as if memorizing its contours. It was long and narrow, and much larger than any I'd seen before. The wood looked ancient, and the glass holding the sand was milky and yellowed. "It's always all about time, isn't it?" Ruby said. "No time for this, no time for that. Time is always running out. It's just so tedious."

"So what are you planning? If that hourglass is supposed to tell you when we're out of time, I can answer that one. We're out. Now."

"Don't be funny dear. Of course that's not what it's for."

"Okay, then what?"

"For stopping time, of course!"

And ten minutes later, back at the lodestone, that's what she did.

I think I'd been expecting some sort of earth shaking incantation - vibrating walls, howls of wind, maybe glowing orbs dancing all over the field of magnetite. Seemed to me like stopping time would require something along those lines. I mean a blood sacrifice wouldn't really have surprised me given the enormity of such a thing. But it was nothing like that at all.

What most people, myself included - yes, even though I'm a born-witch, I'm not above all the stereotyping -

what most people think of, when thinking of spell casting, is something much more awe-inspiring than what actually tends to take place.

It's ninety percent intent. In many ways, the thing that separates witches from mortals is nothing more than our finely tuned ability to cast intent. Channel that intent into a laser and send it to whatever the target happens to be. Oftentimes, objects used in spell casting are basically just props to help get the razor sharp focus required to channel.

And Ruby's time stopping spell was no exception. Words spoken softly over the old hourglass, the hum of Ruby's intent vibrating around us, and that was pretty much it...

Well... a gentle breeze *did* begin to whisper through the vines and the magnetite. And yes, the hourglass *did* light up with a ghostly green glow. But lightning didn't strike and that wind never made it to a howl, and the green glow didn't ever come close to erupting in fire.

But it worked, all the same. In the basement, over the lodestone, time simply stopped. And with it the growth of the vines.

Ruby and I walked out of that circle of stopped time, out of the sub-basement, and ascended back up to the lobby. Before we opened the door, she handed me the hourglass.

"We'll take it with us to the vineyard, though I'm not sure what good it will do," she said, placing the piece into my hand.

"I can imagine lots of uses," I said.

"I know what you're thinking Tula, but it's too risky. Stopping time at the vineyard and then just waltzing in and taking care of business isn't how it would go down."

"Why not?" To me it seemed like a damn fine idea. I'd already started to plan the whole scenario in my mind.

"Use your head, girl. If time stopping was a simple, safe thing to do, don't you think witches would be doing it all the time? Like, you see a kid about to get run over by a car - why not just stop time, rush out and pull the kid out of the way, right? Imagine any such catastrophe, if it was that easy we'd all be running around playing Time Lord twenty-four seven, wouldn't we?"

All I could do was shrug. I didn't know where this was going but Aunt Ruby was in teacher mode, so I figured I was about to find out.

"The reason we don't is because like so often is the case with magic, it's extremely dangerous"

"Then why even bring the hourglass?" I asked her.

"Well, if a super skilled witch, one with an intent level of at least silver, is the one doing the casting, there are ways to stop time in a sort of micro targeted kind of way. It's risky though, and *you* certainly wouldn't be able to do it."

But Aunt Ruby could. I knew she'd reached platinum, the highest level possible, and had been the youngest witch in the Northern Hemisphere to have done so. 'Course I didn't know when that had happened. Aunt Ruby's age was a closely guarded secret. For all I knew she'd been around in the seventeen hundreds when our inn was being constructed.

Having her with us tonight could make all the difference in the world. Time stopping or not, she was capable of magic that I could only dream of.

"Tula honey," she said as we stepped into the lobby. "What exactly is your skill level now anyway?"

"Who knows," I told her. "I've never been tested." Our mother wouldn't allow such a thing when we were younger, and now that we didn't need her permission, none of us had bothered with it. Truth was, Mother had done a pretty good job of indoctrinating her daughters into the world without witchcraft. Not a single one of us ever thought about magic as anything other than a passing interest, not really even rising to the level of a hobby. We'd mostly just focused on the bare minimum. Spells and concoctions that we could use easily and readily in our daily lives. Nothing more.

But some things came easy, like my skill with the calling of small animals. I'd been able to do that effortlessly since I was a child. Emmery had a particular skill with water, and Alafair could dream travel at the drop of a hat. But anything that required study and work, forget about it. Not only were we not taught, we were discouraged from learning.

And it stuck.

But now, this case was making me see that my mother had been wrong. People I loved were in real danger and yet I barely had access to the power that might help save them. I felt swollen with regret and longing. Why hadn't I mastered the magic that I was literally *born* to? The very idea of this loss made me feel ill.

I didn't know about Emmery and Alafair, but I wasn't going to be that witch anymore.

I'd master this shit or die trying.

Right now I was worse than a novice, but at least I'd have Ruby with me, and if there was a more badass witch this side of the equator, I'd never heard the name.

A line from my favorite movie ever popped into my head. Wyatt Earp right before the showdown in *Tombstone.*

In the words of old Wyatt, kind of paraphrased and made my own..."*I'm coming, you punk-assed bastards, and hell's coming with me.*"

Chapter 30

Victor and John were waiting when we got back up to the lobby. I could see white bandaging peeking out from the neck of John's shirt, and a large gash on his cheek was covered in one of those butterfly bandages, but his eyes looked clear and focused.

Mauled to hell and back, but at least he's recovered from my frog-tropic intervention. Score one for the froggies. And he wasn't high anymore. I wasn't sure if I was happy about that or not. I kind of liked easy going trippin' out John. A nice change from the whole Eliot Ness Mr. FBI guy thing.

Victor, for his part, was sprawled out on one of the sofas, sucking on what looked to be a bag of plasma. *Snack time.*

Ruby looked at both men, then at me.

"Introduce me dear," she demanded, and so I did. Then she insisted on having a look at John's injuries.

"Decent work, even for an amateur," she sniffed. "Doctors nowadays rely too much on WebMD if you ask me. Always with the little iPad's in their laps and that nonsense. I wouldn't trust them with a hangnail."

The cougar bite looked particularly awful, though most of the skin surrounding it was intact. Luckily for John, the cat had only bitten, and not torn. I figured that the sound of the whistle had caused the beast to simply let go. Otherwise he'd have been missing a sizable chunk of shoulder.

When Ruby was done, she carefully re-wrapped the bandages, then turned her attention to Victor, but with none of the warmth she'd shown to John.

"I didn't think vampires were allowed at the inn," the glower she sent my way made me feel like something from the bottom of a shoe. "What is this business, Tula? How did this *thing* get in here?"

"This *thing*, as you so rudely address me, was of course invited," Victor said. "How else could I be here at all?" Victor was looking at Ruby as if he'd like to suck on her for a bit instead of the plasma bag.

"So you presume me to be stupid?" Aunt Ruby asked him. "Everyone knows your kind doesn't need an invitation. That myth was debunked centuries ago." Then she turned to me and continued. "Your mother would be horrified."

"Victor... well, he's different," I told her. "He..." I was trying to remember what it was about Victor that set him apart. I'd been told, but for the moment, it escaped me. It was true, we *didn't* allow vampires, but Victor was an exception.

"February 29," Victor offered. "Leap year."

"Yes! That's it," I told Ruby. "Victor was turned on a Leap Day... I don't know the year." In fact I knew almost nothing at all about Leap Year vamps period. None of us did. Channeling our thoughts in that direction resulted in nothing but a vast, impenetrable fogging of the brain. There was some powerful magic that kept us from being able to even *think* on their origins.

"And I'll never tell," Victor said to us with a smile. "Vampires never do. But being a Leap Year initiate, you witches can't refuse me. Ever. Just be glad I'm not one to take advantage," he added, looking pointedly in my direction. "Otherwise..."

"Hell's Bells," Ruby whispered. Her eyes had suddenly gone from cold to frostbite. "Leap Year vampire! I've never seen one of you before. You know what this means don't you, young man?"

"Yeah, yeah, yeah. I know. You'll kill me if you get a chance, etcetera, etcetera. Send me to the depths of hell, dance at my funeral, spit on my grave, and all that jazz. Are you done yet?" he asked her.

"You've been warned."

"Ok. Well you can't refuse me, so now comes the part where I tell you not to kill me. End of story."

"We'll see," Ruby told him. "We'll just see."

I was acutely aware of time flying by, and I didn't need Ruby's fancy hourglass to tell me that we were running out of it. I told them all as much. Ruby and Victor continued to shoot each other looks that would have scared the living shit out of anybody with a brain, but in spite of the electrified hate in the room, I could tell we were finally about to get down to business.

About to make some plans.

Which immediately started my skin itching and a big knot was forming in the pit of my stomach. I was allergic to planning. And it was an affliction I came by honestly. Though our mother was around at least from time to time, to a great extent, us girls had been raised by our grandparents, and Grandaddy Whitlow had always cautioned us about the folly of planning for anything. He would laugh at folks who saved their money or even had the audacity to fill the gas tanks on their cars. "They must think an awful lot of themselves," he'd say. "Being so sure they'll be able to spend that money or run that gas out their cars." Filling up at the gas pumps or watching a saving account swell was in his opinion, just asking for trouble.

I didn't consider myself a true believer in fate as a concept, but he sure as hell taught me not to tempt it. And by any definition, planning did just that. I didn't really know if the old adage about God laughing while men make plans was true, God might not laugh, but I knew a little sprite named Fate that did. She laughed her ass off and I was kinda on a first name basis with the hussy.

But my discomfort aside, I knew plans were required, and I'd just have to suck it up and roll with it. At least Ruby was the one in charge and if anyone could beat Fate at her shitty little game, it would be her.

Ruby knew just about everything there was to know about druid lore, and gave us all a rundown on the forest gods they worshipped, and at least in this case, had somehow managed to conjure. How a group of bonafide old school Druids had come to settle in Henley-on-Hale without us Whitlows even knowing would have to be examined at a later date. Right now we just needed to figure out a way to kill them and their monster.

Ruby was very careful to make sure we all understood that Druids would normally be some of our most natural allies. But Moncrieffe and his ilk had apparently decided on the dark path. It wasn't unheard of. Some families of true born witches had done the same. It was rumored that even a Whitlow or three had dabbled in the dark arts. I looked over at Ruby as she continued speaking. I'd heard plenty of stories that she herself was one of those Whitlows, but had seen no real evidence that it was true. There was the story of Cousin Priss being fed to Ruby's pigs. But that was just a story. Who knew if there was any truth to it? I only knew that right about now, having someone on board who knew a little bit about the dark side was a plus.

We very well might need it, and if that's what it took to get my people back, I'd dance with the devil himself.

Ruby had stopped speaking and it was Victor's turn. He outlined everything he'd learned while his fog-self had drifted around the vineyard.

It boiled down to a simple equation. Destroying the skulls plus killing the bad guys equaled us getting our people back and Gwyneth being released from the vines that were slowly killing her and her baby. It sounded pretty straightforward – all in a day's work kind of thing – and then John asked the question that had been on my lips since we started.

"How are we going to *find* the skulls, much less destroy them?" he asked. "It's not like we have days to figure this out. We have hours." As he was speaking, I couldn't help but think about him, the day he'd shown up on my doorstep – a button-down, Special Agent by the book kind of guy. Now he was sitting here discussing evil druids and forest god's as if he did it every day. Like taking out the garbage or something.

"We don't have to *find* the skulls," Ruby said. "There's really only one place they could be. Well, only one *reasonable* place. Mortals are uniquely lacking in imagination, so if there was a need to hide a thousand skulls and the perfect place was right there in one's backyard so to speak, I doubt these Moncrieffes would go to the trouble of creating a brand new one. Do you?"

"So where are they?" I asked her.

"There's an old mine shaft in the woods behind their property. It was part of the old Linder line, dug out ages ago, back when old man Linder sunk his entire fortune into the belief that there was copper under the mountain. And he actually found some, just a little. Not enough to amount to much as it turned out. But it's still there, and the entrance is just at the edge of the woods. Right behind the vineyard. As far as I know the mine itself is still intact."

"She's probably right," Victor said, looking at Ruby with a hint of grudging admiration. "If I needed to hide a thousand magic, screaming skulls, an old mine is perfect. I'd jump on it."

John and I looked at each other. "That's what the surveillance cameras are for," he said. "They're monitoring that entrance."

I thought about my electronic jammer. Thought about how Moncrieffe and his crew had found John and me earlier. I was pretty sure the jammer hadn't failed or anything, which meant Moncrieffe had other ways of keeping watch. It was troubling, the fact that the man had been so *ready* for us, down to where we'd parked the Land Rover and even *when* we'd be coming out of the woods. And I was pretty sure that I knew what at least one of those ways was.

"The cougars," I told them. "Somehow he's controlling them as well. I think that's how he knew we were there tonight."

"Probably," Aunt Ruby said. "And there may be other safeguards in the woods. Maybe dozens of them. But that doesn't matter, I'm not worried about a bunch of cougars."

Easy enough for her to say, I thought to myself. Until you'd had to take a freezing cold bath with a pissed off mountain lion, you really didn't know beans. I could still smell the stink coming out of that damn cat's mouth, and I, for one, wasn't planning on an encore.

"You need to worry about the cougars," I told her. "One of them damn near killed John tonight as you yourself can see. Next time we might not be so lucky."

"If it came to it, I could handle a dozen cats, Tula. But it's not going to, because we're not entering through the woods."

I wondered if she was going to magic us into the mine shaft somehow, and Ruby seemed to pick up on my thoughts, because she shook her head at me and continued. "No. Nothing like that, girl! Use your head. A burst of magic big enough to ninja us all into that mine is exactly what we want to avoid. Moncrieffe may be human, but from what you tell me, Andrew is far from it. He'd know we were there. I'm sure they have people stationed all around that entrance and we'd have a fight on our hands almost instantly."

"Okay, then what?" Victor asked. "You know I could do this by myself. I can vaporize and be in and out of there before they know what hit 'em."

Ruby looked at him as if he'd just crawled out from under a rock and said: "*You?* These people are holding an innocent young boy and his mother. Not to mention my *niece*, my *blood*. Do you honestly think I'm about to risk their welfare on the likes of you? Leap Year, Leap Day, I don't care. You're still a vampire. I'd die first."

"Okay, suit yourself," Victor told her. "So what's your plan? Enlighten us."

Ruby reached into her bag and pulled out a rolled up tube of paper and a felt marker. She laid the tube down on the coffee table and began unrolling what I instantly recognized as a map of the county. She then took her marker and circled a spot near the outer edge of the county line.

"There's the vineyard," she said. "And here..." She circled another spot just behind the first one. "That's the entrance to the mine shaft." She bent over the paper and after a moment drew another circle that was roughly an inch away from the first two. From the legend at the bottom of the map, I estimated the last circle was about a mile east of the vineyard. Looking at the map and the circles, I tried to bring to mind what was in the general area where she'd placed that third circle.

Finally it hit me.

"That's the Bentley Cemetery." Even thinking of the place sent cold chills down my spine. If the Whitlow's had a nemesis in the county, it would be the Bentleys. Nowadays the two families were in the midst of a truce that had held for the last hundred or so years, but back in the day, the Bentleys had even burned a few of us. Right there in the same place where that wretched graveyard stood.

I'd just about rather take another bath with a mountain lion than go anywhere near the place.

But that wasn't even the worst of it. As part of the truce, we'd agreed to a spell that basically stripped us of our powers if any Whitlow dared step foot on Bentley soil.

"We can't go anywhere near that place, Ruby. You know this."

"We can and we will. There's a cave there, and it leads directly into that mineshaft."

"But..."

"No buts. We're doing it."

"We'll be powerless," I argued. That wasn't such a big deal for me, I was pretty much powerless on a good day. But I'd counted on Ruby being my big gun, my nuclear option, and now she was about to piss that all away.

"I agree. It's not ideal. But we don't have time to waste coming up with a better plan."

Okay, I thought. It wasn't so bad. As soon as we were off Bentley land, we'd be good to go.

"How far into that cave, tunnel, whatever, will we have to go before we leave their property?" I asked.

She wouldn't look at me when she answered. Just kept herself busy rolling up the map and tucking it back into her bag. Finally she raised her head and looked me in the eye.

"When the Linden family sold the mine, they sold it to the Bentleys, if you must know."

Oh. Shit. The mine belonged to the Bentleys. Then I thought of what Ruby had said earlier.

"But you said the Moncrieffes owned the land."

"Well yes, they do."

I was just about to let out the breath I'd been holding when she added, "But the Bentleys kept the mineral rights."

"Does that—"

Ruby raised a hand to halt me mid-stream. "If you're about to ask me what that means in terms of us, our powers..."

"Yes! That's exactly what I was going to ask. Will we have any or will we be defenseless?"

"I don't have the answer to that," she said, shaking her head, momentarily at a loss. That was a new thing. Ruby was *never* at a loss. Seeing her that way terrified me.

"I just don't know," she added. "I wish I did."

Chapter 31

I was back at home gathering up everything I could think of that might be needed for our trip back to the vineyard. For a brief moment I even considered bringing our rabid chainsaw Larry Joe, but then thought better of it. Fifty-fifty chance when push came to shove it would side with the bad guys anyway.

As I made my preparations, it struck me that the house seemed dreadfully empty, silent like a tomb, like no one had ever lived inside its walls, or like someone had, but maybe they'd recently died. That's how big a hole was left by Alafair's absence. And not just absent as in not at home, but absent like she might very well never return.

I choked back a sob and wiped unexpected tears from my eyes. My little sister was a humongous pain in my backside. Constantly into shit she shouldn't be, frequently embarrassing, always stubborn as a mule. Everyone knew she'd argue with a stump, and being in her presence for fifteen minutes could often feel like an hour. She was that good at wearing you down.

And apparently brave as hell. She'd offered herself up without even telling a soul. I was so proud of her I was about to bust, yet at the same time, I wanted to wring her neck. She'd compounded our problems to say the least, and she should have known that Vicki would never let anyone take her place by Caleb's side.

But really the main thing I was feeling at that moment was that Alafair was mine, warts and all - no pun intended, in case some of you really believe that warts and witches go hand in hand. I loved the little shit, and I was determined to have her back. Along with Caleb and Vicki.

John had said he was going to go back to the cabin to check in on Gwyneth and his dad, Ruby had gone up to Willowbrook to fetch a few more things, and Victor - well, who knew what he might be doing. Certainly not putting together a trick bag. Vampires didn't need a bag of tricks, they *were* a bag of tricks.

We'd all agreed to meet at Bentley Cemetery. It had been decided that Moncrieffe and his goons were probably watching the inn, so leaving from there was out of the question. We also had to assume that our homes were being watched, so getting out of the house was going to require a bit of subterfuge. Unlike Ruby and Victor, both of whom had the ability to just kind of magic themselves from one place to the next, for myself and John a more traditional means was required.

The two of us would be sneaking out of my house, hoofing it through the woods for about a mile, where Sheriff Blaylock had arranged for a deputy to pick us up on the roadside and take us on to the graveyard.

I hoped that would be enough. Moncrieffe wasn't stupid. He would assume we'd try something, but if he didn't know we knew where the skulls were located, and didn't know about the other entrance to the mine, we'd have a bit of a jump on anything he might have up his sleeve.

That was the hope anyway.

I was in the process of shoving a fold-over cheese sandwich into my mouth when John knocked on the front door.

I let him in and told him to have a seat while I finished my sandwich. I looked at the time and saw that we had a few more minutes to kill, so I asked him if he wanted me to fix him one as well.

"No, I grabbed something while I was at the cabin," he answered.

"How is Gwyneth?" I thought about the reaper that had been lurking in the corner by her bed, wondered if it was still hanging around. Prayed it wasn't.

"She was actually sitting up in bed, if you can believe it. I don't know what was in that concoction your aunt sent, but I'm grateful."

"And the vines?"

"The vines are still there, just like before, but they haven't advanced. It kills me to even look at her, and to be honest, I wonder if it wouldn't have been better if she'd stayed unconscious. She's just... terrified, if you want to know the truth. I think Dad's already had to sedate her."

Of course she'd be terrified. Who wouldn't be? To wake up and find that half of your body was sprouting greenery like some backyard shrub would kind of do that to a girl. Ruby seemed convinced that destroying the skulls would kill whatever had hold of Gwyneth as well. I hoped she was right.

At any rate, knowing that the woman's condition was still improving took one bit of worry off my mind, which was a blessing. Getting through this night without any of us losing our lives was enough to worry about, thank you very much.

"Look," John began. "I have to tell you how grateful I am. And sorry. Very, very sorry to have gotten you mixed up in all this. I never dreamed that this would end up putting your family at risk. I hope you know I'd never have knocked on your door that morning if I'd thought anything like this would happen."

"I don't believe that, John. And I hope it's not true," I said. "I hope you'd have moved heaven and earth to save your sister. I'd have done it for mine, and I wouldn't have given a shit how many people had to get put at risk to make it happen. And I'd hazard a guess that Gwyneth at her worst is an epic sister compared to either of mine, both of whom are glorious pains in my ass, so please tell me you don't mean that."

"Well," he grinned. "When you put it like that, I guess you're right. Maybe I would have. But that kid, Caleb. If I'd known he'd get dragged into this, I'd have never involved you."

That I could believe. Having Caleb at risk was a game-changer, even for me. If I had to choose between him and Alafair, I honestly had no idea where I'd come down on that. So I decided not to think about it. Some things, I'd learned, were best left unexamined.

"We're going to get all three of them out of there alive. That's the only option. Caleb, Vicki, and Alafair. They're all coming home."

"And Andrew?" The words were spoken softly and when I looked at him, his eyes were unreadable. Should I tell him Andrew was probably as good as dead? That even if we didn't kill him this night, that the man was already lost? Did I even know that to be true?

"I don't know about Andrew," I finally said. "If we can save him, we will."

He looked back at me as if he knew I was only speaking words I thought he probably wanted to hear.

"Okay," he said, the message in his eyes a hard one, and plain for anyone to see. "But if he has to die to save my sister or any of the others... kill him. Don't even hesitate. If it comes to that I'd do it in a heartbeat.

"Let's not even go there til we have to..."

"No, listen. I saw him tonight. I know I was stoned out of my mind – thank you for that, by the way – but I *saw* him. Whatever that thing is, it's not Andrew."

"No..."

"And it doesn't need to live."

Then he picked up his pack and stood.

"You ready?" He asked me.

"Are you sure you're up for this?" I looked at his bandaged shoulder. It had to be hurting like hell.

"Yep," he said. "Let's go. Nothin' more fun than having a pretty girl take a stroll through a graveyard with you in the middle of the night."

Then he had the audacity to actually wink at me.

I didn't know whether to hug him or knock his teeth out.

I did neither.

Instead, I winked back at him and then made both of us invisible. I would only be able to hold such a spell for about three minutes, but that would be long enough to get us out of the house, through the backyard and into the woods. If we ran like hell.

I wasn't Ruby, but I had a few tricks up my sleeve.

After that we'd be on our own and completely visible to anyone bothering to look, until we met up with the deputy.

I sent out a wish to the universe and anyone who was listening to let that be enough.

Chapter 32

Bentley Cemetery was as austere and bleak as the family it serviced. For the last two hundred years the land had welcomed the Bentley dead, and none others. You had to be born to the family or related through marriage for the privilege of one day being planted in this particular piece of earth.

The cemetery grounds lay at the end of a dirt road, surrounded on three sides by dark, menacing forests. Just inside the gates, at the top of a steep hillside, stood a tiny chapel, squarish and plain, tucked in beneath the branches of two towering oaks. I know the description seems lovely – pastoral even – but it was anything but. The little church seemed savage in its stinginess, and guarded; so devoid of anything that might make it beautiful that it was easy to imagine its builders were those who favored brutal, unflinching righteousness. The two oaks towering above it didn't seem majestic, but more like threatening sentinels, branches lifted against the darkened sky.

Above the door leading inside the little place of worship was a rough wood sign that said simply "Bentley Church". No denomination was given, which probably seemed strange to any outsider who might have wandered there, but I knew the Bentleys had their very own way of looking at such things. The family had their own path to what they believed to be heaven and salvation, and had no need for instruction or intrusion from other forms of established religion.

To say they belonged to the "hellfire and brimstone" club would be an understatement. But for all their rigid rules and self-righteousness, I knew them to be a murderous lot, and dangerous to the extreme.

As I looked out the back window of the cruiser, I wanted to be just about anywhere else in the world, wanted to sit right there in the cop car with Blaylock's deputy and let Ruby and the rest of them finish this wretched job.

But I opened the door and put my foot out onto the rough gravel.

On Bentley land.

Immediately I felt something leaving me. Leeching out of my body like the very air itself had become some giant invisible sponge. I'd expected to feel something along those lines, but even so, the sensation was just about overwhelming. I'd never imagined I had that much magic to *lose* in the first place, but judging from the way I felt, I wondered if maybe I'd been wrong. Maybe I was filled to the brim with it. Or maybe even the loss of a little bit of it was just this devastating.

With an effort of will, I put one foot in front of the other. With John at my heels, I headed toward the plain wooden gate, opened it, and stepped inside.

The cemetery was large, probably covering at least two acres, and to my eyes at least, looked to be pretty well full up. Soon the Bentleys would need to clear out part of the woods to add more space to the thing.

Though there must have been well over a hundred graves, there wasn't an ornamental headstone to be seen, just stumpy little rectangles of stone and marble, varying heights, all uniformly gray and forbidding. In the scant moonlight they reminded me of squat little soldiers, ugly and mean and solid.

The place was particularly solemn, as if the family had determined that the dead might be distracted from their rest by any piece of frivolity or beauty.

It was quiet as a tomb and I couldn't help but wonder if even the ghosts had bolted. If so, I wouldn't have blamed them, I knew I'd do the same if by some mischance I'd come to be buried in such a dark, forbidding piece of earth. Though that was hardly going to happen. The Bentleys would bulldoze the place before they'd allow a Whitlow interred in their precious, saintly soil.

I pulled the flashlight out of my bag, flipped it on, then stabbed the light into the darkness ahead.

"Turn that damned thing off, Tula!" It was Ruby, coming toward where John and I stood, marching over graves as if they weren't even there, Victor right behind her. I was wishing the two of them would take some care. Everyone knew it was bad luck to walk over a grave, but there they both were, stomping over the Bentley dead with zero concern.

I flipped off the light and waited for her instruction.

"It took you two long enough to get here," she scolded.

I knew we were at least ten minutes ahead of the time we'd all agreed on, but decided not to point that out. Instead, I asked her if she'd figured out where the cave was, and if the entrance was clear.

"I didn't need to find it, Tula. I went right to it. I've been in the thing a half a dozen times over the years. And yes, it's clear."

"Okay," I told her. "Let's get going."

"Don't turn that light on again," she cautioned. "Unless you're keen to feel some Bentley buckshot in your butt. It's not like we got permission to skulk around their property, and we sure as hell aren't welcome. Just stay close and keep quiet."

Which is what we all did. Our little group silently marched through the graveyard, then into the woods until we finally came to a natural opening in the side of a steep rock cliff.

Single file, with Victor in front and John bringing up the rear, we stepped through.

It was much darker inside the cave than it had been in the woods, which wasn't surprising given that we were without even a sliver of moon to light the way.

We were about six feet in when Ruby gave the okay to turn on our flashlights, which we all did, including Victor, even though he had no need for such things. As a vampire, he could see as well in pitch darkness as he could in a bright, well lit room.

I felt not a tingle of indication that my powers were returning, not that I'd expected them to. I knew we had a ways to go before we'd be clear of Bentley land. And then with the issue of the family still owning the mineral rights at the mine, it was possible they wouldn't return until we exited the mine shaft itself. Needless to say, if that's how things played out, it would be a very bad thing indeed. If we met any kind of resistance at all, we'd have to rely on nothing but our wits and our weapons.

Well, and a vampire, of course. But even though Victor said he was fully on board, and seemed to be sincerely excited at the prospect of raining down some fury on the Moncrieffes, I still had my doubts that he'd stick his neck out much if it came right down to it.

But then again, he didn't even have to be here, yet here he was, at the head of the line no less, leading us through the tunnel. I thought about last year, when I'd kissed him. Sure, I'd been drunk and certainly not myself, but in truth I'd never regretted it. Even now, I could feel the attraction. There was something so alive about Victor, especially when you considered how well and truly dead he was.

John would have been an obvious choice for a smooch partner, had I wanted to be kissing on somebody. Tall, dark, handsome, *human*. And alive, very much alive. There was something to be said for having a pulse. And a part of me *wanted* to be attracted to him, I knew I should be, and probably would be, but there was one thing about John that was absolutely disqualifying. He was a cop, and Whitlow women didn't pair up with cops. Sure, FBI was on the fancy side of the spectrum, but still, he was law enforcement. Centuries of your people being drowned and burned at the stake would tend to generate a healthy grudge against such types.

So Mr. FBI, handsome, kind, and smart as he seemed to be, just hadn't been on my radar in that way. But in spite of that, I knew I'd developed a certain affection for the man. And more than a fair amount of admiration. How could I not? He'd been mauled by a mountain lion, still had to be in tremendous pain, but here he was, marching with the rest of us to what could well be his death.

All for the sake of others.

We were more than halfway through the tunnel when I discovered that breathing was becoming difficult for me. At first I marked it down to exhaustion, or maybe some weird claustrophobic reaction. But with each halting step, it became more and more difficult to draw air into my lungs. I was about to mention this to the others when suddenly, there came a low rumbling, and a shower of rocks fell down from above, followed by a shout coming from the head of the line.

Victor.

His sudden shout had turned into a howl of pain. When I was finally able to pin him in the beam of my light, I could see that he was clenching the side of his head, and smoke was curling up between his fingers. For a minute I was so stunned by what I saw that I failed to react. Maybe I'd expected to see blood, but did vampires even bleed? I didn't know, but this kind of burning was something I associated with vampire exposure to sunlight, and there was damn sure no sunlight down in this pitch black hole.

"Victor!" I shouted, increasing the speed of my steps, trying to catch up to him, but Ruby was ahead of me and reached him first.

"It's the fungus," Victor moaned. "It was all over those damn rocks that fell. Whatever you do, don't touch the wall or the ceiling. The shit is everywhere."

Fungus? I turned my flashlight beam onto the walls of the tunnel. They seemed to be a mixture of blasted rock and dark red clay, but time and wear had smoothed and blended the two components to the point that it was hard to tell where one ended and the other began. Most of the surface was covered in a green shimmering growth that on first look resembled moss. On closer inspection, however, I could see that it was something entirely different, unlike anything I'd ever seen.

Like moss, it grew low and fuzzy, but that's where the similarities ended. Protruding from the clumps of green fuzz were sharp, needle-like teeth.

And they were moving, snapping.

"What the hell is that?" John was standing beside me, reaching his fingers out toward the wall.

Slapping his hand away, I whirled on him. "Are you crazy? Don't touch that shit."

"I... wasn't going to," he said. But I could see that was exactly what he'd been about to do. Even in the dim light, the longing in his eyes shone bright. The idiot *wanted* to touch the stuff.

"It's doing something to him," Ruby warned. "Don't let him look at it."

I grabbed John by the arm and pulled him back away from the wall of the tunnel.

"Look at me John. Look at *me*, not at the wall." I was having trouble forming the words. It was all I could do to force the air in and out of my lungs, much less speak, and a weird kind of thudding was going on inside my head. Like some tiny little creature had crawled into my brain and brought along a big bass drum. Pounding and pounding until it felt like my skull would explode.

"But..." he began, his face already drifting back in the direction of the fungus.

"Blindfold him," Ruby snapped. "Right now. Because he's human, the fungus is affecting him in a different way. It's mesmerizing him, I think." I could tell from her voice that she was having the same breathing problem as me. Her words were raspy and barely audible above the pulsing clamor inside my head.

"What the hell am I supposed to blindfold him with?" I gasped.

Victor was up from the dirt floor, one hand still clasped to the side of his head.

"Hell's bells," he said. "Hang on."

Then he was holding both hands in front of his body and I watched as the nails on his fingers elongated until they no longer resembled nails at all. They were claws – long, pointed, and *sharp.*

With a quick swipe of his hand, the lower part of his shirt separated and fell to the ground. He picked it up and thrust it in my direction. Taking the scrap of fabric, I quickly tied it around John's head, then adjusted it until his eyes were fully covered.

"Ruby, what is this shit?" I asked her.

"I don't know, but it's slowly killing us all." Her tone was matter of fact, as if she'd just told me it was dark outside or something equally inane. The fungus hadn't surprised her. I wondered why.

Victor shook his head. "Not bothering me. Not unless I touch it anyway. Then I think it would probably set me afire." He reached up to his head again, where narrow tendrils of smoke were still oozing from the gash.

"We have to get out of here," I told them.

I shoved John in front of me and took up his position in the rear. Ruby was ahead of him, with Victor still in the lead. I watched as Ruby reached back and grabbed John by the hand, and then we were all moving again, but much too slowly. I knew that if we didn't get out of the tunnel soon, I, for one, would be hitting the dirt. My lungs couldn't take much more.

And I was hearing things as well. The thudding inside my head now had some company. Whispers, furious ones, layered one voice on top of another. I had no clue what was being said, but I had the distinct impression that something was being planned. That whatever was inside my head doing all that whispering had an intent beyond just driving me mad.

Moments later, I realized that my hand had gone to the knife at my belt. I suddenly had an insane desire to pull the knife and shove it between John's ribs. I could almost feel the resistance of the sharp blade meeting the fabric of his jacket, then skin, then the give when it plunged through. Feel the blood as it welled from the wound and gathered around the hilt. Then I could see myself, in slow motion, moving from John, to Ruby, then Victor. Letting my knife play with each and every one of them in turn.

I shook my head and with a huge effort of will banished the scene from my mind. But the allure of it was still there, threatening to pull me in, drag me down under its hellish, suffocating pull.

What is wrong with me?

I looked down at my hand and the knife that was somehow out of its sheath. I let go as if scalded, watched as it fell to the dirt, then somehow, trancelike, began to walk on. The fact that I'd just discarded one of my weapons was registered and acknowledged, but in a

225

remote kind of way. Like I was watching someone else drop the knife, walk over it, and leave it behind.

It meant almost nothing at all.

I was lost. Suffocating. I was still there, but someone else, *something* else, was driving the bus.

"Please..." I whimpered. But no one heard. Or if they did, they didn't respond.

I wasn't sure if my feet were even moving, but figured they must be, because John was still right in front of me, Ruby in front of him, and Victor leading us all. If I'd stopped, then so had they.

I wanted to call out again, scream even, but there was simply no more air.

As I fell to the ground, I figured this was what dying felt   like.

Chapter 33

I woke to the sound of dripping water and the smell of mold and rot, something wet and cold running into the corners or my eyes. I shook my head, cracked my eyelids.

High above me there was row after row of weathered timbers, slow drips of water leaking through the slats. I could hear the muffled sound of heavy rain and booming claps of thunder, and the wind was howling, blowing so hard I could see the timbers of the ceiling vibrate and sway.

My first thought was, *this roof is gonna fall in on me*, my second, *where in the hell am I?*

My third thought, *I can breathe.*

Then it all came rushing back. The tunnel, suffocating, John acting all weird and scary. *And me too. Thinking about stabbing him... And his eyes, before you put the blindfold on...*

I'd seen evil there.

I propped myself up on my elbows, looked around the cavernous room, tried to get my bearings.

The walls were more dirt and stone, just like the tunnel, only this space was huge, and split down the middle by something that looked kind of like an old railroad track, only not quite. The rails were closer together, so not meant for a train but something else, something smaller.

Minecarts. That's what they were for. Minecarts to haul the copper from the excavation site back up to the surface. Which meant I was somewhere in the mine.

The room was dimly lit by a kerosene lantern hanging on the wall opposite me. I could see a wide wooden double hung door, and occasional flashes of lightning seeping through the cracks.

But what I didn't see was Victor, Ruby, or John.

I was alone. Any scenario that removed them from my side wouldn't be a good one. For a moment, absolute terror flooded through my veins.

What the hell had happened? I remembered starting to fall, then everything had gone black. I had no idea how I'd come to be in this room or who had dragged me here.

Other than the din of the storm, and the drops of water hitting the dirt floor, the room was silent. Like a tomb.

Not beneath the earth though. Above ground. I could see lightning through the cracks in the door, and hear the wind outside, neither of which would be possible if I'd been deep in the belly of the digs. That, at least, was a plus. Presumably, beyond the big door were the woods and the vineyard, so this had to be the opening to the mine.

Was I a prisoner?

I put my hands in front of my face, moved my feet back and forth. Apparently no one had bothered to tie me up, so that was good. I allowed myself to be a little optimistic. Maybe I wasn't a prisoner.

Of course, if that door was locked, binding me wouldn't have been necessary. I might as well be sealed in a drum. No way was I going back through that tunnel with its scary acid spitting, mind bending moss. Options didn't seem to be something I had a lot of, but regardless of that simple fact, a plan of some sort had to be formed.

Step one, find out if I'm locked in.

Picking myself up off the dirt floor, I made my way over to the door, pushed against it, only to discover that there wasn't an inch of give. I'd expected as much but it would have been stupid to not even try. I thought about shouting out, but assuming that anyone who heard me would be one of the bad guys, it was probably better if they believed I was still out cold.

I turned around with the intention of heading back in the direction I'd come, hoping that maybe someone had been careless enough to leave my bag behind, and that's when I saw them. They'd been directly behind me as I'd lain on the floor.

Skulls. Eye sockets empty and leering, mouths spread as if caught in mid-scream. There were so many of the horrible things that I'd be a long time trying to count them all, but surely at least a thousand. The gigantic stack of bone began on the dirt floor, then stretched the full width of the wall which I guessed to be around twenty feet, and continued upward, all the way to the ceiling.

So this was it. The big bad we'd come to destroy. It was the most hideous thing I'd ever seen. A shrine, obscene in its majesty, a wall of tortured, anguished souls. Its power would be monstrous.

Ruby had said she had a plan, and it occurred to me that it better be a good one. Otherwise we'd all likely die here. I wondered where the hell Ruby had gotten to. Was my witchy aunt even still alive?

I walked over to the wall of skulls and put out my hand to touch one. I don't know what I'd expected.

Cold smooth bone? Certainly.

Distaste? Absolutely.

Fear? You betcha.

But I never expected the mouth to open or the hissing scream that came out of it, a sound so piercing that it nearly burst my eardrums.

The scream, more a wail actually, bounced off the surrounding walls and echoed throughout the huge empty chamber. Quickly I withdrew my hand and immediately the ear-splitting cry dialed itself down a notch. The hissing continued for a few moments more, then with a clack of bone against bone, the hideous mouth closed and the thing was silent.

Note to self: Do not touch those damnable things.

All the skulls were completely free of flesh as far as I could tell. So at least none of them were fresh. For whatever reason, that thought alone calmed my nerves just a bit. But looking at all of them, stacked and crowded together like a bunch of finely balanced blocks, brought an immense sadness. Once upon a time they'd been people living their lives, probably assuming that when death claimed them, their remains would find some sort of resting place, either deep in the earth or scattered upon it. Certainly none of them would have dreamed of becoming part of this insane altar to some bygone god.

The urge to just smash the thing to bits was strong. But I resisted it. I had no idea what Ruby's plan was, so not a clue what to do.

I needed to find her and the others. With that thought in mind, I searched around on the dirt floor in hopes that by some miracle my bag would be there, but of course it wasn't. In fact, there didn't seem to be anything in the room at all other than the kerosene lantern, the skulls, and myself.

And the rails.

The things were old and rusty, twin strips of iron bracketed on each side by rail ties, here and there slats of wood crossing from one side to the other, kind of like a flat ladder laid out on the ground.

As I looked at the way the little railway was put together, it occurred to me that there had to be nails. Maybe even big long ones, considering the size of the crossties. The wood was rotting away in places, so maybe I'd be lucky enough to prize one out.

I knelt down on the ground and began to examine the wood with my fingers and sure enough, it wasn't long till I felt the flat round top of a protruding nail head. Pushing it from side to side, I could feel it giving beneath my fingers. After a minute or two of this motion, I had the nail out and lying in the palm of my hand.

It was indeed a wicked looking thing. At least six inches long, and even after what surely was many decades, the rusty old piece of iron still had a nice sharp point. I shoved my new toy down into the front pocket of my camos, then noticed that the wood slat that had been at the other end of this nail was now cocked to the side a bit. It had come loose from the tie. I reached down and gave a tug, but the thing didn't budge. It was still well and truly attached at the other side, so I stood up, went over to the opposite end and put my foot down to brace it. Then using both hands and all the strength in my body, I grabbed the slat as close to the other end as I could reach, which was just a little more than midway.

Probably not going to get me enough leverage.

Trying to remember everything I learned in my one and only yoga class, wishing I'd paid more attention, I stretched my tendons and muscles and maybe even my bones. I stretched until it felt like everything inside me was probably going to rip in two and somehow managed just a few more inches.

And then I braced my foot and pulled. My back and arms were screaming with the effort, but finally I heard a satisfying crack and the wood broke free.

Oh, and that baby didn't just break, but was kind enough to do it in such a way as to leave a nice sharp point at the end. Basically, I now had myself a spear. I held the lovely piece of oak up to my face and decided that it could probably kill a man if I used it just right. So, between the wicked rusty nail and this fantastic spear that I'd accidentally made for myself, I was no longer weaponless.

I'd already determined that at least some of my powers had returned as well. Certainly not a hundred percent, but I figured I might be able to manage a little something witchy if I really poured myself into it.

My eyes went to the locked door. Could I open it? I didn't know, but it was past time to try, but first I had to make sure that Ruby and the others hadn't been taken further into the mine.

I walked over to where the iron rails disappeared into the darkness. They presumably continued on deeper into the mine itself, but the light didn't extend far enough for me to make out much beyond the first few feet.

I walked over to where the lantern hung against the wall, pulled it from its hook and moved back over to the opening. It was smallish, just about tall enough to stand beneath and wide enough for the cart to pass through with a walking path to either side.

Lantern in hand, I stepped through.

I'd only taken a few steps when I discovered that venturing further was out of the question. With the light from the lantern, I had a clear view of about forty feet of shaft, ending in a wall of fallen rock and debris. A cave-in, from who knew how many years ago, had blocked access to the rest of the mine. And between where I stood and the wall of fallen rock, there was nothing. Just emptiness.

Well, not counting the bats.

The walls and ceiling were teeming with them. Forget about a thousand skulls, there must have been fifty thousand bats in that shaft, all of them trembling in excitement at the unexpected light invading their dark little hidey hole.

Quickly – not wanting to find out what a swarm of thousands of pissed off bats looked like – I backed away until I was once again inside the room with the skulls and the firmly locked door.

I stood there for a moment, trying to catch my breath, heart thudding against my chest. Then I heard a screech of rusty hinges, and the door opened.

A tall figure loomed in the shadows on the other side of the doorway. For a moment I didn't know what I was looking at, but then John walked in, carrying a big scary rifle. I was no expert on weapons, but I thought it might be an AK-47 or maybe an M-16. I thought to myself that I'd never seen such a beautiful sight.

"It's about damn time," I said, and I could feel the grin splitting my face, at the same time wondering how he'd gotten his hands on that kind of firepower.

Then he raised and leveled the thing straight at me.

And   he   wasn't   grinning.

Chapter 34

"Back up against the wall," John snarled. "Now. And you can drop that little spear while you're at it." He'd moved a few more steps into the mineshaft, and I could make out a large shadow following at his feet. It was a cougar, a cougar with a torn left ear. The same one that had attacked him in the creek just hours before.

When he came to a stop, the cat began pacing back and forth in front of him, its glowing amber eyes fixed in my direction.

"What the hell is this?" I asked him. "What are you doing?"

I didn't know where the words came from, I was that shocked at what I was seeing. John pointing an AK-47 at my middle wasn't part of any kind of scenario that seemed possible. Time seemed to slow for a moment – no magic hourglass necessary. I was dimly aware of what sounded like a string of firecrackers popping off somewhere in the distance, then the boom of what could have either been thunder or maybe a shotgun. I could tell by the look on his face that John registered the noise as well, but his eyes never wavered.

"I guess you've just become our new hostage. You can thank your friends for that."

"What do you mean, *our new hostage?* You're with them? How...? Your sister..." It couldn't be. Yet there he was, not only holding a gun on me, but being guarded by the cougar. Then it occurred to me that maybe he'd completely lost his shit, maybe the fungus had done something to his brain.

"John, it's the moss, the fungus. It's done something to your mind. Put down the gun. Let me help you." I took a step toward him, which brought a deep snarl from the throat of the cougar.

The cougar... the fungus didn't explain Moncrieffe's little feline trailing at his feet. I knew I hadn't been out of it long enough for him to somehow make friends with the cat that had just tried to kill him. And anyway, the idea that he'd cozy up to the beast after what it had done to him was ludicrous, to say the least. But I was grasping at straws at that point. Trying to latch onto anything that might explain away his behavior. Anything except the obvious, of course.

That he'd been in on it from the start.

The words he'd spoken earlier... that I was their new hostage...Could that mean that the others had been freed?

No, that was just wishful thinking. Surely he was just talking out of his head. He couldn't know whether anyone had been freed because he wasn't part of Moncrieffe's crew. Even with everything I was witnessing, I wasn't quite yet ready to believe that John was part of this crazy cult, or even worse, that he'd managed to trick us all so thoroughly.

John was shaking his head back and forth, his lips drawn into a tight, thin smile. "There is nothing wrong with my mind, Tula. I admit, for a few minutes in that tunnel I thought I might be a goner, but no. I'm fine. Just doing what has to be done."

He motioned again with the rifle. "Get back against that wall and drop your little spear."

I stood my ground. He'd said I was a hostage, so it wasn't likely he'd just start blasting away.

"How could you do this to your sister?" I spat the words, now certain that there was nothing at all wrong with his mind. He was part of it all, that much was crystal clear. Should have been from the minute he pointed the gun at me, but I hadn't wanted to see it.

"It wasn't supposed to be this way," he answered. "No one knew she was pregnant. If not for the pregnancy, she'd have been drawn back to the vineyard, just as Andrew was. If things had gone to plan, she'd be here with him right now, taking her rightful place by his side."

"I don't understand..."

"Morning sickness. Although hers didn't happen in the morning, as is often the case. But that's neither here nor there. The nausea brought on by her pregnancy apparently caused her to vomit up the wine. The nectar from the Green Man was in it, of course, and unlike Andrew, she didn't get her proper dose. Then, as if that wasn't bad enough, she wandered out here alone in the middle of the night, sticking her nose in where it had no business being. And... well, the vines did what the vines do. They protected the vineyard. The God."

"How are you involved in all this?" I asked him, not that it really mattered, at this point I was just trying to keep him talking while I accessed what little of my power that had returned. I didn't care how he answered. He'd had a hand in, or at least known that Caleb would be taken, all while pretending to be the worried brother, the devoted son. The hate that was suddenly burning inside me was breathtaking in its magnitude.

"Nosy Miss Tula. You want all the answers don't you?"

"I'd like to know why you even came to me for help when obviously you've been a part of this from the very beginning."

"Going to you for help was never part of it. That was my father's idea. But once he insisted on it, I had no choice but to go along. I did all the necessary follow up – checked you out through the Marshal's office, got the recommendation from McMahan, made all the arrangements. Then, as it happened, Moncrieffe had his eye on the inn and the lodestone, so getting you out here and under their control was kind of like icing on the cake."

"You don't know my family," I laughed. "It would take a lot more than holding me to get them out of your way."

"We'll see," he said.

"But why?" I asked him. "How did you become involved with Moncrieffe in the first place?"

"Why does anybody do this type of thing? Money and power are part of it, but for me, it goes deeper. One of the first cases I worked out in California involved Moncrieffe's uncle Roger. Roger introduced me to the nectar and all it could bring. I became stronger, smarter, better looking even – though I never lacked in that department if I do say so myself. But the biggest benefit is adding decades to the human lifespan. Near immortality." As he spoke, he moved closer to the

238

kerosene lantern, and in the glow I could see his eyes literally glittering with malice.

"I suppose you still have more questions?" he asked me.

I did, but that could come later, and the answers would have to come from someone other than him, because I decided right then and there that I was going to kill him. But to do that I'd have to get the cougar first, and obviously I'd need a better weapon than a rotted piece of wood and a rusty nail.

I'd need that gun. Not that I even knew how to shoot it. Hopefully it was gonna be basically a point and shoot kind of thing. If not, I had no idea how one of those monstrous things worked. But getting it away from him would be a step in the right direction.

At the risk of stating the obvious, I stated the obvious.

"You know you're a walking dead man. If I don't kill you, my people will. If not Ruby, then Emmery, Alafair, folks in town. They'll be lining up to take you out. Why don't you give me that gun? It's not too late to make this right." It really was way too late, but he didn't have to know that.

"You actually think you have the upper hand here? Even now?" He threw back his head and laughed, a big booming laugh that seemed to bounce off the dirt walls before disintegrating into a fit of giggles.

He was mad. Insane. Bat shit crazy.

Bat shit...

I knew what I had to do. But I needed to keep him talking. Just a little more time. I could feel the power building inside me, I was almost there...

239

"Your cabin, it's not even a mile away from the vineyards," I said. "I'll bet if I checked the property records I'd see that Moncrieffe is the actual owner," I didn't give a shit about who owned that damn cabin, nothing could possibly matter less. I was just trying to engage his attention, anything that might buy me a few more minutes of distraction.

"Yea, I was really hoping you wouldn't think to do that. It was a detail that worried me. Snuck up on me if you want to know the truth. The cabin was the one thing that tied me to the vineyard. I should have installed Gwyneth and my father elsewhere. But by the time it occurred to me, well, by then it was too late to do anything about it. But I gave you no reason to check on the cabin's ownership, and of course, you didn't."

"And the cougar?" I asked. "I saw her attacking. I was there. I *saved* your ass. Now she's your buddy. How did that happen?"

"That business in the creek was unfortunate. But purely an accident. The cats are bonded to the Moncrieffes, not me. As soon as she bit though, she knew. She tasted the nectar living inside my blood." He reached down with his free hand and gave the big cat a scratch behind its mangled ear. "She's a fighter this one, as you can probably see. She could have easily killed both of us. But that wasn't the plan."

"But you want to kill me now." As I was speaking to him, inside my head I was building my intent, letting it flow through every fiber of my being. Drawing in the magic, then sending it outward. In a very specific direction.

The power had its own voice, and it was calling out softly. Not yet loud enough to be heard, but I could feel it growing. Soon it would penetrate the darkness and find its mark. Moments, even.

The cougar sensed it. She was pacing frantically back and forth in front of John, her body shuddering with anxious snarls coming from deep inside her throat, her features a fixed mask of hate. People who say that cats have expressionless faces have never seen a pissed off cougar.

"I must say, I don't particularly want to kill you," he mused. "I'm not looking forward to it. But it's probably going to come to that. I don't see any other way."

"And my people? Caleb, Vicki, my sister? Ruby? What's happened to them? Where are they?"

"Ah, Ruby. The whole point of taking the kid was not so much about getting Gwyneth. We figured that wasn't going to happen. He wanted Ruby here, even more so than you."

I laughed at that, then said, "Moncrieffe should be careful what he wishes for. Real careful."

"Possibly. I guess we'll find out. The god told us that if we had the boy, the crone – your Aunt Ruby – would show herself, and she did. He told us we'd defeat her, and we will. We must. You see, Ruby holds almost all the power of the Whitlows. Even though your mother was chosen by your precious Lodestone, she doesn't have half the power of your aunt, or if she does, she never learned to channel it. Your aunt can turn the lodestone over to us. And I think she *will* before she stands by and watches any of you die."

If they actually believed that then they didn't know Ruby. She'd sacrifice every single one of us before she'd see that happen. And even if she wanted to, she couldn't. The power of the lodestone wasn't hers to give. Sure, Ruby could use it to a certain extent, but it belonged to only one. And that was my mother.

"Where is Ruby? And the others? Are they still alive?" I didn't really expect him to tell me, but then he did exactly that. Obviously he felt like I was no threat at all.

"You'll be happy to know that your meddlesome aunt and that vampire friend of yours have freed your sister. *And* the boy and his mother. But they're here, somewhere on the property. We'll have them in hand soon enough. And now we have you, a brand new hostage. I like our odds."

He was still holding the AK-47 steady, still pointing it dead center of my chest, and he didn't know it, but he'd just given me the green light I was waiting for. If Ruby had our people, this shit was about to be over. And that was all I needed to hear.

I let go of the power then, gave it everything I had, which admittedly wasn't much, but as I heard the movement of thousands of tiny wings, I knew it was enough.

The bats came. A mass of them, all at once, exiting the depths of the mineshaft, bursting out of the darkness like a huge screeching black cloud. They landed on John and the cougar, and as soon as they did, I started moving toward the gun.

The cougar, seeming to sense my intention, crouched down on its haunches and sprung. But as fast as it was, the cat didn't have the speed of my dark, screeching friends. One minute the cougar was a giant ball of teeth and fur hurtling toward me, then suddenly it became a mass of writhing black bodies, thousands of them, screaming madly as they engulfed the beast in midair.

The cougar immediately fell to the ground, and the last I saw of it, the thing was running through the open doorway, still enveloped by a dark cloud of squealing, biting bats.

I turned my attention to John. Somehow, even with the bats swarming his entire body, he'd managed to hang onto the AK-47. It was dangling from his left hand, blood dripping onto it from what I figured were likely hundreds of bites from the tiny vicious teeth.

Underneath the cloud of small, muscled bodies, I could hear his strangled screams. I reached out and took the gun from fingers that didn't resist, as if he had no awareness that his hand was even on the thing. Likely John no longer even knew he was still in this world. I had a fleeting moment of sadness when I realized that he wouldn't be much longer. The bats would do their work.

I'd grown fond of the man, and wrapping my head around what he'd proven himself to be wasn't an easy fit.

I slung the strap of the firearm over my shoulder and stepped out of the mineshaft into the sweet open air.

And didn't look back. Let the bats have their midnight snack.

I headed out into the night. The storm had passed and I could see a small sliver of moon. Each step toward the forest carried me further away from any regret I'd felt over causing John's death. Thinking of the enormity of his betrayal brought me to only one conclusion.

The monster is getting off easy. He'd earned his ending, no question of that. By the time I entered the treeline I felt nothing but rage. And I embraced it, let it fill me, let it spread into every particle of my being.

Rage was good. Rage was *necessary*. The killing likely wasn't done.

At the sound of hurried footsteps coming from the darkened vineyard, I raised the big rifle and pointed it into the darkness, found the trigger and wrapped my finger around it, hoping that was all it would take to engage the thing. I was dimly aware that it probably had a safety, but figured John probably would have already disengaged it. He'd have wanted to be ready to rock-and-roll at the drop of a hat.

Tensing, ready to shoot, I trained the gun on the dim figure that was quickly moving in my direction, weaving its way through the trees and brush.

"Put that damn thing down, Tula." The words came from pitch darkness, but I instantly knew who spoke them. It wasn't like that particular stretch of North Carolina woodland was teeming with Irishmen. Right then it seemed to me that lilting brogue was the most beautiful sound I'd ever heard.

Victor.

He stepped out of the treeline, came up to me and put his hand on the rifle barrel, nudging it down toward the ground. "You okay?" He asked. "Did they hurt you?"

"I'm fine. No thanks to you and Ruby," I snapped, forgetting that I was glad to see him, thinking only of how I'd woken to find them both gone, while I was locked in that horrible place all alone. "Why the hell did you leave me back there?"

"Look, it wasn't like we wanted to," he answered, quickly averting his gaze, trying to hide the guilt written all over his face.

Good. He should be feeling a bit of shame.

"It all happened so fast," he continued. "We had seconds to get out of there. And you were out cold, but otherwise okay."

"So you both decided to just stroll out of there and leave me to my nap? My nap in the dirt with all those godforsaken skulls looking on? Lots of things could have happened to me in there, and none of them good." I was really wound up by then, the enormity of the fact that they'd left me was beginning to sink in and I wanted some answers.

"It wasn't like that at all," he said. "Like I told you, it happened fast. One minute Ruby and I were in the mineshaft, trying to fight off a good half dozen of Moncrieffe's goons, and that was with Ruby having almost zero witchery at her disposal. You remember, the Bentleys own the mineral rights, so she was still feeling the effects of the loss of power."

I knew that was true. Summoning those bats should have been fairly easy, even for me, but it had taken all I could do to make it happen. And it sure as hell hadn't happened quickly.

"Then somehow the fight spilled outside," Victor continued. "Then down the hill. Which is when we heard a kid screaming somewhere off in the distance, and that's where we headed. Toward the screams. And that damn John, you need to know, he's not what you thought... I'm gonna kill that son of a dog –"

I looked back over my shoulder at the opening to the mineshaft, and Victor's eyes followed my gaze. "You?" He asked quietly.

"Done and dusted," I whispered. Then, though I was terrified of the answer, I asked the question, "Where's Caleb?"

"Well, as of about ten minutes ago, he, along with his mom and Alafair were with Ruby. She's taking them to meet the sheriff in the parking lot, then I guess he's taking them back to the inn." he said. "Everyone's fine. A little shaken up, but otherwise tickety-boo."

Caleb, Vicki, and Alafair were free. Hearing those words was like a huge boulder being lifted from my body. I wanted to know how, but that could wait. I also wanted to know who the hell says 'tickety freakin' boo', but that could wait as well.

"What about Andrew and Moncrieffe?"

"We haven't found either of them, but I think we dealt with all of Moncrieffe's crew, so wherever they are, the two of them are on their own." He went on to tell me that when he and Ruby had broken into the main building where Alafair and the others were being held, Moncrieffe had been there but had escaped into the woods while they were putting down the rest of the guards. Right now the man could be anywhere, but more than likely he was trying to connect with Andrew.

"We've got to find both of them," I said, and started to head on through the woods, only to be stopped by Victor grabbing me from behind.

"Whoa! Ruby said for me to keep you the hell away – get you out of here."

"What? Why?" I asked. As far as I was concerned we couldn't leave without dealing with those two, but Andrew in particular.

"What about Gwyneth?" I demanded, thinking of the poor woman and her baby, the reaper who even now was probably inching closer and closer to her bed. I would *not* let the greedy thing have them. And Dr. Wheaton... I'd taken his son...

And I'll be damned if I see him lose his daughter too.

I moved to pull away from Victor's grasp, intent on getting on with whatever lay in store, but he simply increased his hold on my arm, pinning me in place.

"Have you never heard the term 'live to fight another day'?" He asked. "I'm supposed to take you back to the inn. Ruby said we'd regroup there. Figure out what's next. Things are way more dangerous than she anticipated."

I was wondering if I was going to have to try and call the bats down on Victor, thinking it might take something that drastic to get the vampire to let me go, when suddenly the wind that had been snaking gently through the tall, slender pines seemed to gather itself, and within seconds that nothing little wind became a full-blown squall.

The change was sudden and intense and electrifying. Magic was in that wind, and I had a pretty good idea that Ruby was behind it.

I was having a hard time holding my body upright against what I was sure must be hurricane-force winds, and could see that Victor as well was barely holding his ground. The vampire was semi crouched, feet spread, doing his best to remain standing. As I watched him, I was vaguely aware that the color of the night had changed. Everything was now awash in a spectral greenish glow.

This is Ruby. And she's in trouble. Or maybe making trouble. Either way, I knew I needed to be there.

"Victor!" I shouted over the wind. I was about to tell him that we needed to get the hell on our way when I noticed he'd raised his arm up into the wind, pointing his hand toward something behind me.

I turned to look, and at the bottom of the hill, out near the edge of the vineyard, the entire forest seemed to be trembling. Up and down, then side to side, as if some giant hand had grabbed the edge of the forest floor and was shaking it out like a dirty mat. And the green glow was there as well, only much more intense.

I looked at Victor, and he at me, and then we both started running. Directly into the cutting wind, as fast as our feet would carry us, we ran downward, straight toward that hellish green glow and whatever awaited us inside   it.

Chapter 35

Once Victor and I entered the forest, we were lucky enough to find ourselves on a well-worn path. It was narrow, the pines and bushes on either side were close enough to reach out and touch, but mercifully free of the vines that seemed to cover everything in sight. And the weird green glow that had seemed - and still did - so frightening was actually helping us. The woods weren't nearly as dark as they should have been.

We were about fifty yards in - what I judged to be about a third of the way to the bottom - when I became dimly aware of something or someone moving through the trees on either side of us. I couldn't get a good enough look to tell who or what it was, because every time I turned my head and peered into the darkness, there was nothing. Then as soon as I focused my eyes back onto the path, the movement would begin again, subtle, but unquestionably there, barely glimpsed from the corners of my eyes.

There were no ifs, ands, or buts about it. Something was following us - stalking us, really, something like a cat after a mouse. Exactly like a cat...

Cats. Could it be the cougars? Maybe. But I had my doubts. Whatever this was seemed bigger, taller.

And coming closer every minute, closing in on the edges of the path. Whatever strange game our stalkers were playing with us, they seemed to be tiring of it. Coming in soon to finish it, whatever it might be.

Coming in for the kill? A part of me wanted to dare them to try, but the other, saner part of my brain, the part that wanted to live to see the bottom of the hill, decided to just run faster.

Victor was a good twenty feet ahead of me, and occasionally I could see him turn his head, as if making sure he still had me in sight. Which I appreciated, since he could have literally made himself into vapor and been down the hill in seconds. Or maybe not, maybe he simply floated when he was in that state. I really had no idea. Either way, I was happy not to be alone.

I picked up my speed. All at once that twenty feet that separated me from Victor felt more like twenty miles. I wanted to get closer. *Needed* to get closer. I was suddenly certain that dozens of eyes were now on us both. I was almost close enough to reach out and touch his black leather jacket when Victor froze in his tracks, holding up his right hand in the universal signal for 'stop.'

Standing very still right in the middle of the path, Victor moved his head from side to side, listening, looking, then very slowly he turned his body full circle, all the while his eyes focused hard on the forest.

"Something's out there," he finally said. "I don't know what, but there's more than one."

"I know. Do you think it's cougars?"

"No, I could smell a cougar. Whatever this is smells just like the woods. It doesn't really have a scent of its own."

I was worried about whatever was stalking us, but even more worried about what might be happening at the bottom of the hill, keenly aware that minutes were ticking by, minutes that might make a huge difference, depending on what we found there.

I was just about to tell him we needed to get going, regardless of what might be in the woods, when I suddenly saw one of the bushes move. And not in an ordinary kind of way. Not in the way that branches might bend or sway when the wind hit them. More like a slow, jerking kind of movement. *Forward.* By at least a foot or two.

They're coming for us. The damn bushes are somehow coming for us.

And then it was as if some silent signal had gone out, and I could see other bushes crowding up along the side of the path, all of them edging closer and closer, their movements awkward yet disturbingly resolved. Then I remembered the bushes on the creek bank when John had been attacked by the cougar – well, pretend attacked as it turned out – I had that same vague sense that they had been moving toward me. Or at least slightly changing position when my back turned.

It seemed that we had more to worry about in these woods than cougars. We had bushes and shrubs that somehow possessed *intent.* Maybe even some weird kind of intelligence.

Victor had apparently seen them as well. "Shite," he whispered, his brogue once again as wide as the Mississippi. "What now? You know I hate forests. The US has way too damn many trees and shrubs and all the like. When I get out of these godforsaken woods I don't care if I never see another tree. Maybe I'll go back to Ireland. Irish vegetation at least knows how to behave. Manners

251

is what it's about, none of this creeping up shite." Then he grabbed my hand and tugged me forward and we were running again, this time not even bothering to be careful, not even looking at the path. We were both intent on just getting the hell out of those woods.

And then suddenly, we were.

And what I saw almost made me want to go back inside them.

Alafair, Vicki, and Caleb were trapped inside a green glowing vortex of whirling leaves and sticks and vines, their eyes wide with fear, their mouths open in silent screams. And all around them particles of green and gold swirling light. And they weren't alone. Andrew – The Green Man, god, monster – whatever the hell name you chose, he was with them. And worst still, he had little Caleb clutched by the neck, hanging from one of his gnarled, obscenely oversized hands. Even from a distance I could see that the boy was in dire need. Unlike the others, whose eyes were bright with fear and shock, little Caleb's eyes were vacant, indifferent, as if they beheld only a stark, silent, void.

Nothingness.

Please, please, don't let him be dead... And then it hit me. Maybe they all were dead. I saw not a flicker of awareness from any of them. Including Andrew himself. They all seemed to me like marionettes, frozen in some strange, dark dance of air and light.

The sound just outside the vortex was near deafening, the wind around the thing howling like some insane, angry banshee. I looked over at Victor and saw his lips moving, though I couldn't hear a word. Finally, he simply pointed. Standing off to the right, about twenty feet

252

outside the glowing maelstrom of wind, was Ruby. In her hands was the old hourglass she'd taken from the basement before we left the inn. She was holding it up at chest level, and I could see a green stream of blinding light radiating from its base, outward, like horizontal lightning.

The hourglass is powering the vortex.

Careful to stay well beyond the beam of light, Victor and I rushed to Ruby's side. Without ever taking her eyes off the hourglass, she shouted, "Get back to the mineshaft – fast! You've got to destroy the skulls. I've frozen time, but I won't be able to hold it for long."

"How long is long?" Victor shouted back. "It'll take a bit of time to set the C4."

"No!" Ruby yelled. "Forget the C4."

And then she told us what to do. It seemed so simple that I was sure it would fail. I took one last look at the people I loved most in the world, then turned and began running back up the hill. Back to the mineshaft.

And back through those monstrous things in the woods...

Chapter 36

We were almost to the mineshaft when we saw them. Maybe twenty more steps and we'd have been there. Not exactly safe and sound, but at least maybe carrying out the one mission that might save us all.

The mad, uphill dash had left me breathless, gasping for air that felt like razors tap dancing inside my weary, heaving lungs. I was barely keeping pace with Victor, but I was managing it, because I could literally see the end in sight. The door to the mineshaft was *right there.* Just a few more feet...

And then there they were. I instantly knew that the creatures now lining up to block our path were the same shapes that had been stalking us earlier as we'd hurried down the hill. Now they'd lined themselves up like some weird, impenetrable hedge, a mass of vine covered shapes, somehow merging together, effectively blocking our way.

Beneath the vines and forest brush that covered their bodies, there was a hint of human form, but they were blanketed so heavily in flora that it was near impossible to tell where one creature ended and the other began, much less get a clear idea of what might be hidden beneath.

I immediately thought of Gwyneth. Was this what she was becoming? Was this the hell she would be facing if we failed tonight?

No! We're so close....

Keenly aware of the need to *hurry*, a part of me wanted to just charge right through the things. Whatever they might be, whatever threat they posed was surely not as great as the threat we'd just left behind.

We only have minutes....

If Ruby's spell broke... I couldn't even think of what that might mean. Foremost in my mind was the image of Andrew holding little Caleb by the throat, and my sense that the young boy was near death. And here we were, stopped cold.

I turned to Victor, who was slowly inching closer and closer to the barrier which incredibly, *seemed* to be creeping closer to us.

"Where's a sling blade when you need one?" He whispered. "Better yet, a good ol' Irish briar axe."

"What do you think?" I asked him. "Should we plow on through?"

I was whispering as well, somehow positive that the things were sentient, and likely capable of understanding what was being said. I also had the distinct impression that blocking our path wasn't the only thing they had in mind. Menace was coming off them in waves – the damp night air was saturated with it.

"We could try to go around them," Victor said, taking a few small steps to the right of the path, easing up toward the treeline. Immediately the barricade shifted in the same direction, and when it did, I could feel something shifting within me as well. It was sanity, looking for a place to hide. Until all this was finished, there was no room for something ordinary as a healthy mind. The only way to beat this thing, all of it –

The Green Man, the vineyard, these obscene things on the trail – was with madness.

As if in echo of my thoughts, the madness appeared, and even notched itself up a bit. A squirrel skittered out from the woods onto the path, its little body freezing in fear as it became aware of the sudden exposure. Like lightning, and with an oddly feminine grace, a vine covered arm reached down, grabbed up the furry little body, then pulled it into the vines.

Eating it. Just as they would eat us.

"These damn things are fast." I heard Victor speaking, but it was like his voice was coming from a thousand miles away. I'd stepped outside of what was real, what was immediate. I was like some kind of primitive amoeba. Pure instinct. Survival. And not just my own and Victor's.

"Tula!" Victor shouted, snapping his finger in front of my face. "Did you hear a word I said?"

I stood there, transfixed, my eyes still glued to the monstrosities blocking our way.

"I can fly us from here to the mineshaft," he said.

"What? Since when can you do that? Fly?"

"Always, but I need fresh blood to do it." To my horror, I could see the vampire focusing his eyes on the soft skin beneath my jaw. "Just a little would be enough," he continued. "It's not that far."

Hell no, that's not gonna happen. No way was I gonna stand there and let a vampire have a little nibble. Not to fly or anything else.

Without even knowing I was going to do it, I charged the tangle of vine and brush, my fingers digging in, pushing, tugging, *ripping.* I was dimly aware of being bitten and clawed, the teeth monstrous and sharp, the claws like hot iron spikes as they dug into my skin.

My wounds were like burning ice, but I didn't care, I was so outside myself that my own agony barely registered. Not in that moment. It was as if some *other* girl was inside the furious mass, some *other* girl was slowly being bitten to death.

I could feel hands – human-like hands – what felt like dozens, grabbing at me from within the vines. And I could hear whispers, almost like the rustling of tiny wings, issuing from the mass of vegetation. Allowing my eyes to follow that sound, peering into the dark teeming foliage, I saw faces. Ghastly, but still vaguely identifiable as human, those faces almost brought me to my knees.

My blood was flowing from countless wounds now, and I was weakening with every passing second. With each breath I took, I had to wonder if it would be my last, if the next slashing claw would find the soft tissue of my throat. Or if those hungry, scythe-filled mouths would converge to eat me alive.

They're killing me...

If Victor hadn't been there, I believe that's exactly what they'd have done, but he saved me. With what seemed to be no effort at all, the vampire jumped – almost flew – over the tops of the writhing mass, then from the other side, he reached in and pulled me free.

Then we were off again. Moving so fast I was barely aware of my feet hitting the hard-packed earth. I strained my ears, listening for something following close behind, but my ragged breathing and the pounding and thudding of my heart inside my chest was the only thing I could hear.

And then we were at the opening to the mineshaft, rushing through, Victor hurriedly slamming and bolting the door behind us.

Without the benefit of the bright green glow that had covered the forest, it took my eyes a few moments to adjust to the darkness. I almost tripped over John's body, still sprawled on the floor right where I'd left him. I could see one of his eyes open and staring, the other socket empty, a big gaping hole where the bats had done their work.

His death hadn't been an easy one. Horrible evidence of the bats was all over his body. His shirt and pants were only tatters of cloth, savagely ripped and torn, bits of bloodied flesh visible through the shredded fabric.

Victor pulled a flashlight from his pocket and shoved it into my trembling hand. "You'll need this," he said.

I turned it on and cast the beam down onto John's body. What had seemed horrible in darkness was shocking and beastly in the light. Beneath his one remaining eye, I could see the tear tracks that were etched in the blood and dirt covering his cheeks and chin. And the look in that eye… It shone with abject terror. And more than that – loneliness. I had a sudden image of John, lying there on the dirt floor, life leaving his body with each and every wound. He must have known he was dying. Had he felt alone? Afraid? The thought of it filled me with shame.

I did this to him. In that moment, it didn't matter that I'd had to, that he'd been moments away from killing *me.* Right then, I wasn't seeing the evil. All I could see was Gwyneth's brother, Dr. Wheaton's son. And a man I'd come to think of as something of a friend…

"Don't you dare," Victor said. "Don't you even think about feeling bad. He had it coming, and we have more important things to do than cry over the likes of him."

He was right, of course. I knew it. But still, I was sure that I would never forget the sight of his bloody corpse, lying in the dirt of that mineshaft. His flesh filthy, bitten, and torn. I'd carry that image with me for the rest of my days.

Finally I looked away, determined to focus on what we were there for. Carefully stepping over John's body, I made my way over to the gigantic heap of skulls.

"Grab one," I told Victor, motioning toward the towering wall of bone.

"I don't suppose it matters which one we take," he murmured, laying his hands on the skull nearest to the bottom edge. Kind of a risky choice, I thought. Better to take one from the top lest the whole thing topple down. But the disgusting pyramid of bone never even wavered as he pulled the selected skull away from the rest.

"Crazy, isn't it?" he said, gesturing toward the wall of skulls. "Here I had pockets full of C4, thinking I was going to have some fun tonight blowing this lot to hell and back."

But Ruby had said to take *one* skull, so that's what we were going to do. No explosions, no witchcraft. Just good old basic math.

"We gotta go," I was in a hurry to put this whole nasty business to bed.

"Wait," Victor said, looking down at John's body lying in the dirt at our feet. "Reckon his skull counts in the math? Maybe we should cut off his head? Throw it out the door?" Victor's eyes had taken on an excited shine.

The idea of beheading John's corpse was obviously one the vampire found to be exceptionally appealing.

But I wasn't up for any corpse desecration. Not if it could be avoided, and I was pretty sure John's skull would make no difference. It wasn't part of the *wall.*

But why take chances? In the end we spent a few more precious minutes dragging John's body outside the mineshaft.

Everything had taken longer that it should. I could only pray we weren't too late.

* * *

Mercifully, as we ran back down the hillside, there was no sign of the creatures, nothing skittering about within the trees. Maybe they were there and just hiding. I didn't know, but they made no effort to stop us.

I had no clue as to what the awful abominations might be, but they were connected to The Green Man and the vineyard. That much was plain. Before she'd lost consciousness, Gwyneth had told John that a vine had bitten her. Maybe the same thing had happened to those things in the woods. Then again, John had lied about so much, maybe everything he'd told me about what had happened to his sister was a complete fabrication.

But there *was* something decidedly human about them. I thought of the one that had snatched and eaten the squirrel. It had seemed distinctly feminine – there was even the suggestion of breasts underneath all the vines. And while I'd been trying to shove my way through them, I'd felt hands and fingers that seemed human.

But the claws...

Those things weren't simply long fingernails. I looked down at my arms, covered in deep, bleeding gashes. No, human nails hadn't done *that*.

I shivered, thought again of poor Gwyneth – maybe on her way to becoming one of these creatures. They were...

Vine people?

It seemed a ridiculously lame thing to call them, but I'd had the disadvantage of being up close and personal, and that was as apt a description as any.

As we ran, I glanced over at the skull swinging from Victor's hand, white bone gleaming in the tiny sliver of moon penetrating the forest.

This had better work. Ruby had said: *"Get one of the skulls from the heap and take it outside the mineshaft. If the literature is right, in order to maintain The Green Man, it takes a thousand skulls. Not nine hundred and ninety-nine, not one thousand and one."*

That was it. Get one skull. Butsurely this wasn't the end of it. No way it could really be this easy.

"I think it's working," Victor shouted as he ran. "Look around. The glow's fading."

I let my eyes sweep down the hillside. He was right. The glow *was* fading, almost gone in fact. Only the slightest bit of green mist still hung over the trees. Maybe one skull really had done the job.

As we moved further down the path, I was struck by the silence. It felt very much like running through a living, breathing tomb. Not even the chirp of insects broke the night.

And then the moaning began. Chilling in its urgency, it was the sound of anguish, heartbreak, and fear. It was coming from all around us, close, somewhere off inside the trees. I somehow knew the pitiful bellowing was coming from those awful, vine-covered mouths, but had no idea what it might mean.

As long as it didn't interfere with us getting back to my people, I didn't much care.

Finally we reached the bottom of the hill, leaving behind the forest and those horrible, anguished wails.

And right there in front of me was my family, my people. No longer trapped and as far as I could tell, they seemed to be unharmed. Vicki was slumped but standing, little Caleb clutched tightly in her arms. Alafair and Ruby were sitting down on the grass, the figure of a fallen man on the ground between them, his head in Ruby's lap.

Then the man turned his head and I could see that it was Andrew, alive, and free, and human.

Before I had the chance to even wonder about how that had come to be, from behind me, back near the trail, I heard an awful weeping. A chorus of it. Reluctantly, I turned back to that godforsaken forest, and saw dozens of naked, battered people streaming out of the trees. Men and women, some of them quite young - children even - stumbled from the woods into the clearing, their bodies filthy, their hair wild and full of leaves and twigs. Some still had bits of vine protruding from their skin.

As they continued to come forward, I noticed their movements were uneven and halting, as if they barely understood how to use their legs, but every second seemed to bring a bit more awareness, as if they were awakening from some awful dream.

Watching them was like watching a drunken march from the very bowels of hell. And they'd all been people, just like Gwyneth, presumably just going about their lives. Then one day, through some terrible misadventure, they'd all had some brush with Moncrieffe, and become those terrible creatures. But no longer...

The sadness, coupled with the sight of them all finally free, brought the sting of tears to my eyes.

"I won't pretend to understand what's happening here," Ruby said. She gently put Andrew's head down in the soft grass, then stood and wrapped me in an uncharacteristically affectionate hug. "But it's all good, so dry those damn tears. You know I can't stand that kind of sentimental nonsense."

"They're free," I told her. "The creatures... I think whatever it was you did to Andrew, somehow freed them as well. I think they're all like Gwyneth." I didn't know if they'd been bitten by vines, but it seemed obvious that they'd somehow been infected with the same vile substance that she had, which, I suddenly realized, probably meant that Gwyneth was free as well.

"Yes," Ruby answered. "I think you're right."

As we all watched those poor, ravaged people, my tears began to fall in earnest. Ruby could just bite my ass. If ever there'd been a time for tears, this was it. A feeling was swelling within me, a feeling I dimly recognized as pride.

We did it. Son of a bitch, we actually did it.

I could feel the beginnings of a release for myself as well. The stress that I'd been under for the past couple of hours was unwinding, I could feel my muscles start to relax, and my heart rate and breathing were now approaching something like normal. For the first time that night, I felt like myself, instead of some frightened, cornered, animal.

Then, from the corner of my eye, I caught movement over by the side of the main building. Something or someone was emerging from behind it, and as the figure moved from the shadows, I could see that it was a man, his movements shuffling, his body bent by age.

The old man came to a stop between a tired, paint blistered wooden shed and the outer edge of a row of vines. He went inside for only a moment, and came out holding a big, red container. I wasn't sure, but it looked to be a gasoline jug. The shed seemed like a place where gardening implements might be stored, so would of course have gas for the mowers and other lawn and pruning equipment.

I didn't like the looks of that. Anyone laying their hands on a can of gas at a time like this could only have one thing in mind.

The figure took a couple of steps forward, stopping just inside the glow coming from one of the many security lights attached to the main building.

I began walking toward the shed; Victor, Ruby, and Alafair right on my heels.

We were about twenty feet away when I finally realized who the old man was. I *knew* this guy. But not as this wrinkled, stooped, troll of a man. When last I'd seen him, he'd been vibrant, cosmopolitan, walking and talking with an arrogant kind of ease, and at least forty years younger.

Victor had recognized the man as well, and whistling low, he whispered, "Devil break my bones, if it isn't that son of a dog–"

"Yes," I said. "I reckon your bones are safe, Victor. That's Moncrieffe."

I had no idea what had caused his sudden aging, but assumed it had something to do with the same magic that had transformed Andrew and the poor wretched people in the forest. I thought about John, what he'd said about the nectar of the vines, how he'd experienced physical enhancements, and wondered if – for Moncrieffe anyway – the magic had been even more powerful. Maybe even powerful enough to transform a very old man into a younger, more vigorous version of himself.

If that was true, there was no telling what Moncrieffe might be willing to do to restore it. I began walking toward the advancing figure. No way was I letting him get anywhere near Caleb.

Moncrieffe saw us coming, I was sure of it, but he showed absolutely no concern. He simply stood there, calmly, watching us advance. When we'd gotten within a dozen feet or so of the shed, he pulled the cap from the jug of gasoline, then proceeded to pour the entire contents over his body, then around himself in wide sweeping arcs, flinging aside the empty container when he was done.

Okay, so the asshole wants to burn himself alive. And I'm supposed to actually care?

I didn't.

Moncrieffe could burn himself straight back to hell and I'd just beg the devil to leave open the door. Leave the light on too. Hell, I'd even hold the door. So if this was supposed to be some kind of threat, he'd found the wrong bunch of folks to give a shit.

He walked up a little closer to where we stood. Did he actually think we were crazy enough to just stand idly by while he set us on fire?

But I soon discovered that wasn't what he had in mind.

"I'm going to burn the whole thing down," he said.

"As long as your sorry ass burns with it," Alafair spat. "Hurry up and do it! Do you need some help, you worthless piece of shit?" She and Ruby had moved out front, and I could see the only thing stopping her from charging in like a maniac was Victor, who held her firmly from behind.

"This whole Green God thing was all about keeping sorry assholes like you from aging, wasn't it?" Alafair screamed. "You would have killed a little boy for that shit."

"I would have killed a dozen of them," Moncrieffe replied. "But there's so much more to it than eternal youth. More to this piece of land than you could know. More to it than you'll *ever* understand."

At that moment I noticed a slight movement from his hand and then, like a vision from hell, he burst into flames. Seconds later the shed exploded, hot tongues of fire leaping out in every direction.

By the time we'd all ran back to the gates, and the relative safety of the parking lot, the entire vineyard was a living, breathing inferno. I didn't quite get why Moncrieffe had taken himself out as he had, but wondered if it might have something to do with protecting secrets.

Or maybe he thinks he's not gonna stay dead... thinks that maybe he has a way back...

Seemed out of the realm of possibility, but a week ago so had something as absurd as a Green Man, and vines that could grow out of bodies. As a witch – someone who had a natural inclination to find most things believable – much of all this had strained credulity, even for me.

I was happy though, at that moment. Us safe in the parking lot, watching as the whole damn place burned to the ground. It seemed to me to be a proper ending for this whole sorry mess. And those poor wretched people that had stumbled from the woods. They'd followed us to the parking lot, and according to Ruby, all of them were present and accounted for.

One of us was going to have to head back to town to arrange transport to get everyone the hell away from this god awful place. But that was small shit. Details. The important thing, the thing I wanted to savor for just a little bit longer, was that the good guys won this one. All things considered, I was feeling pretty awesome.

Below where we stood, I could see that the fire in the vineyard was spreading, almost all of it was now in flames. And then I suddenly remembered... *everything* wasn't safe and sound.

"Oh no!" I shouted. "The dogs. We have to get the dogs." I prayed we weren't too late. Knew they could have already either burned or died from the smoke.

I rushed down the hill, dodging fire as I ran, with Victor following and Ruby shouting from behind for us to stop. But I kept going, running as fast as my feet would take me.

Finally we made it through to the outside of the locked kennel.

The dogs were there, some of them in bad shape, maybe even dead, just lumps of fur lying on the ground.

I started speaking to them. Not just with my voice but with my power. I'd never tried to summon anything as large as a dog, but I was damn sure going to try.

I was exhausted but somehow it seemed as if my exhaustion was feeding my intent, I could feel a strength there that was new to me. It seemed bigger, more focused than ever before.

Then one by one, they woke, all except one.

Victor ripped the lock from the gate of the kennel and the dogs began coming out, slowly at first, dazed and frightened. I held onto my intent, focused it, and the magic found its way to them. They began to make their way through the fires, gingerly at first, then faster until finally they were all headed up the hill toward the parking area and breathable air.

All except the one dog that still lay on the ground, unmoving...

"We gotta get out of here, Tula," Victor urged, grabbing hold of my arm, trying to pull me back.

"Wait!" I pulled away from his grasp, and ran through the kennel to the unmoving form at the back, near the worst of the fire and smoke. My eyes were burning so badly I could barely see, and my lungs felt like they were full of hot coals, but I leaned over and put my hand on the big dog's coat.

Daisy.

She was breathing.

"Victor!" I shouted. "Pick her up."

And he did. He picked up the enormous dog, tucking it under one arm as if she were no more than a sack of potatoes. Then he did the same with me.

"There's only one way we can get out of here alive," he said. "I'm going to have to fly us out. There's too much fire. We'll never make it any other way."

He was right, of course. But not my neck. *Never* my neck. I held out my wrist to him, and the vampire drank. Not much, but enough.

When he was done, I felt my feet leaving the ground and then we were airborne, the three of us flying above the flames, higher and higher, above even the smoke-filled air.

When he sat us down on the gravel lot, I pulled the dog's head into my lap.

She looked up at me with big brown eyes, gave a small thump of her tail, and her pink tongue found my hand and gave it a small, timid lick.

"Looks like you've got yourself a friend," Victor said.

"I hope you're not thinking what I think you are, Tula," Ruby laughed. "If that dog goes with you, Emmery's going to have something to say about that, I'll bet. What with her cats and all."

"Emmery and her cats can kiss my ass," I said. "This one's going home with me."

Then I looked at Victor, and leaned over and whispered into his ear, "Thank you." I will admit to being sorely tempted to say something else, something like '*and you're coming home with me too*' – I mean there he was all handsome and covered in soot and blood like some avenging angel. And of course there was that beautiful smile. But then, that would have been the

269

ultimate tempting of fate though, wouldn't it? And I kind of felt like I'd done enough of that of late. For now at least, I'd settle for what had turned out to be a very good night indeed.

My family was safe, and I'd found a dog and something like a – and I couldn't believe I was thinking of a vampire in these terms, but there it was. He was a hero. Newly found, probably newly minted. I was pretty sure the Irishman wasn't exactly used to being the one who saved the day. And all in one's night's business.

Not   bad.   Not   bad   at   all.

Chapter 37

The next few days were crazy, even for us Whitlows. There was a lot to arrange in terms of covering up what we'd done at the vineyard. Even though it had all been necessary, explaining that to a bunch of law enforcement types wouldn't do. Luckily we weren't without friends in high places, so in the end the whole thing was put down to a fire, and if that story didn't perfectly dot every I and cross every T, well, those friends of ours made sure that no one was looking at that too closely.

Still, the entire thing had required a lot of running around and calling in favors and hand holding all the way around. But eventually, the whole episode was all tied up in a neat little package, and done with.

When it was all said and done, nine people were dead, and none of them ours. Nine evil, murderous bastards. To me, that felt like success.

Of Moncrieffe, there was no sign at all. Though we'd all seen him burn, none of the charred remains that were recovered from the fire matched up to his DNA.

So that was still a mystery. The fire investigators that had come down from Charlotte said it was possible that his body had simply burned to ash.

Maybe... But maybe not. I had a bad feeling that somehow, someway, the asshole was still out there somewhere.

I'd gone by to check on Liz Montgomery and was very happy to discover that she'd decided to sell her property to her neighbors, the Gilliams, who'd had their eye on the place for years. She'd already found a little house in town and was busy packing. I was relieved to see that Liz seemed happy and content to be starting a new chapter in her life. She'd even confessed that maybe she'd reached the age when living in the middle of nowhere was just more trouble than it was worth.

The meeting with Dr. Wheaton and Gwyneth had been hard. Having to tell them that John was gone, that Gwyneth had lost a brother, and Dr. Wheaton, a son. It had been a thoroughly miserable business. I'd wanted to tell the both of them the truth of it. It had been just right on the tip of my tongue, I'd been that eager to give them what John truly deserved – the hatred of these two innocent people.

He deserved that in spades.

But of course I couldn't, because Dr. Wheaton and Gwyneth *didn't* deserve it. It was better they viewed the man as a hero who fought a dark force all the way up to the bitter end, sacrificing his own life to save his sister's.

Any other story would have been unthinkable.

I knew it would be hard for them. But they'd be okay. The vines invading the poor woman's body were dead and gone, she'd be good as new in no time. And then there was the baby to look forward to. Hopefully it would restore some joy to their lives. They were strong, good people, and I'd added them to my list of responsibilities. I'd be checking on them. A lot. They were now and forever within the Whitlow fold.

At least they had Andrew back. He was weak, still barely able to walk, and mercifully had no memory at all of what he'd suffered.

As for John. Well, he'd been good. Good at deception, and his acting was right up there with the greats. I'd never seen it coming, not a whiff of it.

Maybe I should have. Maybe he wasn't quite as sad and worried about his sister as he should have been. Maybe he'd been a little too lucky with the cougar. Looking back, the thing hadn't put up the kind of fight it was capable of. It could have ripped his shoulder right out if it had wanted to, rather than simply taking a little nibble. Or it could have bypassed his shoulder all together and gone for his neck. That would have been the end of him.

But yeah, anyway. He'd fooled me. Fooled us all. But maybe not completely. I like to think my mad desire to kill him inside the tunnel was my inner witch starting to figure it all out. Maybe it wasn't just the monstrous moss doing its work on my brain. Maybe on some level I *knew.*

I like to think that's the case. So that's how I'm going to file it away.

And not just in my head. You see, I keep an actual file of every single case that comes my way. Both large and small, all of them eventually have their own special folder. The problem with this case is that it ended up with so many legs. Maybe it's gonna need some sub files. It turned out to be a lot more far-reaching than what I was used to. So many moving parts.

I'd set up a new office for myself. I'd taken Ruby's advice and kind of made The Library my own. And right next to the glass cabinet where Nelson – Ruby's favorite little creature – lives, I'd put my own cabinet. This one was about five feet tall, made from scuffed gray painted steel. It had five rolling drawers that I was slowly filling with folders, folders containing files. The Carolina Files.

I picked up a black felt marker and pulled a large manilla folder from a box of them I'd placed on the floor beside me.

With something kind of like reverence, I laid the folder out on the polished oak table. This would be the very first one created in The Library. Soon I'd have the power of the lodestone, soon this space would be mine and mine alone. In the meantime, Mother was on the other side of the world, and I wasn't going to let this place go to waste another moment longer.

I bent over the folder, the marker held poised in my hand as I thought about the case. Thought of Andrew, John, the Moncrieffes, the Green God. Victor, Ruby, and my sisters. How they'd all played their part. And then there was Gwyneth. Poor Gwyneth.

With a flourish, I wrote a single word and marveled at how much meaning a single set of letters could hold.

One word, sitting there all alone on the empty folder.

Invasion.

* * *

Less than two miles away, Violet Winters, dressed in her cheerleading outfit, walked hurriedly through the woods. There wasn't a game that night, but he'd asked her to wear it, so of course, she'd obliged. She liked wearing it anyway. It made her feel like someone else. Someone *better*. There was a power in that. And Violet loved power above all else.

She was very near the lake now. She could smell it on the wind. The closeness of it excited her in ways she'd never dreamed.

Darkness was falling on Lake Sylvie, and deep beneath the dark, still water, something woke. It whispered, and as she had so many times before, Violet listened...

A NOTE FROM WILLA BLACKMORE...

To find out more about Violet Winters, join Tula Whitlow as she attempts to uncover the gruesome secrets lurking in the shadowy depths of Lake Sylvie in *Undertow, Book Two of The Carolina Files*.

Thank you so much for reading *Witchwood- The Carolina Files Book One.* I hope you enjoyed it. As a writer, creating adventures for Tula and her sisters is an absolute blast, and I consider it a huge privilege to be able to bring them to readers.

If you're ready to embark with the girls on their next adventure, *Undertow - The Carolina Files* is available now.

If you're interested in updates on new releases or freebies, you can follow me on Facebook HERE.

If you have the time, I'd be forever grateful if you'd post a rating or review. It's especially helpful for new authors such as yours truly!

Once again, thank you so much for reading, and I sincerely hope you'll be hanging around for the rest of the series!

276

Want More Carolina Files?

Thank you so much for reading Witchwood! I hope you enjoyed it. If you'd like more from Tula and her sisters...

Click HERE to go to UNDERTOW – The Carolina Files Book Two

If you'd like to follow me on FACEBOOK, or join my mailing list, here's a link: http://www.facebook.com/WillaBlackmore

If you liked this book, I'd be forever grateful if you'd take the time out of your busy day to drop a short review. Thanks so much!

Also by Willa Blackmore

Willa Blackmore is the author of two supernatural urban fantasy series: The Carolina Files and the soon to be released Babineaux Chronicles. She has written professionally as a non-fiction freelancer for many years but her love has always been fiction. Willa lives right in the corner of North Carolina, Tennessee, and Georgia with her large extended family, more cats than she needs, and her ever loyal poodle mix Bernie.

Undertow - The Carolina Files Book Two

https://www.amazon.com/dp/B093DZSDM2

Thank you!

Masquerade: The Carolina Files Book Three

Coming This Fall!

Furies - The Babineaux Chronicles Book One

Coming This Fall!

Made in the USA
Monee, IL
07 September 2023